One la

Judy checked the sleeping girls for the last time, pulling their blankets up, smoothing their hair back, thinking with a pain that ripped right down the middle of her how much they would change in a year, how much they would learn and grow. And Dan, already noticing girls, would experience the ups and downs of adolescence without her. She had loved them from the very beginning, but now it was more than that. Over one beautiful coastal summer their lives had been woven into hers. They were tied to one another—they would be torn by the separation.

"Judy?" Dan's voice, groggy with sleep, came out of the dark. "I knew you'd be leaving in the morning, and I wanted to tell you—" he paused on an audible constriction in his throat, and Judy felt her own close and tighten "—how great it's been having you here. It's been almost like...as good as...before Mom died. I'm gonna miss you."

Judy wrapped her arms around him and simply held on, too full of emotion for a moment to speak. "I love you, too, Dan."

ABOUT THE AUTHOR

A native of Massachusetts, Muriel Jensen now lives in Astoria, Oregon, with her husband who is also a writer, two calico cats and a malamute named Deadline. She also has three grown children. Muriel loves investigating restaurants and dress shops— all in the interest of research!

Books by Muriel Jensen

HARLEQUIN AMERICAN ROMANCE
73–WINTER'S BOUNTY
119–LOVERS NEVER LOSE
176–THE MALLORY TOUCH
200–FANTASIES AND MEMORIES
219–LOVE AND LAVENDER
244–THE DUCK SHACK AGREEMENT

Don't miss any of our special offers. Write to us at the following address for information on our newest releases.

Harlequin Reader Service
901 Fuhrmann Blvd., P.O. Box 1397, Buffalo, NY 14240
Canadian address: P.O. Box 603,
Fort Erie, Ont. L2A 5X3

Strings
Muriel Jensen

Harlequin Books

TORONTO • NEW YORK • LONDON
AMSTERDAM • PARIS • SYDNEY • HAMBURG
STOCKHOLM • ATHENS • TOKYO • MILAN

To my children, Mike, Pat and Kathy,
the most precious of my life's blessings

Published October 1988

First printing August 1988

ISBN 0-373-16267-7

Prologue

"I'm very impressed. Culver Middle School's teacher of the year, two years in a row?"

"I had two great classes in a row." Judy Cassidy smiled modestly at the middle-aged woman in the navy wool suit sitting across the table from her. "They made me look good."

Glenna Kramer glanced up from the biography Summer Nannies had provided and removed her glasses, fixing keen blue eyes on Judy. "You're being unduly humble, Judy. I checked your references before I asked you to meet me for lunch. Your principal raved about you as a teacher and a person. Your landlady had high praise for your tidiness and reliability. And, Dana Berny at Summer Nannies said she considers you her best."

"Miss Kramer—" Judy pushed her half-eaten salad aside, determined to be frank "—Dana is my friend, and I think she was trying to build me up just a little. The truth is, this would be my first assignment for Summer Nannies. I work hard at being a good teacher, but I've never been a nanny before. I love children, so I think I could do a good job, but I don't want you to hire me thinking I'm an experienced nanny. I'm not."

She looked at Glenna with honest brown eyes. Judy's quick smile was set in a face that was bright and wholesome. It was difficult to explain what caused an instant rapport with another human being—some emotional reaction to qualities and traits one recognized in oneself, or some subconscious connection that had less to do with likenesses than with admiration for obvious differences. Judy saw both in Glenna Kramer.

Glenna was a woman whose feet were firmly set on the path of old-fashioned values and strong principles, a direction she herself always tried to follow. But while Judy was very much a contemporary woman—adventurous, determined, focused on achievement of a goal—Glenna had admitted she'd always thought of herself as a wimp.

She had expressed doubt that such a well-educated, self-confident young woman as Judy would understand the cowardice that could attack a middle-aged woman who had never married. Having spent most of her life caring for ailing relatives and aged parents, she had never lived alone, never loved a man, never gotten in touch with the real Glenna Kramer. She had awakened one day to discover that some intrinsic part of her hadn't developed, and that she was now, at fifty, afraid of the world.

But that wimp had finally taken a step toward emotional independence and had signed up for a three-month tour of Europe—alone. She told Judy there were moments when she still couldn't believe she'd done it.

"What did Mrs. Berny tell you?" Glenna asked.

Judy refilled their coffee cups from the pot on the table. "That you keep house and care for your widowed brother and his three children, that you're going to Europe for the summer and need someone to take over your duties while you're gone." Judy put the pot down and added as an afterthought, "On the Oregon coast, I think she said."

"Manzanita. A beautiful little place on the beach." Glenna sighed and smiled. "I went to help Mitch out two years ago when his wife died. Despite the fact that I'm twelve years older than he is, we've always been good friends and, well, it's been a good arrangement. He's a wonderful man, and the kids are great. But sometimes I think I depend on them too much."

Judy smiled at Glenna, touched by the wavering courage she saw in her eyes, understanding it. Her mother had been like Glenna, devoted to her family, living for them. She simply hadn't lived long enough to reach the point where she would have questioned what had become of herself, the individual.

"A trip to Europe sounds wonderful," Judy said, toasting Glenna with her coffee cup. "I'll be going to Oxford in September to get my master's degree."

"Mrs. Berny told me. That's why you hired on at Summer Nannies—to make extra money before you go." Glenna sat a little straighter, satisfied. "I'll have to take special notes and photos while I'm in England so that I'll have lots to report back to you."

"I'd love that."

Glenna frowned. "Did I mention that you're hired?"

"No." Judy laughed. "You didn't."

"Well, you are."

Chapter One

"I don't want French toast."

The preference was stated plainly, unequivocally. Mitch Kramer looked down into his almost-four-year-old daughter's determined blue eyes and suggested, "Pancakes?"

Katie shifted her plastic, bear-shaped bottle from the crook of one elbow to the other. "Nope."

"Cereal?"

"No."

Mitch pushed the milk, eggs and bread aside and reached down to lift the child onto the counter. He pulled down her pink T-shirt that said TERRIFIC KID in lavender letters and thought with a private smile that it should say TERRIFIC FINICKY KID. He looked into the eyes he always had trouble holding firm against and asked, "What would you like for breakfast?"

"'Strami," she replied instantly. Apparently it was a choice to which she'd given considerable thought.

"I second that."

Mitch glanced over his shoulder at his fourteen-year-old son, who had endorsed the motion without removing his eyes from the sports page spread out before him on the table.

"Thanks, Dan," he said dryly.

"Sure." Without raising his eyes, Dan gave his father a careless wave to indicate that thanks weren't necessary. Mitch turned back to Katie.

"You can't have pastrami for breakfast," he said reasonably. But he knew the child's response even before she made it.

"Why not?"

"Because it isn't nutritious."

"You eat it." Katie used the weapon she already understood was difficult for a parent to fight. Then added for good measure, "I've seen you."

"I'm not still growing," he replied patiently.

Dan glanced up from the paper. "At least, not taller."

Mitch turned to the boy again, this time with a threatening look. Dan grinned, going back to his American League stats.

"You're not supposed to have meat for breakfast." Liz, Mitch's middle child and possessor of all motherly knowledge, spoke from in front of the utensil drawer several feet away. She was gathering knives and forks to set the table. "It clogs your batteries."

Mitch thought a minute. "Arteries?"

"Yeah. Those things that make your heart go. They get full of junk when you eat meat for breakfast." She looked at her father judiciously before crossing to the table with the silverware. "I told you that."

Indeed she had. For an eight-year-old, Elizabeth had firm ideas about what her family should and shouldn't do. Occasionally she reminded Mitch so much of her mother that he had to stop and stare. She had the same long, soft brown hair that ended in ringlets the color of old gold. Her eyes were lighter than Katie's, the very same hyacinth shade Mandy's had been. It was hardest for him when she laughed; the hearty, unrestrained sound might have been a recording of his wife's delight over something simple.

In the two years since Mandy's death, he had learned to cope with the loss. Raising his three children and keeping his construction business going when the economy was bad had left him little time to consider his loneliness. His children were warm and loving; his parents and his sisters had been there to help every time he'd thought that he needed it; and he counted his employees among his closest friends. He had more than any man could ask for. As far as he was concerned, the night-time loneliness was a small price to pay for having shared a beautiful relationship with a very special woman.

"We're having French toast," Mitch told his youngest firmly.

Katie's lips pursed into a wry quirk. She was accustomed to being overruled. "Lizzie isn't the boss," she pointed out with a glare at her sister. "You are."

He lifted her off the counter. "Right. And I say we're having French toast. Go wash your hands." He gave her a noisy kiss before setting her on her feet.

Holding fast to what remained of her planned menu, Katie asked plaintively, "Can we have grape Kool-Aid to drink?"

Mitch broke eggs into the square pan, knowing if he looked at her he'd laugh. "Nope. Orange juice. And milk."

With a sigh, Katie walked off to the bathroom. Mitch breathed a sigh of relief.

"Hey, Dad," Dan said, folding the newspaper in half and coming to the counter to hold it under his father's nose. "Look. Somebody in Cannon Beach has a motorcycle for sale cheap!"

Mitch glanced where Dan's finger pointed and nodded, pouring milk into the eggs. "Good."

"Can you buy it for me?"

Whipping up the milk and eggs, Mitch thought he really had to hand it to his son. The kid was no quitter. They'd had this same conversation at least ten times a week for the past six months, and Dan never stopped trying, even though the reply was always the same.

"No."

"Why not?" The question that followed was also always the same, but the answer bore repeating.

"Because I like you in one piece."

"Dad..."

"No, Dan."

"All the guys have 'em."

Mitch frowned. "Bill Cosgrove doesn't have one. Kenny Farmer doesn't have one. Dusty Carter—"

"Dad, I'm not a kid anymore." Dan handed him the loaf of bread. "I work after school. I do all the stuff around here you ask me to do."

Mitch stopped working on breakfast and leaned against the counter, looking down at his son. Just as the girls resembled their mother, Dan took after him with his dark hair and eyes and long, sturdy limbs. He was good-natured and reliable, but single-minded, with a temper that could rise without warning. Mitch wryly recognized the latter traits as other things they shared in common.

"You're absolutely right," he conceded, "and I appreciate your eagerness to work and your dependability. That's why I'd rather have you unbroken. In another year you can get your learner's permit, and if you do well, I'll be glad to help you get a car. I'd rather see you in a car than on a motorcycle."

Dan emitted a long sigh and leaned his elbows on the counter. A year was a long way into the future, but Mitch knew that the prospect of a car minimized Dan's disappointment over his father's negative attitude about the bike.

"A Ferrari?"

Mitch dipped a slice of bread in the egg-and-milk mixture, then dropped it onto the hot griddle. It sizzled and spat, and man and boy leaned back out of reach. Mitch smiled down at his son. "How about a secondhand Toyota?"

Dan shook his head. "Be reasonable, Dad. How would it look if your astronaut son drove around in a used Toyota? Do you expect Chelsea Miller, the foxiest woman in the freshman class, to be seen with me in an old Toyota?"

A second slice hit the griddle after Mitch turned the first. "If you treat Chelsea well and she truly cares for you, she'd ride with you on a moped. And I heartily endorse the astronaut dream, Dan. But it'll be fifteen years before you can realize it, what with college and all the other steps you'll have to climb first. By then you'll be able to afford your own Ferrari. You could even buy one for me."

"You'll probably have your license revoked by then," Dan retorted, stepping strategically out of reach, "because of your advanced age."

Liz stepped between them before Mitch could wield the spatula. "Daddy, if you don't hurry, we won't have the table cleaned up before the nanny gets here."

"That's another thing," Dan said, coming closer once again, his manner mildly aggressive. "What do we need a nanny for, anyway? I watch Katie and Liz all the time when Aunt Glenna's gone and you're at work."

Mitch nodded, putting the browned French toast in the warm oven and more dipped bread on the griddle. He gave his son a serious glance, understanding the boy's resentment at being watched over. "That's right. But school let out yesterday for the summer, and Aunt Glenna left the day before for three months in Europe. You'll be working four hours a day at the market until September. Who can I trust with the girls while you're gone?"

Put that way, Dan understood his father's dilemma. "She won't expect to baby-sit *me*, will she?"

"Think of her as the job foreman. She'll probably expect to pass judgment on where you'd like to go and with whom. I'll sure she understands your routine."

"How long's she gonna stay?"

"Until school starts and Aunt Glenna's back and things get back to normal."

"What's her name again?"

"Judy," Liz replied, taking a pitcher of juice out of the refrigerator. She put it on the table, giving her father a moody glance as she poured carefully. "She's a teacher when it isn't summer."

Mitch had read aloud to the children the biography Summer Nannies had provided. Liz never forgot a thing. He suspected that she wasn't pleased about the nanny, either, though she'd been less vocal about her disapproval then Dan.

"She's probably old and crabby," Dan prophesied pessimistically.

Mitch laughed. "You know she isn't. Aunt Glenna went to Spokane to interview her in April, and she said she was pretty. And she's only thirty-two."

"Thirty-one," Liz corrected. "She taught fifth grade and coached volleyball, and she likes to paint stuff. Not houses and not pictures, but boxes and plates and things." For once at a loss for a detail, she frowned up at her father. "What do they call it?"

"Rosemaling," he replied. It had been listed as a hobby in the nanny's biography. Never having heard the word before, Mitch had helped Elizabeth look it up. The dictionary had informed them that it was a Scandinavian peasant style of decorating objects with painted or carved inscriptions or floral designs. Liz had found the craft, if not the woman, fascinating. "Lizzie, would you check on Katie? She's been in the bathroom a long time."

Liz ran off to check on her sister, and Dan looked skeptically at Mitch. "The nanny could be young and crabby."

Mitch pulled the plate of toast out of the oven and added the last two pieces off the griddle. "Your aunt seemed to think she was very nice. Give her a chance, Dan. I'm not crazy about the idea of bringing a stranger into our home myself, but I'm in a tight spot here. You've got to help me out. Anyway, I don't think she'd be in the nanny business if she was crabby. Get the butter and the syrup, will you?"

"Daddy!" Liz's shout stopped Mitch halfway between the stove and the table.

"Yeah?" he shouted back.

"Katie's shoe is stuck in the toilet!" There was a moment's pause. "And she's in it!"

Mitch looked heavenward in supplication, then handed the plate to Dan and hurried off to save his daughter and his plumbing. Envisioning the sort of nanny required by his dear but lively and curious family, he got a mental image of a large woman in fatigues and a helmet, blowing a whistle and shouting orders at the top of her lungs.

MANZANITA WAS NESTLED on a mountainside that sloped gradually from the highway to the ocean. Narrow roads wound around hills covered with scruffy pines and an intriguing collection of old and new homes. Judy Cassidy guided her Reliant down one of the roads that stretched all the way to the beach. She had no map, but she had memorized the address, 237 Beachfront Lane. If logic could be trusted, she should find her charges on the road that fronted the water.

The air through the open window of her car was pungent with the smell of pine and a delicious oceanfront freshness. Judy inhaled deeply and felt the clean air revive her. The drive from Spokane had given her more than eight hours to think about the job she'd taken for the summer.

Every other June through August for the past ten years, she'd tutored or been a camp counselor. Those jobs had been fun and enough of a change from teaching fifth grade that she'd returned to the classroom in the fall, renewed and enthusiastic. But this fall would be different.

In September she would be returning to the classroom, but as a student. A thrill ran through her as she thought about *where* she would be. She, Judith Kaia Cassidy, was going to study at Oxford. She had been dreaming for ten years of getting her master's degree in European history, seriously planning it for five. Last year, she'd applied for her sabbatical and admission to Oxford. The approval had come through a short two months ago, and the excitement was still new. She laughed softly to herself as she concluded that it would remain fresh until she stepped on British soil. Then the result of all those years of planning, the realization of the dream would become reality.

Planning the sabbatical with Dale Fitzgerald had made the entire project that much more special. She and Dale had taught at the same school in Richland, Washington, and though Judy had eventually moved to Spokane, they'd maintained a close friendship. When they'd met in summer school in Seattle two years previously, Judy had told Dale her sabbatical plans and he had suggested going also to get his degree in languages.

The real excitement had begun at that moment and had been building ever since. Judy had never really believed that Dale would follow all the plodding steps required to make his plan to join her a reality, but he had. And now, while awaiting the fall, he was off to Newport, Rhode Island, to race his sailboat, and she was on her way to be a summer nanny.

"Teachers are perfect for this kind of work," Dana Berny, a former teacher and Judy's good friend, had insisted. "So many families lose their regular baby-sitters during the summer because of vacations or changing schedules. But teachers are usually free from June to August, and they know how to deal with children. They're perfect for summer child care."

As far as meeting her own personal needs for the summer, the job couldn't be more perfect. She would be fully occupied for three months. The time would fly, and she would be earning a generous wage. Before she knew it, it would be September and time for Dale to pick her up for **the flight to New York and then London. She fought a** resurgence of excitement and tried to concentrate on house numbers.

Two thirty-seven. She braked to a quick stop in front of a rustic two-story white frame house nestled in a grove of brushy pines. A blue pickup with lumber in the back and a bumper sticker that read THIS VEHICLE PRO-

TECTED BY SMITH AND WESSON was parked in the drive-way. In front of it was a late seventies station wagon. A ten-speed bike leaned against the front-porch railing, and a tricycle lay on its side in front of the house in the broad area that was sand rather than lawn. A well-worn wooden sign over the door said KRAMERS. The atmosphere was charming, though she'd love to get at that sign with her paints.

Judy breathed a contented sigh, grabbed her Kenya purse and got out of the car. She started up a sliced-stone walk to a screened-in porch that ran the width of the front of the house. An old green porch swing with a cal-ico seat cushion stirred lazily in the midmorning breeze.

Inhaling the warm salt air, Judy started up the steps. She had liked Glenna Kramer so much when she'd been interviewed for the job that she was sure she'd like her brother and his children. The house looked cozy and comfortable, and she liked the lazy, resort atmosphere of the town itself. This job promised to be a pleasant way to pass the time until September.

As Judy raised her hand to knock on the screen door, she heard a commotion from within. There were chil-dren's high voices and a man's brief shout. Then there was silence. She started to knock once more, but aborted the action again when she saw the running figure of a boy. Leaning forward to peer through the screen, her hands on either side of her face blocking out the light, she watched him race through the living room to a door. He disappeared, then reappeared carrying a huge toolbox.

"Pardon me," Judy said quickly as he hurried past her, straining under the weight of the box. The boy stopped and squinted toward the screen door.

Judy tugged at the door, found it unlocked and pulled it open. "I'm Judy Cassidy," she said. When the young man simply frowned at her, she added, "From Summer Nannies. Is your father home?"

"Oh, hi." The boy started off again toward the direction of the commotion. "We're all in the bathroom. Katie's stuck in the toilet."

Unsure whether that was an invitation to follow him, Judy found herself unable to resist. She trailed the boy through the living room and down a corridor to a green-and-apricot bathroom. It took a moment for her to make sense of the scene there.

A child's face caught her eyes first. It was pink and cherubic with dark blue eyes. A riotous tangle of curly platinum hair topped it. A soft hum issuing from its little pink mouth, the face rested on a man's broad shoulder. If she remembered correctly what Glenna had told her, the child must be Katie, and judging by her serenity, she must not be upset by her dilemma. One of her very short legs, clad in jeans, stood on one very long leg stretched out to brace the man kneeling in front of the toilet.

Muscles rippled under the man's white cotton T-shirt when he leaned farther forward. The action tipped the child backward, and she calmly took a tiny fistful of his thick dark hair. Judy noted his tight, narrow hips in the well-worn jeans.

A girl of about eight—she had to be Elizabeth—was standing in a claw-footed bathtub, the only place from which to get a complete view of the goings-on in the crowded bathroom.

The boy dropped the toolbox to the floor with a bang. "Why don't we just flush her?" he asked.

The calm child suddenly let out a wail and swiped at her brother with a plastic baby bottle clutched in one hand.

"Cork it, Dan," the man said without looking up. He held up a hand. "Give me a wrench."

"You're gonna pull up the john?" the boy asked incredulously, rummaging through the box.

"Got a better idea?"

"I guess we've tried everything. Her foot's really stuck. But as soon as you get that up she'll have to go to the bathroom."

"Dan . . ."

"Okay. Okay." The boy slapped the wrench into the man's hand.

"Have you tried pulling her foot out of her shoe?" Judy asked.

Three pairs of eyes looked up at her. The man turned as far as the child clinging to him would allow. His eyes were hazel under a strong brow. A hank of dark hair fell over it. She saw his mind shift from the crisis at hand to an analysis of who the intruder was.

"The nanny," she said. "Judy Cassidy."

Mitch closed his eyes for a moment. The whole family gathered around the toilet bowl was not the first image he would have chosen for her to see. "Hello." He gave her a harassed half smile. "Yes, we did try to pull her out of her shoe, but it's really wedged in there. Dan's and my hands are too big to get at the Velcro fastener, and Liz doesn't have the strength to pull hard enough."

Judy came to kneel beside him, forcing herself into the narrow space. She pushed the sleeves of her sweater up. "Want me to try?"

With a firm grip on Katie, Mitch distanced himself from the crisis to study the pretty face at his shoulder. So this is what nannies look like today, he thought, interest suddenly overtaking his concern with the problem. It was no wonder the somewhat old-fashioned profession was making a comeback.

Dark-chocolate eyes shone at him with a mixture of amusement and an interest in him at least as lively as his in her. Short, dark hair with cherry-wood highlights waved away from her face in a sort of fluffy, flyaway casualness that took time and care, if what he remembered about sharing a bathroom with a woman held true. She had a perfect nose, a pointed chin and a consummate confidence that left him little recourse but to reply, "Why not?" If she could to it, which he frankly doubted, he'd be ahead. If she couldn't, he wouldn't have lost anything.

Judy pulled a topaz ring off the third finger of her right hand and passed it to Liz, who was still standing in the bathtub. "Hold that please, Elizabeth."

Mitch moved aside to let Judy kneel in front of the bowl. With one hand on the child's chest, he braced her and kept her weight off Judy. Immersing her hands in the cold water, Judy found the heel of the child's canvas shoe and, with her fingers, followed the foot into the drain. The toe of Katie's shoe was wedged firmly into the opening.

Judy looked up at her employer. "Have you considered cutting the back off the shoe?"

"No!" Katie wailed. "Don't cut Big Bird!"

"She just got them yesterday," Mitch explained, patting the child reassuringly. "They have Big Bird on the toe and on the heel. She was trying to wash them. That's how she got stuck. I was saving cutting it off as a last resort."

He waited for her to laugh at his reluctance to employ the obvious solution. Instead she sat back on her heels and rested her wet hands on the side of the bowl.

"Right." She turned to look over her shoulder at the young man she had followed into the house. "Dan, isn't it?"

"Yeah," he replied.

"Would you look in my purse for a small zippered bag? It has yellow flowers on it. I think I put it down by the bathroom door."

"This?" He indicated her large, straw Kenya bag with the toe of his Reeboks.

"Yes."

He rummaged through it, frowning. "This is worse than Dad's toolbox," he grumbled. Then he held up a bag.

"That's it. There are tweezers in it."

He found them and handed them to her. Immersing her hands in the water once again, Judy caught the end of the Velcro tab in the tweezers and pulled. She lost her grip on the tweezers and they flew out of her hand, falling into the bowl. She groped for the small tool before they slipped into the drain, caught them and tried again. She felt the barest give and applied more pressure. The tab gave a little more, then there was the unmistakable ripping sound of Velcro separating from its bonding material. The fastener closest to the instep was loose.

Judy held firmly to the heel of the shoe. "Try to pull out of it, Katie."

The small foot under Judy's hand wriggled but remained stuck.

"Look . . ." Shifting position, Mitch began to make a suggestion, but she wasn't listening to him.

"Try once more." Judy felt the heel of Katie's sock slip out of the shoe and shouted in delight. Katie squealed and with another wriggle was free.

Dan and Liz applauded while Mitch, both surprised and grudgingly impressed, pulled Katie up into his arms. He removed her wet sock and held her foot up to inspect it. Except for a little redness and a mild swelling on the instep it appeared unharmed.

"Does it hurt, Katie?" he asked.

"No." She wiggled it to show him. "But Big Bird?"

Judy reached into the bowl and wrenched the shoe out of its captivity. She held it aloft triumphantly, and there was more applause.

"Okay." Mitch put Katie on her feet. "Liz, help Katie with fresh socks and shoes, please, and put Big Bird in the laundry. Dan, will you put my tools back and pour some coffee?"

As the children disappeared, talking and laughing, Mitch helped Judy to her feet with his dry hand.

Pleased to be able to begin her job on a note of success, Judy smiled up into his eyes. But what she saw in them gave her a moment's pause.

Unused to having even such small matters taken out of his hands, Mitch was dealing with what he realized was an adolescent case of injured pride. Being bested with charm and a dazzling smile made him feel even more guilty about his resentment.

Before Judy could analyze the confusion in his eyes, he had yanked a green bath towel off the rack and offered her one end while he dried his hands on the other. His smile and his voice were slightly ironic as he said, "Welcome to the Kramer residence, Miss Cassidy."

Chapter Two

At opposite ends of the bath towel, Judy and her employer measured each other.

Judy saw a very handsome man. On his feet at last, Mitchell Kramer topped six feet, was sturdily built and fit, with biceps and pectoral muscles that filled the soft cotton fabric of his T-shirt. He was tanned from a life outdoors, though the sun had failed to lighten his dark brown hair. His eyes were hazel, a curious gold-to-green shade. His nose was straight and strong, his square chin a statement of self-sufficiency.

Mitch Kramer bore little resemblance to anyone's father that she had ever met, and even less to the summer employer she had imagined. He was gorgeous, but he wasn't sure he liked her. Judy read that as clearly as though it were another feature on his face.

Judy remembered his sister telling her that he was "a strong man" and acknowledged with a private smile that that probably meant a man who liked to take charge. No doubt she had offended him by freeing his daughter when he'd been unable to do it. She looked at him levelly, refusing to appear apologetic.

Mitch rested his hands on his hips and looked back at Judy Cassidy. He appreciated women who were confident and competent, as long as they didn't challenge him to prove that they were. He controlled a loud, big-fisted construction crew, and everyone in it recognized him as boss. It was easy to consider another well-muscled, six-foot man as competition, but this steely-eyed challenger probably weighed less than his fourteen-year-old son and didn't quite reach his chin. Mitch felt his usually formidable presence waver.

Then Judy said with sudden frankness, "I'm sorry, Mr. Kramer. I meant to help, not to interfere." Her smile held a hint of humor. "Shall I put Katie back in the toilet?"

A laugh escaped from him before he could stop it. She had read his mind and was teasing him about it. He looked silly and, after a moment's consideration, decided that he deserved to.

"Thank you, but I'd prefer to try to live with the fact that your solution worked better than mine." He swept a hand toward the hallway. "Shall we talk over coffee?"

When they reached the kitchen, there were two steaming mugs on a round table to one side of the large, well-equipped room. Dan stood near the table buttoning a clean shirt.

"I've got to get to work, Dad," he said, snatching his baseball cap off a kitchen chair.

"Right. Miss Cassidy, this young man who was rummaging in your purse is my son, Daniel. Dan, Miss Cassidy."

Judy offered her hand, and the boy took it. His grip was firm and his smile a trifle shy, though his eyes were bright and full of controlled mischief.

"He works at the grocery store in town every afternoon. He grabs lunch there, but he's usually home for dinner. If he makes other plans, he'll let you know."

Dan nodded. "You workin' this afternoon, Dad?"

"Yeah. I probably won't be home till late."

"Okay. See you then. Bye, Miss Cassidy."

Judy waved as the boy backed away toward the living room. "Call me Judy, Dan."

The boy nodded, waved and hurried away. Judy turned back to Mitch Kramer to find him holding a chair out for her at the table. The chivalrous gesture pleased her. She was seldom accorded such refinements in the teachers' lounge. And it was nice to know he didn't hold a grudge. She thanked him and sat, pulling a coffee cup toward her.

He moved his chair back from the table to allow him to stretch out his legs. "Are you prepared to start today, Miss Cassidy?" he asked. He reached for his cup and brought it to his lips. His voice was quiet and smooth.

Judy nodded. "If you like."

"I know this is a day early, but during the toilet bowl crisis—" he smiled "—I got a telephone call from the site. Seems we have a problem with a water line."

She nodded again, indicating that she understood his problem. "Then go, by all means. I can cope."

"You understand that cooking is part of your duties, as well?"

She hesitated just a moment before saying, "Yes."

He caught the small pause and frowned. "Your bio said you could cook."

"Well . . ." She lingered over the word and finally smiled honestly. "Not brilliantly, but if you don't require Cordon Bleu quality, I can cook."

He didn't look particularly pleased by her admission. She continued, "I explained it to your sister. It's just not one of my gifts. I've had a nutrition course, though, and I've supervised enough lunch periods in the cafeteria to know what kids like and what they hate. I'll see that the children get something palatable from all the food groups.''

He put his cup down and sat up in his chair. Judy expected a complaint about her lack of culinary skill, but instead he continued to list details of the children's routine. ''The kids are used to eating at six. Liz and Katie spend a lot of time across the street with a family that has girls close to their ages. They're not allowed on the beach without an adult. Dan obviously gets around a lot more, but I like to know where he's going and with whom. You'll get to know his friends, they're around a lot. Excursions on motorcycles or in cars are out.''

Judy nodded. That all made perfect sense.

''On the whole,'' he went on, ''they're great kids. But infractions of the rules will happen. You can handle them however you think best, but I'd like to know about it. The girls should be easy enough to deal with, but Dan can get testy when he's crossed. If you prefer, you can leave him to me. My work number is on the bulletin board by the phone. You can call me at any time for any reason.''

She nodded again. An accessible parent was a precious commodity to teacher or nanny.

''Questions?'' he asked.

''Yes. Are you usually home for dinner?'' Considering his apparent disapproval of her inability to cook, she considered it a logical question. ''Or will you be eating out?''

He studied her for a moment, and, seeing that the question was more of a tease than a taunt, he grinned. ''I'll see how the kids fare. If they remain healthy, I'll try coming home. For now, don't count on me. I often work late, catching up on paperwork in the trailer on the site. If I'm going to be home, I'll try to let you know. Would you like to see your room?''

Before Judy could reply, Liz shouted from the top of the stairs. "Daaad!"

Mitch closed his eyes, bracing himself. "Yeah?"

"Katie dumped the flowers. There's water all over the place!"

As he shook his head, Judy mentally applauded his steady nerves. Spilled water was hardly a catastrophe, but on the heels of the toilet incident, it might have rattled her, and she considered herself to be steadier than most.

"Coming," he called back. He stood and indicated the stairs as Judy rose, also. "The girls put flowers in your room this morning. In a very large coffee can, as I recall. Your bed may be under water."

Judy followed as he sprinted up the stairs. In a large room with a breathtaking view of the beach and the sunshot ocean, Liz was on her knees in front of a long oak dresser. With a large flowered bath towel, she dabbed at a saturated patch of deep pink carpeting. Katie held her bottle in one hand and a fat bunch of Queen Anne's lace in the other. At her feet was the toppled five-pound coffee can.

"Is not!" Katie was denying tearfully.

"It is too your fault," Liz retorted. "You got stuck in the toilet, and you dropped the flowers."

"You—" Katie began.

"What beautiful flowers!" Judy interrupted. She took the bouquet from Katie, touched that it had occurred to them to try to make her welcome. "Did you girls pick them?"

Liz looked up from her task to nod warily. "Katie wanted to," she said, quickly denying any hand in the gesture of welcome. "We got 'em from the side of the baseball field."

Seeing suspicion and a mild distrust in the light blue
eyes, Judy smiled, choosing to ignore it. To a child starting the school year, the teacher who replaced a mother
for so many hours every day deserved that look. There
was a lot to be proved before a child would trust whole-
heartedly. She understood, too, that a nanny who replaced a beloved aunt would receive the same watchful
mistrust.

"Well, I love them. Let's fill the can again and see how
they look." She extended her hand to Liz, who studied it
a moment, then took it and got to her feet. "Then we'll
get my bags and work on the carpet with my blow dryer.
You bring the can, Katie. Where's the bathroom?"

"You have your own." Liz led her to the far end of the
room and into a large, airy bath. "This is Aunt Glenna's
room, only she's in Europe."

Mitch followed as far as the doorway and allowed
himself a moment to study the trio gathered around the
sink. He had to give the new nanny credit. Just a few
words had stopped an argument, restored pride and
turned pouts to smiles. Well, at least Katie's pout.

"If you'll let me have your keys," he said, "I'll bring
your bags up."

Judy looked over her shoulder and pointed downstairs. "In my purse. I think I left it on the floor by the
kitchen table."

He ran down the stairs and found the object he'd
watched Dan rummage through in the bathroom. He
pushed aside long leather handles and searched for a ring
of keys.

He pulled out the small bag with the magic tweezers, a
tooled-leather wallet, a Sidney Sheldon paperback novel,
a lint brush and a steno pad with a pen pushed into its

wire binding. Dan was right, he thought. This was worse than his toolbox. In fact, it was worse than his closet.

He moved aside tissues and a checkbook and struck keys. With the feeling of having accomplished something major, he tossed the keys in his hand, found the one with the Plymouth emblem and went out to the small car parked behind his pickup.

He pulled two soft burgundy bags out of the trunk, and was surprised that she traveled light. He closed the trunk and laughed as he realized that it was probably because most of what she needed was in that bucket of a purse. Then he spotted a paint box in the back of the car and pulled it out, as well.

When Mitch put the bags on the bed, Judy and Katie were looking out the window, the child pointing to the field where she and Liz had picked the flowers. With a small yellow blow dryer in hand, Liz knelt on the carpet, working on the spot with frowning concentration. Upon seeing her father, she turned it off.

"Is this everything?" Mitch asked.

Judy turned away from the window with a smile, and Mitch felt it hit him like a puff of breeze on a hot, dry day.

Judy glanced at the two bags and the paint box. "That's it. I think we'll be all right, Mr. Kramer," she said, looking down at the girls for confirmation. They both nodded. "You may go."

The words sounded much more like a dismissal than the expression of control she had hoped to convey. Mitch raised an eyebrow.

"Sorry," she said quickly. "That did sound a little imperious, didn't it? I meant that I know you're anxious to get to the job."

"Thank you." He smiled as though still uncertain about her, then came across the room to kiss Katie and Liz. "I'll be home by nine." He held her keys out to her. "You'll have to move your car and let me out of the driveway."

"Of course." She took the ring from him and started for the stairs, Katie trailing after her. She noticed that Liz was watching them leave with a frown.

MITCH DROVE TO SEASIDE, squinting against the glare of the sun reflected off the chrome and windshields of cars. Well, that had been an interesting encounter, he thought. In the two years he'd been a widower, he'd had little contact wth women except those in his family and the wives of his friends. He felt he had made a reasonable adjustment to the loss of Mandy's physical presence, but all he'd loved about her—her sweetness, her generosity, the entirety of her love for him—still lived inside him, and he imagined always would.

He turned down the volume on the Willie Nelson tape filling his truck with music. He was startled by the fact that he had noticed Judy Cassidy. It wasn't that he felt a lustful longing for her or that she had awakened needs in him that hadn't surfaced in too long. It was simply that he had noticed her—the shine in her hair, the laughter in her eyes, the graceful lines and curves of her obviously well-cared-for body. He'd looked at her and made the conscious observation that she was an attractive woman.

Unsure whether to smile or frown, he recalled her teasing him about putting Katie back in the toilet. Then she'd made that crack about whether or not he'd be eating out. He had asked Glenna to make sure she could cook. Of course, Glenna had come home after the interview so full of praise, she'd probably forgotten to ask about that detail.

He just wasn't used to being teased by a woman. Mandy had never teased him or fought him for control. He was smart enough to know that she sometimes maneuvered situations so that he reached her decision, but she'd never stood toe-to-toe with him and grappled for the final say.

He'd never made a point of putting himself in a position of power, but he'd always had a knack for taking something abstract and turning it into reality. With that ability came people willing to work for him, willing to do things his way because it had been proven to achieve results. When he spoke, blueprints became buildings, and the children complied with his wishes. His wife had contributed her own ideas, but always concurred with his. He was used to being in control.

He smiled as he turned into a back street, then pulled up to the cavernous hole in the ground being dug for the foundation of the Franklin Office Complex. He was probably just hitting his mid-life crisis a little early. So he had noticed a woman, one who liked to take charge as he did. That was nothing momentous.

Life was moving along fairly comfortably at the moment, except for Glenna's absence. He let himself think about his sister for a minute, let himself miss her quiet competence and her skill in the kitchen. Then he pushed thoughts of her aside. She needed this trip, and he could certainly cope until she came home.

If the nanny could help him keep the kids and the house together through the summer, he'd have it made. Then everything would be back to normal. That was a comforting thought.

"WE CAN HAVE ICE CREAM for lunch," Katie told Judy with all-apparent sincerity. "And grape Kool-Aid."

On Judy's instructions, Liz was carefully pulling things out of the suitcases and giving them to her to put away in the closet with a built-in dresser. Liz was quiet but cooperative. Katie sat on the floor, clutching a stuffed cat in her arms—it had been Dale's birthday gift to Judy. Katie smiled winningly. "Daddy said so."

"He did not," Liz was quick to correct. "He said if you ate everything Judy gave you for lunch, you could have ice cream for dessert. We have to have milk with lunch." Liz handed Judy a pile of pastel lingerie. "Milk gives you good teeth and strong bones, you know."

Judy nodded as Liz went on. "Dad said we could have Kool-Aid with an afternoon snack, if you make it. Katie puts in too much sugar. Sugar makes you hyper."

"*She* never puts in enough." Katie stuck her tongue out at Liz, who'd gone back to the suitcase. "It tastes yucky."

Judy smiled at Liz as the child handed her a leotard and tights. She was beginning to see that Liz was not the typical eight-year-old busybody. She was sincerely concerned about her family and took her duties as oldest female seriously. Realizing that she was dealing with something a little more complex than simple mistrust, Judy accepted that Liz probably considered her an usurper and a threat to her position.

"Liz is right." Judy leaned over to pull open a bottom drawer and put her exercise gear inside. "Too much sugar isn't good for you. But I don't think it's much fun to live without any at all." Judy held up her hands. "Toss me the wrist weights, Liz."

Katie got on her knees to inspect them. "What are those?"

"You wear them when you exercise." Judy fitted one on Katie's small wrist, then laughed with her when the weight made her drop her arm. She pulled it off. "It helps you get strong muscles."

Liz approached, looking interested.

"Want to try one?" Judy asked.

After a moment's consideration, Liz held her wrist out, and Judy pushed the weight onto it. Liz flexed her puny bicep in imitation of a weight lifter. Katie giggled and Judy laughed. "Do you go to a gym?" Liz asked.

"I used to at home." Judy tossed the weights into the drawer then pushed it closed. She went back to the suitcase to see what remained, and the girls followed her. "But I brought a video tape with me." Judy pulled it out of her tote bag and held it up. "I'll work out in the mornings before breakfast."

Still clutching the cat, Katie frowned at her. "I watch cartoons before breakfast."

Liz rolled her eyes at her little sister. "There's another TV in the family room," she told Judy, inspecting the tape. "You can use that one. That's where the VCR is, anyway. This is Jane Fonda."

"Right."

Liz gave Judy's face a slow, sharp scrutiny. Judy saw her come to the conclusion that a nanny was a pain, but perhaps a health-conscious nanny could be useful. As though expecting to be denied the privilege, Liz asked with a tilt of her chin, "Can I work out with you?"

Progress, Judy noted as she pulled makeup, curling iron and other toiletries out of the tote. She walked into the bathroom, the small parade following her. "Sure. If you want to." She lined makeup and cologne on the countertop and stored everything else in the small cabinet under the sink.

Katie put herself between Judy and Liz. "Me, too?" she demanded.

"Of course. We'll have our own exercise class." The trio moved back into the bedroom. Judy stored her two cases in the bottom of the closet and put her paint box on a small desk in a corner of the room.

"Is that your rose..." Unable to remember the rest of the word, Liz finally abandoned it. "Your paint stuff?"

"Rosemaling." Surprised, Judy turned from the desk to look at her young charge. "How did you know that?"

"It was on the paper that told us about you."

"Oh, yes." Judy nodded, remembering the bio sheet. But she was still surprised. "And you know what that is?"

"Dad helped me look it up," Liz explained. "It's painting and carvings with flowers and hearts and stuff."

Judy had no trouble picturing the man helping his bright daughter add a new word to her vocabulary. It was easy to see how much he cared for his children and what an open and easy relationship they had.

"You can help me work on something sometime," Judy promised. Splashing paint always made a child forget his or her troubles—and doubts. "Now we'd better try to round up something for lunch."

After grilled cheese sandwiches and fruit, Liz and Katie took Judy across the street to meet their friends, two red-haired little girls who were busy disassembling a tricycle.

"Should they be doing that?" Judy whispered to Liz, frowning at the pile of parts.

"Their dad's a mechanic," Liz explained as they waved and walked away. "They're always taking something apart."

She led the way to a baseball field and showed Judy the deep border of Queen Anne's lace that had provided her bouquet. Dandelions and snapdragons grew there, as well.

"I'd like to have a garden," Liz said, kicking sand as they walked home along the beach. "But Dad says nothing will grow in the sand around our house."

"What about cactus?"

The girl frowned. "Cactus are ugly. I want flowers and green things."

"Flowers really do best outdoors in the sun, but you could have a plant in a pot in your bedroom."

Liz stopped, squinting up at Judy. "But if things can't grow in sand, they won't grow in sand in a pot will they?"

"You have to get some potting mix."

"What's that?"

Judy considered explaining the special components and nutrients, then decided a simple answer was best. "Dirt," she said.

Katie, still clutching her bottle, was fascinated. "You can buy dirt in a store?"

"It's a special kind." Judy took Katie's hand when they reached a clump of rocks and the child chose to go over them rather than around. "With special stuff in it for plants that live indoors."

"We used to have ivy," Liz said, following Katie, arms outstretched for balance. "On the wall in these pretty pots on both sides of the big window in the living room. It died..." Liz hesitated. A small frown appeared between her eyebrows, and then it was gone. "After Mom died. We all kept forgetting to water them. Daddy broke the pots."

Unsure what to say, Judy kept a firm grip on Katie, an eye on Liz, and waited quietly. "I broke something, too," Liz confessed.

"Oh?" Judy swung Katie to the ground when the rocks gave way to sand, and offered Liz a hand as she jumped down. "What was that?"

"Mom's picture."

"Well..." Knowing Liz was sharing an important confidence, Judy kept her eye on Katie, who ran ahead of them to inspect a sand dollar. "Sometimes breaking things makes you feel better when you're angry or hurt."

"I was mad," Liz admitted quietly, "because she went to the hospital and didn't come back. She said she would, but she didn't. Breaking the picture made me feel better for a minute." She looked up at Judy as though trying to decide whether or not to continue. When Judy didn't coax or prod, she added voluntarily, "Then I missed having it. Daddy had given it to me, and I was afraid to tell him I'd broken it."

"Did you?"

"Yeah." Liz smiled, the sunny, heartwarming smile of a child at peace with a difficult world because someone had helped her to understand. Then she sobered before going on. "That's when he told me what he did to the pots. He got me another picture. I'll show it to you. Aunt Glenna made me a frame for it."

The mood of the conversation changed almost instantly from gravity to contained excitement. "We're going to Bend in August. Me and Katie and Dan. Daddy's too busy to leave. Our Aunt Jackie and Uncle Bill have a ranch there, and we get to ride horses and swim in their pool and do lots of fun stuff."

Katie fell into step between Judy and Liz as they headed back to the house. Liz went on to explain in detail her aunt's plans for their visit the second and third weeks in August.

Able to listen and let her mind drift, Judy thought about her employer, left alone in his prime to raise three busy children and deal with a demanding world without the comforting arms of the woman he loved. She had to admire the job he'd done with the children. A teacher's job would be only half as difficult and twice as rewarding if there were more parents who gave their children the time and understanding he obviously did.

Was he seeing a woman now? Or several? Did he really work late at night, or was that an excuse to let off steam with his crew or trip the lights with a lady? What kinds of things did he like to do for recreation, she wondered?

The girls began to run, and Judy quickened her pace, reminding herself that she was here to do a job, not to gather data on her employer. What he did in the evening was none of her business. Quiet, complex men made her nervous, anyway.

Chapter Three

By evening Judy was convinced that she was beginning to get the job of nanny under control. Dan was home on time, and all three children praised her dinner of spaghetti and salad. Dan even had seconds. After dinner he went to the baseball field with friends, and Judy and the girls cleaned up the kitchen and loaded the dishwasher.

"How come Dan doesn't have to help?" Liz wanted to know.

"Because he has a job," Judy explained, pouring powdered soap into the built-in cup. "He's been working all afternoon. He deserves a little time to himself, don't you think?"

Liz frowned, declining to comment. Katie handed Judy her small bowl with a picture of Snoopy on the bottom. In her other hand was the ever-present bottle.

Judy placed the bowl in the machine, then pointed to the bottle. "Do you want to give me that so we can wash it, too?"

"No." Katie looked horrified. "Aunt Glenna just puts it under the faucet."

"But it had milk in it. Bacteria...germs grow in milk. We have to wash it so that it doesn't make you sick."

"No." Adamant, Katie now held the bottle in both hands behind her back.

"She won't give it up," Liz told Judy. "Daddy and Aunt Glenna have tried everything. She'll just scream until you give it back."

Judy considered the belligerent but teary-eyed little girl. "Will you let me wash it in the sink then, with hot water and soap?"

Suspicious after Judy's initial suggestion, Katie eyed her warily. Judy lifted her onto the counter near the sink. "You can sit right here and watch me do it."

Katie handed over the bear-shaped bottle reluctantly, looking prepared to jump into the sink after it should Judy make a suspicious move.

"The dishwasher would do a much better job of this," Judy explained as she scrubbed the bottle, "because the hot water would kill all the germs. But this will do it pretty well. When we go shopping for Liz's plant, we'll look for a pretty cup you can use when you're ready to part with this bottle."

Katie gave her a measuring look, apparently realizing with a child's insight that she was being carefully handled. Judy pinched her chin with a sudsy finger. "But we won't rush you. We'll just have it around for when you're ready."

When Judy had rinsed and dried the bottle, Katie took it back and tucked it possessively into the crook of her arm.

The telephone rang, and Liz stood on tiptoe to answer it. "Hi, Daddy!" she said, twirling the cord around her index finger. "Yeah, everything's fine. If it's okay with you, we're gonna go shopping tomorrow and buy a plant and a pretty pot for my room and a cup for Katie."

Continuing to fill the dishwasher, Judy kept an ear on the conversation. Liz listened a moment and said, "She took it away, but just took it to wash it. She wanted to put it in the dishwasher, but Katie wouldn't let her. So she washed it in the sink. She's gonna buy Katie a cup to use when she finally stops drinking out of her bottle. Yeah, Katie's right here."

Judy groaned silently, wondering if her employer was convinced that the busybody nanny was trying to cure Katie of her bottle dependency on her first day of employment.

Smiling, Katie reached up to take the receiver from her sister. "Hi, Daddy. Fine. We walked on the beach, and we had sketti for dinner." She, too, listened a moment. "I think so. Wait." Katie looked at Judy. "Have we been good?"

Judy smiled, closing and locking the dishwasher door. "Yes, very good."

"Did you hear that?" Katie asked into the receiver. "She said, 'yes, very good.' Is it almost time for you to come home?" Katie listened again, then looked at the large round kitchen clock. "When the little hand is where? Okay. Yeah, Judy's right here. Bye, Daddy."

As Judy took the telephone, the girls ran into the living room to turn on the television.

"Hello," she said politely.

"Miss Cassidy, is everything all right?" Judy could hear voices and activity in the background.

"Yes, fine," she replied. "The girls have been wonderful."

"Dan get home for dinner?"

"Yes. Right on time. He's at the baseball field with..." She probed her mind for the names of the friends she'd been introduced to. "Kenny Farmer and ... Sandy..."

"Dusty?"

"That's it. Dusty Carter. He promised to be home by nine."

"Good. Well..." He paused to reply quietly to something he'd been asked on the other end of the line. "Sounds like you have everything under control."

She heard the smallest trace of irony in his voice. Determinedly she ignored it. "Yes. Things are going well. I forgot to ask you about bedtime."

"I'm loose about bedtimes in the summer. The girls might or might not go to bed before I get home, and Dan's always up for the late movie. I should be home by nine. Good night, Miss Cassidy."

"Good night, Mr. Kramer." Judy hung up the phone, surprised that he hadn't asked her about Katie's bottle.

DAN WAS DRAPED sideways in an overstuffed chair when his father came home just before nine. Liz ran to the door, trailed by Katie, who'd been fighting sleep for the past hour, determined to greet her father.

Judy looked up from the sketch pad in her lap when Mitch walked into the room, his hand on Liz's head, Katie slung over his hip. She felt awkward, unsure what was required of her at this point. Should she disappear and let him spend some time with his children? Or would he want her to stay to put them to bed?

"Hi, Dad," Dan said from the chair without looking away from the television.

"Hi, son." He rapped Dan lightly on the head as he passed his chair. Halfway into the room, he sniffed the air. "Fresh coffee?" he asked, obviously pleased at the prospect.

"Yes." Judy smiled, happy that she'd done something right. She had thought it was something he'd enjoy, coming home so late. "Shall I pour you a cup?"

"Please."

He followed her into the kitchen, sinking into a chair, Katie straddling his knee. He looked tired but gorgeous, Judy thought, determinedly keeping her eyes on the task of getting a mug and pouring coffee. Dishevelment added a dimension of sexuality to his dark good looks.

"Judy wanted to get the Germans out of my bottle," Katie reported, holding her bottle up for her father's inspection. She was leaning sleepily against him. "But I wouldn't let her. Is it okay if they're still in there?"

Mitch looked at the bottle, then up at Judy as she brought his coffee. A smile teased at his mouth. "Germans?"

"I tried to talk her into letting me put the bottle in the dishwasher to get the germs out of it."

"Ah." He smiled, looking boyish and dangerously sexy at the same time. "Dan's convinced she'll be taking her bottle to the junior prom."

Judy brought sugar and cream to the table and sat opposite him, leaning toward him on folded arms.

"About the cup," she said earnestly. "If you don't think it's a good idea—"

"The cup?" It took him a moment to follow her. "Oh, yeah. Liz said something on the phone about buying Katie a cup."

She explained her theory. "And maybe if it's somewhere visible, she'll want to use it more than she'll want to keep her bottle."

He considered that a moment and nodded. "Nothing has worked so far. Maybe that will. It's worth a try. And Liz seemed excited about getting a plant for her room."

"It's fun to watch things grow." She indicated the child now sound asleep in his lap. "Children and plants. Would you like me to put Katie to bed?"

Mitch shifted Katie so that she looked more comfortable. "No, I'll just hold her for a while and finish my coffee."

He'd like to invite Judy to remain across the table from him, Mitch thought. He'd like her to have a cup of coffee and tell him how she had fared with his children and what she thought of them. Then he remembered that she'd been watching them since midmorning after a very long drive. It was now after nine. She had to be exhausted.

"You can go, Miss Cassidy. I'll put the girls to bed. Thank you for making the coffee."

Had she been dismissed or excused? Judy wasn't sure. The position of nanny was a problem that had been faced by innumerable women for several centuries. The nanny was not a member of the family, yet was required to be present as long as the children were. She felt as though her status were somewhere between that of domestic and a relative in disfavor. She wanted to be there to do her job, yet she didn't want to intrude upon the familial relationships. The position required a delicacy she hadn't anticipated and wasn't entirely sure how to handle.

Mitch noted the confusion in Judy's eyes as she said good-night to the girls and Dan. With a frown he watched her walk toward the stairs. Complicated woman, he thought, and communicating with her was tricky. But the children seemed to like her, and that was what counted.

JUDY WAS UP at six the following morning, grateful to find the house quiet. She didn't know what time Mitch

Kramer rose, but judging by the silence, he was neither stirring around in the kitchen nor showering. Dressed in black tights and a turquoise-and-black leotard, Judy made her way quietly to the family room, tugging on her wrist weights, her exercise tape tucked under her arm.

She had just put the tape in the VCR and turned the sound down to barely audible when the girls appeared, whispering and giggling. Liz wore shorts and a tank top, and Katie was still in cotton sleepers. They were sleep-flushed, their hair tumbled. Katie's eyes were bright and full of laughter, Liz's still watchful, reserving judgment.

"I thought you were going to watch cartoons," Judy teased Katie quietly.

The child's shoulders hunched up as she giggled. "Lizzie says it's heal-thier to do robics with you."

Though she knew her workout would suffer from their company, Judy felt the affection for them that was already growing inside her and was happy they had chosen to join her.

She positioned a child on each side of her, an arm's width away, and directed them to keep their eyes on the television. "Don't overdo," she directed, stretching her arms. "Stop if you get tired. And save questions for the breaks, okay?"

The warm-up stretches were easy. The girls found those fun and their pliable little bodies moved easily and with unconscious grace. Just beginning to perspire, Judy tried not to resent their flexibility. With much comment and laughter, Liz and Katie followed her through the preliminary aerobic moves. Then the serious work began. The quick movements and the bending and stretching were breath-stealers, and Judy made a point of concentrating on the music to ignore her discomfort. Imagining herself in some slinky Paris original helped considerably.

Sipping at a glass of orange juice, Mitch followed the
faint sound of music and the not-so-faint sound of giggles. He stopped short in the doorway to the family
room. The picture Judy presented widened his eyes and
kick- started his body with more efficiency than his usual
jolt of caffeine. As his pulse settled down to a mildly furious pace, he leaned against the doorway and decided
that he'd never seen a more provocative derriere in his
life.

Fascinated, Mitch watched as she jumped, kicked, ran
in place, stretched, bent over. She caught her ankles, her
short, damp hair reaching toward the floor. She closed
her eyes, groaning as she extended into the stretch, then
opened them and saw him. He did not try to pretend that
he hadn't been staring. In fact, he was thinking that '*attractive woman*' didn't begin to cover it.

Judy stared back at him for a moment in her upside-
down pose then unfolded slowly to a standing position
and reached over to turn off the VCR. There was no reason to be embarrassed, she told herself firmly as she
turned to face her employer. She was wearing more than
most women wore at the beach. But even upside-down,
she had noted a distinctly appreciative look in his eyes.
He had looked anything but mysterious.

Mitch would have guessed that it would be difficult to
look cool and controlled while breathing hard in tights
and a leotard, but Judy managed. Taking a towel from
the chair, she wrapped it around her neck, sheened with
perspiration, and dabbed at her cheek with one end.

"I'm sorry," she said. "Did we wake you?"

"No, of course not." He indicated the girls with his
juice glass. "I heard them giggling and thought I'd better see what they were doing. I wasn't sure you'd be up
yet."

"Hi, Daddy!" Katie ran to him, wrapping her arms around his thigh.

"This...is...good...for...your...batteries," Liz puffed, jogging toward him.

"Arteries," he corrected.

"Oh, yeah." Liz stopped, collapsing against his waist. "We're gonna do this...every morning."

Mitch leaned down to hug both girls.

"Can we go have our juice?" Liz asked.

"Sure." He released them and pushed them gently toward the kitchen. "But leave some for Miss Cassidy."

"It's okay to call her Judy," Katie informed her father. "She said so." Then she added with little-girl authority, "And she could call you Daddy."

Liz groaned despairingly and pulled her little sister from the room. "You are so dumb!" she exclaimed as she closed the door behind them.

"Maybe you'd rather call me Mitch," he suggested with a laugh as he sat on the arm of the sofa. "I apologize. I didn't mean to interrupt your session."

He appeared to settle in for conversation, and Judy stood uncertainly in the middle of the room, fiddling with the end of her towel, unsure just what he wanted. "That's all right. That was probably all the girls should do anyway."

Observing her uncomfortable stance, Mitch gestured to the sofa. "Do you have time to talk for a few minutes?"

"Of course." Sitting on the middle cushion, Judy put her hands in her lap and waited.

"Is your room comfortable?" he asked.

She nodded. "Oh, more than comfortable. Thank you."

"Do you have everything you need?"

"Everything."

"Last night," he said cautiously, "I thought I detected some...problem...or confusion when I came home. Did you have trouble with the kids?"

"No," she denied quickly, making a nervous gesture with her hands as she remembered how unsure she had felt of her next move. Uncertainty was a new feeling for her. "It was just, well, it's kind of a silly problem. I mean, I've never been a nanny before and..." She looked at him with sudden urgency. "Your sister did explain that to you?"

"Yes," he replied. "But she trusted you, and I trust her."

"Okay, well." Relying on that quietly spoken vote of confidence, she cleared her throat and went on. "I guess I'm just not sure what my position is. I mean, when you come home, should I disappear, or should I stay—" she groped for a word "—handy if you need something? I hate to intrude if you need private time with your children, but on the other hand, you did hire me to..."

He was watching her with an expression that showed he was as amused by her problem as he was interested in it. She could certainly understand that; she was speaking less clearly than Katie. She shook her head despairingly. "I'm not making any sense, am I?"

"I think I understand." He nodded, suddenly taking the matter more seriously. "Can't you just think of yourself as a member of the household?" he asked. "You're entitled to be wherever the children are, whether or not I'm here. If I need privacy, I'll let you know. Just make yourself at home. With my sister gone, your presence is making it possible for me to be at my job at a very critical time. We're pleased to have you."

She smiled ruefully. "I don't think Liz is."

Again he seemed to understand. "She does her best to mother us. I suppose she feels a little threatened. But she's a sweet kid. She'll come around." Glancing at his watch, he whistled and took a bill out of the pocket of his chambray shirt. "For the trip to Seaside," he said, handing it to her.

She shook her head, trying to hand it back to him. "For a plant and a clay pot? I can take care of—"

"And a cup for Katie. And don't think the girls are going to let you go by the bakery without stopping. If there's change, keep it for later excursions." He got to his feet. Judy followed. "I'd better get moving. I'll be late again. Drive carefully. And keep your eye on Katie. She can disappear in a flash."

Mitch opened the door and stood face-to-face with a disheveled Dan in brightly colored shorts and a pink T-shirt.

"When's breakfast?" Dan asked through half-closed eyelids. Then he spotted Judy standing behind his father in tights and leotard. His eyes opened and stared. Mitch put his hands on Dan's shoulders as the boy tried to lean around him for a closer look. "I think I'm in love, Dad."

"Mmm." Mitch exchanged a grin with Judy. "Yesterday it was with Chelsea Miller."

Still staring at Judy, Dan puckered his brow thoughtfully. "Arabs have lots of wives."

"You're Irish and German," Mitch pointed out.

Dan straightened and looked disgustedly at his father. "And who's fault is that? Just can't count on you in the crunch, Dad. Aren't you late?"

"Yeah." Mitch moved into the kitchen and filled a commuter mug with coffee. "Judy and I were talking."

"Uh-huh." Dan looked with mock suspicion from his father to Judy. "Behind a closed door, I noted. What would Brenda say to that?"

Mitch frowned at his son, pulling car keys out of his pocket. "Don't forget that you're due at the store at nine this morning." He headed for the front door, cautiously sipping at his cup.

When the screen door slammed behind Mitch, Dan turned to Judy. "I suppose running away with me is out of the question?"

Judy patted his shoulder. "I have to take a shower, and you have to go to work. Maybe another time. Have some juice. I'll be down in fifteen minutes to fix breakfast."

LEE MADISON WAVED a clipboard in front of Mitch's nose. "Better look at this," he said tersely as Mitch took the board. Then he turned to walk away.

"What's the problem?" Mitch scanned the invoice.

"Read it!" Lee barked over his shoulder. "It's self-explanatory."

"Look!" Mitch grabbed his foreman's arm and yanked him back. "We can't work like this, Lee. If you've got something to say, spit it out."

Lee's blue eyes flamed in a grimy, sweat-streaked face as he glared at Mitch and yanked his arm free. "What does a man say to the friend who's making time with his wife?"

Mitch's eyes hardened, and temper rose in him with hot force. He had known that was what Lee would think, had even known that was what Brenda intended, but hearing the words spoken aloud caused a reaction in him he hadn't expected.

"I'm her friend, as well as yours." Mitch made himself speak calmly. "She needs someone to talk to."

Lee studied him evenly, eyes dark and grim. For an instant his anger wavered, then he shifted his weight and shook his head. "You paying me thirty-two dollars an hour to stand here and talk?"

Mitch tightened his grip on the clipboard to avoid making a fist. "No, I'm not. Get to work."

As Lee sprinted back to the excavation, Mitch considered the dangerous traps one could fall into when trying to help a friend. He thought about Brenda Madison, his foreman's estranged wife, who was undermining a valuable friendship by using him to make Lee jealous.

Her intention had been transparent to him from the beginning, and he had chosen to take a watchful role in Brenda's plan. Glenna had warned him against it, but Lee and Brenda were his friends, and he hated seeing them draw further and further apart.

Suddenly, superimposed on his thoughts, was an image of Judy Cassidy in her leotard. He concentrated on it a moment, before grumbling impatiently at himself and heading for the trailer to look over the invoice.

Chapter Four

"You mean Buns and Bosoms Brenda?" Liz asked Judy. They were in a garden shop in Seaside, selecting a flowerpot in which to transplant the three small starts of philodendron in their shopping basket. The child's candid assessment of the mysterious Brenda had other shoppers turning around and grinning.

"Liz!" Judy scolded while trying not to laugh.

"Well, it's true," she replied, her hyacinth eyes all wide and innocent. Judy was pleased to note that the child seemed less cautious of her today. "She has bosoms out to here." She exaggerated wildly by putting her small hands a foot away from her chest. "And she walks like this." She proceeded to demonstrate by swinging her tiny, jeans-clad bottom in an impossible arc.

Katie giggled hysterically, and it was all Judy could do to maintain her own composure.

"She wears these dresses that show *everything*!" Liz added with dramatic intonation, then returned her attention to a selection of glazed, hand-painted pots. She took down a small one. "She used to be married to Lee, and she was nice then. Now she comes to see Daddy a lot, and she acts different. He says they're working on a project together. Do you think this one would be big enough?''

Judy turned her mind from cynical speculation on the nature of the project and looked up at the array of pots. She reached over her head to take down a long, window-box shaped container.

"What about this?" She held it down for Liz to inspect. "Philodendrons love to sprawl and hang. Who's Lee?"

"Daddy's foreman. It's big. Do we have enough money?"

"This plain big one doesn't cost any more than the decorated small one. And we can paint it and make it look even prettier than those."

Liz considered that with a suspicious smile. "Really?"

Katie slapped her bottle against Judy's leg. "I want one, too."

"You won't take care of it," Liz accused.

Katie folded her arms, her fine, platinum eyebrows drawing together. "I want one."

Judy took a small round pot off the shelf and handed it to the child. "How about that one? And a philodendron like Liz's?"

Katie grinned her approval, and, with her bottle in one hand and a plant in the other, led the way to the checkout counter.

At a small gift shop on the busy main street that ran perpendicular to the beach, Katie pretended disinterest in the selection of a cup. While Judy and Liz inspected a shelf of brightly colored mugs, she sat on the floor, staring earnestly into the face of a stuffed bear leaning against a display.

Rejecting all the mugs with simple initials, funny sayings or flowers, Judy finally spotted one she thought would be perfect. A string of rosebuds bordered a depiction of animals at a tea party. A lion in a dress coat and bow tie presided over a table where mice toasted each other with demitasses, a rabbit with a bow in her hair chatted with a cat holding a parasol, and a pig and a frog, both in morning coats, held an earnest discussion over their tea. In the bottom of the cup, the cat with the parasol awaited discovery when the contents were consumed.

"Isn't this perfect?" Judy handed it to Liz, who turned it in her hands and smiled. "Katie, come and look."

"I'm busy," she replied, still in conference with the bear.

Not to be discouraged, Judy bought the cup. Then the trio headed for the bakery.

"Maple bars!" Katie chinned herself on the counter and ordered for herself. "Three of them."

"Make that one," Judy corrected, smiling apologetically at the clerk as she pulled Katie off the display case. "And a cheese croissant. Liz?"

"A cinnamon roll. And we should take home apple fritters for Dan and Daddy."

The order placed, they sat at a small round table and admired their purchases. Katie stared at her small clay pot while Judy and Liz exclaimed over the mug. Katie glanced their way, Judy noted, her eyes covetous as they went over the fanciful, colorful mug. Then she turned away to replace her pot in the sack and concentrate on her maple bar.

They were home by lunchtime and spent the afternoon on a blanket on the stretch of beach near the house, deciding on a pattern to paint on Liz's flower box.

"It should have pink it it, 'cause my room is pink," Liz said as the three went into the house, dragging beach towels and blanket. "And purple, 'cause I love purple."

Only half listening, Judy was trying to remember what she had seen in the refrigerator and the cupboards. She should have given more thought to dinner, but they'd had such fun in the shops at Seaside and then on the beach that it had slipped her mind, which wasn't entirely attuned to cooking, anyway.

"They're not traditional in rosemaling, but I've got both those colors. That'll be easy. And we can use silver and a little—oof!" She'd been making a beeline for the kitchen, her eyes still adjusting from the outside glare to the quiet shadows of the house, when she ran into something tall and angular. Strong hands took hold of her arms to steady her, and she looked up into quiet hazel eyes.

As she collided with him, Mitch was aware first of all of the fragrance of a coconutty sunscreen. Then he noticed the smell of salt and sand—and the indefinable scent of woman. The subtle muskiness of Judy's warm body piqued his nostrils and made him hold her arms several seconds after she'd regained her balance.

He saw that her nose was now covered with freckles. Tortoise-shell combs held back the sides of her short hair, curly little tendrils of rich brown brushing against her cheekbones. Shiny grains of sand clung to her cheeks and her bottom lip. Wearing a yellow halter top and white shorts, she could have been Liz and Katie's older sister.

In a gesture he couldn't stop, though he tried hard to make it casual, Mitch ran a thumb over her bottom lip, brushing off the sand. Then he dropped his hands as sudden confusion and a nagging little pang of guilt startled him out of his trance.

"You ladies have a good time?" he asked, taking a step back.

"Wait'll you see the neat stuff we got!" Liz exclaimed.

The girls ran upstairs to get their purchases, and Judy couldn't quite decide what to do with the queen-size blanket draped over her arm. She had to do something with it, to prevent herself from touching her hand to her mouth where his thumb had been. Under his interested gaze, she gathered it up in her arms and saw sand fall to the carpet.

"I'll vacuum that right after I've fixed dinner," she said, hurrying past him into the kitchen. She deposited the blanket in the service porch and washed her hands. Mitch followed her to the sink. Her confusion helped stabilize his own curious reaction to her.

"What's on the menu?" he asked, leaning against the counter.

Judy looked into the refrigerator, then the cupboard. "Well," she said, frowning, "we could have hot dogs and pickled beets, or bacon and garbanzo beans. With alphabet soup." She offered a tentative smile to her employer. "And we bought apple fritters for dessert."

Uncertain if his continued silent study of her represented simple attention or displeasure with her poor plans for dinner, Judy sighed and smiled again, this time apologetically. "I guess I wasn't exactly tending to business today. We had a fun afternoon, and I forgot to take stock of the cupboards. I'll go shopping tomorrow and promise to be better prepared in the future."

The sounds of running and laughter filtered into the kitchen as the girls ran down the stairs with their purchases.

With a sudden smile, Mitch tilted his head toward the sound. "They're your first order of business, and they seem to be pleased with how the day went. And you weren't expecting me home anyway. I was supposed to have a dinner meeting tonight with the owner of the building we're putting up, but he cancelled."

Liz and Katie backed Mitch up against the counter, holding up their flowerpots and plants.

"And I have a new cup," Katie announced, pulling her father along to the spot on the hutch where Judy had placed it.

Mitch took the cup down and inspected the design. "It's very pretty. When are you going to use it?"

Katie looked up at it as Mitch replaced it on the shelf. "I can't use it and my bottle at the same time."

"That's true."

"Maybe tomorrow."

"Good."

"Did you see the kitty inside?"

"Yes, I did."

"She has a parachute." Katie informed him. "That's like an umbrella for the sun."

"A parasol," Mitch corrected, enunciating the last syllable. "A parachute is for jumping out of airplanes."

"We going skydiving?" Dan demanded as he wandered into the kitchen, the slam of the front door reverberating through the house. "I can't believe there's going to be some action around here at last. What're you doing home, Dad?"

"Change of plans," Mitch explained, putting up an arm to block a mock punch Dan aimed at him. His fist landed in the man's hand with enough force to make Judy grateful Mitch had intercepted it. "We're going out to dinner. Pizza?"

"Yeah!" The girls agreed excitedly. Mitch pushed them gently toward the stairs. "Okay. Go with Judy to get changed. Dan and I'll be in the car."

"We're not going skydiving?" Dan asked in feigned disappointment as Judy followed the girls.

Mitch hooked an arm around his son's neck and pulled him toward the door. The boy pretended to struggle. "Dan, who in his right mind would jump out of a plane that wasn't on fire?"

AT PASQUALE'S PIZZERIA outside of Manzanita, Dan and Liz sat on opposite sides of a video game, with Katie kibitzing. Sharing a carafe of rosé wine, Mitch and Judy faced each other across a rough wooden table. The smells of tobacco and beer, and the taunting spiciness of the many pizza garnishes filled the room.

Mitch studied Judy in her soft white sweater and jeans. The combs were gone from her hair, which curled away from her face in fluffy, attractive disorder. She wore shiny white square earrings and seemed to have completely lost that gamine look she'd had when she walked into the house from the beach. She looked capable again, though more relaxed than she'd been yesterday and this morning. That very particular self-sufficiency was not something he was used to seeing in a woman's eyes, at least not those women who interested him, and he felt a need to discover why it was there.

"Your bio says you've been teaching for nine years," he said.

She pulled her eyes away from the children, who were arguing over the score. "Yes." She felt the impact of his good looks as she turned to him. Weren't fathers supposed to be fiftyish and a little paunchy? She smiled. "I

love teaching. I'll probably still be teaching when I'm
ninety and using a walker.''

He looked into her sunny expression and shook his
head. ''It's impossible to think of you as ninety. It's even
hard to think of you as thirty.''

''Thirty-one.''

''Right. Has there never been a boyfriend or husband
to try to separate you from this dedication?''

She sipped at her wine and shook her head. ''It can't
be done. My course was plotted a long time ago.''

Mitch considered her over his wineglass. ''I imagine
you were as capable a little girl as you are a woman. You
probably decided to become a teacher at five years old
and determined then and there that nothing would stand
in your way.''

''Close,'' she admitted, laughing. ''I was seven. I told
my mother, and she started saving for my education.''
Judy sobered slightly and looked into her glass, a smile
of reminiscence on her face. ''Now *there* was a capable,
determined woman.''

Sensing that she would stop there if he didn't prod,
Mitch said quietly, ''Tell me about her.''

Judy pushed her wineglass out of the way and folded
her arms on the table, still smiling. ''I suppose to anyone else, she might seem unremarkable. But to Mike and
me, she could have been president of the United States.''

''Mike?''

''My twin.'' Mitch nodded, and she went on. ''Mom
was half-Norwegian and half-Irish and was brought up
in a little fishing village in northern Washington. Our
father, a logger, died before we were old enough to store
memories of him.''

She drew a deep breath but continued to smile, as
though something about that revelation required more

comment. Then, with an inclination of her head, she decided against it. "My mother raised us by herself, cheerfully, instilling in us the belief that we could do whatever we wanted to do."

"Where's your brother now?"

"In Virginia. He's a nuclear physicist."

Mitch groaned. "I don't even understand my digital watch."

A giggle that completely surprised him escaped from her. "I know. He's given up trying to explain to me what he does. When we get together, we always talk about other things. Anyway, our mother was a seamstress in a garment factory all the time we were growing up. She did well because her work was finer and done more quickly than everyone else's, but piecework is a demanding way to make a living. The factory was hot and unventilated, the hours long, fringe benefits few. I worked there as a sort of gofer a couple of summers in high school, and I came to really appreciate how hard she worked for us."

Judy shook her head, as though trying to shake off sadness. "She died right after I started teaching. She never seemed to mind what she had missed. She had Mike and me, and because we had dreams, she had dreams." Judy paused a moment, and her eyes focused on Mitch. "Or is it because she had dreams for us that we have dreams? I was never sure which came first."

He smiled gently. "I doubt that it matters, as long as you both had them."

She nodded. "I guess not. But she lived *for* us, and not for herself." Her expression firmed, and he began to understand what had given her her strength. "I have always felt driven by that. That kind of generosity is hard to comprehend, even when you're the recipient. You know, Glenna reminds me of my mother." She played with the folds of a napkin, glancing up at him as he watched her. "She's about the same age and has that same—I don't know—sweetness, I guess it is, of someone who lives her life for others. During the two hours she interviewed me, she talked about the children and you and a little about . . . about your wife. . . ."

Judy hesitated. Not wanting to explore the subject either, Mitch waited for her to go on.

"But not a word about herself." For a moment Judy carefully examined the fan she had pleated out of the napkin, then smiled at Mitch. "You'd be gratified to hear her talk about you. She thinks you're Robert Redford, Frank Lloyd Wright and Pope John Paul II, all rolled into one."

He laughed aloud. "A slight exaggeration. I doubt that the pope swears." Anxious to divert the conversation from himself, he began to ask a question but was interrupted by Liz, who was pleading for more quarters. He gave her one. When she began to protest that one wasn't enough, he said patiently, "Our pizza will be ready any time now. One more game, then I want you guys back to the table. And keep it down," he added as she hurried back to the game. He turned his attention to Judy.

"Glenna said something about your going back to school in the fall."

"To Oxford for my master's in European history." She said it casually, but Mitch got the feeling that she really wanted to shout it out loud and laugh for joy.

He raised an eyebrow. Glenna had mentioned that. He'd gone to Portland State and never longed to roam farther, but he was firmly convinced that those who felt the need should—like his son, whose dream was to be in space. "I presume this isn't a privilege accorded everyone."

She shrugged. "You have to work hard for the opportunity. I'm going with a fellow teacher who's after a degree in languages. He's wealthy and sailing in Newport this summer," she went on, smiling. "But I'm not, so I'm working as a nanny to make money. My school district will pay me half of my regular salary while I'm on sabbatical, and that will help me meet my living expenses. But if I want to see anything of Europe while I'm there and bring back any treasures, I'll need a little more. I've saved some, but not enough to loaf this summer."

"Why European history?" he asked, fascinated by what he was learning about her.

She responded enthusiastically. "Because it's part of what so many of us are. My great-grandparents on my... my father's side were Italian immigrants and full of stories about the old country. My grandfather on the other side escaped from Dublin with a bankroll and a hangman in pursuit." While Mitch laughed and toasted the gentleman, Judy continued. "My grandmother was sent from Norway on a ship, and then overland to her uncle in Seattle. Attached to her coat, there was a tag with his address, because she spoke no English. Can you imagine what kind of courage that took? What strong and exciting people they were. Europe is where they all began."

Mitch shook his head, grinning. "If only you were more excited about it."

Judy laughed. "I'm sorry, but you asked."

"Aren't you guys paying attention?" Dan demanded, leaning across his father to take the stub with the number of their pizza order on it. "They've called our number twice. Dad—" Dan patted his shoulder consolingly "—I thought the legs were supposed to go first at your age, not the hearing."

Mitch grabbed his son by the back of his shirt as the boy turned away. "You know what goes first at your age?"

"The allowance," Dan replied. "You don't have to remind me. Dad, I'm starved."

Mitch let him go and rolled his eyes at Judy. "He reminds me of my father-in-law."

"Oh?"

"Brains and nerve and a line that's made him the biggest name in real estate in Oregon." Mitch poured himself more wine. "He's a great guy, you just have to be operating on all cylinders to be around him."

Questions crowded Judy's mind. Was your wife like him? Did you meet her through him in some connection with your business? But judging by his silence a few moments ago when she had mentioned his wife, she presumed he'd prefer not to discuss her. Anyway Dan was back with the pizzas, and the girls took their places, full of laughter and conversation, swapping mushrooms for pineapple and hot sausage for Canadian bacon. Judy no longer had time to wonder about anything if she hoped to protect her dinner.

"DON'T FORGET PEPSI." Dan looked over Judy's shoulder as he tossed a baseball into his gloved hand with a sound *thwack!* "And cantaloupe. And chocolate. Have you got chocolate?"

At the kitchen table, Judy scribbled feverishly in the small space left at the bottom of her grocery list.

"Peanut butter?" Katie was kneeling on a chair beside her. "And jelly?"

"Green grapes," Liz contributed, leaning over Judy. When Liz saw that she had put an arm around the nanny's shoulders, she quickly drew it back though she didn't move away. Judy pretended not to notice.

"Okay, that's it." Judy pushed away from the table, folding the list and putting it in her straw bag. "If we bring home any more than this, your father will have to build an addition to the house just to store it." She looked doubtfully at Dan's ball and glove. "Aren't you due at work at noon?"

"Day off," he said, heading for the door. "The guys and I are meeting at the field. But I'll be home for dinner. See ya."

"Okay, girls." Judy shouldered her purse, car keys in hand. "On to the market."

"I get to ride in the basket!" Katie shouted, holding the door open for Judy and Liz.

"I get to push it," Liz said.

Two hours later Judy and the girls returned home with every meat, fruit and vegetable known to man, several kinds of cereal, everything else that was on their list and a few things that were not. The bill had startled Judy to a pallor. She hoped her employer wouldn't think she had overspent.

Everything was finally put away, and a ham and potatoes were baking in the oven. Judy was about to suggest to Liz and Katie that they spend an hour on the beach when Dan and his friends trooped in through the back door. The sound of their entrance was at a decibel level that probably registered on the East Coast.

Dan opened the refrigerator door and said in amazement, "Kool-Aid?"

Judy nodded. "Help yourselves. Cookies in the jar, too."

"Aunt Glenna fixes iced tea and health bars."

"They taste like horse food," one of Dan's friends said. Judy guessed that it was Dusty. He bit into an Oreo approvingly, chewed and swallowed, giving her a big smile. "I mean, she's a nice lady and all, but I don't miss her cookies. Welcome to Manzanita, Judy."

"Thanks." Judy turned away from the smudges on the refrigerator door, making a mental note to get rid of them before her employer arrived home. "How'd the game go?"

"Depends on how important winning is to you," Kenny said dryly. "Our ace hitter is spending the summer with his grandmother in Denver. Now we have to go back and lose the second game."

Judy checked the kitchen clock. "Can anybody play?"

"Yeah," Dan said cautiously. "We've got little kids, kids our age, and Dusty's brother is a college freshman. Mr. Corbett, the retired police chief, even umps for us once in a while."

She smiled. Add a beagle and it sounded like the Peanuts gang in action. "Want to put us in your lineup?" Judy indicated herself and the girls.

Dan and his friends exchanged a look of pained reluctance. "Ah, Judy, we . . ."

"Come on." She pushed everyone toward the back door. "It'll be fun."

WITH A TWO-BASE HIT her first time at bat, Judy stole **third while the pitcher was going through an elaborate** windup. She got home on Dusty's powerful line drive.

"You're sure you don't want to run away with me?" Dan asked, obviously impressed as she took her place beside him on the bench.

"Sorry," she replied regretfully. "I've got ham and potatoes in the oven."

"Where'd you learn to hit like that? And steal?"

"I'll have you know I was the pride of St. Clement's School for Girls' softball team."

"And you still remember how?"

Judy looked into his sincerely admiring expression and decided that it was a serious question. "Yes, Dan. As farfetched as it seems, I've maintained the knack all these years."

"Wow." He shook his head in wonder.

Liz struck out, and Katie was walked. Dan explained that previous experience with the child at bat had proved that it was safest not to let her swing. One never knew who would be hit, or by what—the ball or the bat.

The score was tied four to four when Judy hit a line drive all the way to the fence. The hit brought Dan and a plump, bespectacled little girl home. Judy stopped at third to look over her shoulder, aware of some activity behind home plate. But before she could concentrate on it, she heard Dan's shout. "Run, Judy! Run!"

Thinking it would be tight, since the ball was already in a high arc from the outfield, Judy pushed off the bag with every bit of energy she had. She saw arms at home plate go up for the ball. Despite her intense concentration on making it the last few yards, her mind noted the incongruity of the catcher's uniform—dress slacks and brown wing-tip shoes. Hearing the whistle of the ball in her ear, she slid, spewing sand in all directions. She felt her foot connect with the plate an instant before the ball smacked into the catcher's palm.

"Safe!" she heard Dan shout. "She's safe!"

"Damned if she isn't," a familiar voice confirmed in surprise.

There were screams and applause and the sound of dogs barking. As the dust settled, Judy pushed up on her elbows. And found herself looking up into Mitch Kramer's face.

"You slide like a veteran, Judy." He tossed the ball to Dan, then reached down to help her to her feet.

"She was the pride of St. Clement's School for Girls' softball team," Dan informed his father delightedly. "And she still remembers how."

Mitch glanced at his son and at Judy. His eyes were full of laughter and admiration. "Remarkable."

"What happened to the other catcher?" Judy asked. She clearly remembered a chubby red-haired boy at the plate and the sound of his chewing gum in her ear as she swung at the ball.

"His mother came for him," Mitch replied, "While you were rounding third. Lucky I happened along."

Judy smiled with evil satisfaction. "Not lucky enough. I was safe."

"And if you're gonna lend a hand, Dad," Dan scolded teasingly, "I wish you'd do it on our side."

"I did," Mitch said, picking Katie up as she and Liz squirmed their way into the group gathered around home plate. "Had I leaned into that a little harder, I'd have tagged her out. But I gave you guys a break."

"Good story, Mr. Kramer." Judy gave him a skeptical glance as she brushed herself off. "You probably also tell tales about the big fish that got away. Can't you just admit that my slide was faster than your catch?"

"Well, maybe faster than the outfielder's throw."

She smiled sweetly. "Good enough."

Other players began to disperse, shouting goodbyes and challenges for the third game, which would begin after dinner.

"What are you doing here, Dad?" Dan asked. "You taking us for pizza again?"

"No, I had an afternoon meeting with a client, and we still had more to talk about. So I brought her home for dinner. When no one was home, I heard the commotion here and thought I'd check it out." Mitch reached an arm out, and a blond woman in a snug skirt and a formfitting cotton sweater moved next to him. An impressive figure made her instantly recognizable as the woman Liz had told Judy about.

Oh, God, Judy thought. Dinner!

Three cherubic faces smiled up at the woman, who drew back a little against Mitch, as though previous contact with them had made her leery. "Hi, kids," she said with a decided lack of enthusiasm.

"Judy Cassidy, Brenda Madison," Mitch said. "Brenda's building a shop in Seaside. Judy is the children's nanny."

Liz peered around her father's companion at Judy and pointed at Brenda, mouthing, "That's her!"

Judy gave the child a firm stare and offered Brenda a smile. "Pleased to meet you."

She decided that her friendly gesture had been a waste of time when Brenda returned her smile with a cool, speculative look in her bright blue eyes. After a moment's silent challenge, the woman's gaze disdainfully took in Judy's dusty, disheveled appearance, and she laughed softly. "She's sweet."

Still brushing dust off her arms and happy to see that a little of it had blown in Brenda's direction, Judy laughed, also. "I assure you I'm nastier than I look."

Brenda looked from her to the children, still smiling. "You'd have to be."

Mitch, apparently missing the subtle byplay, gave Judy an uncertain frown. "Is there . . . dinner?"

Judy glanced at her watch, praying that the ham had not burned to a crisp yet. She smiled at her employer with confidence. "There is. I put a ham in that should just about be ready."

He looked pleased and surprised. "Great. Let's all pile in the car."

Judy took a step back. "Thanks, but we're really filthy. It's just a block. The kids and I'll just—"

"Nonsense." Mitch reached his free arm out for her and pulled her along as the children ran ahead of them. "If I made the kids walk every time they were dirty, I could sell the station wagon and buy a Corvette."

Chapter Five

"Oh!" Brenda turned the soft, round vowel sound into a flat expression of disdain.

Judy turned away from the salad she was tossing to see the object of the guest's disapproval. It was the finger-marked refrigerator door.

"Looks like you need a maid, as well as a nanny," Brenda said, pulling the door open with the tips of her thumb and forefinger.

Judy looked at her employer in apology, but he seemed unaware that there was a problem. "What we need," he said, handing plates and utensils to the girls, who carried them to the table, "is a guest who doesn't complain. Dressing's on the top shelf."

Brenda looked at her host over the refrigerator door and pursed her mouth as though accustomed to his brutal lack of sympathy for her.

All the way home from the ball field, Judy had expected the preparations for dinner to be an ordeal, particularly with Brenda looking on. But while she and the children were getting cleaned up, Mitch had mixed a pitcher of drinks and washed vegetables for salad. Judy had hurried into the kitchen to find a glass of something limey and refreshing and mildly alcoholic pushed into her hand. Mitch assigned duties to everyone, Brenda included, and within twenty minutes they were all seated at the table.

Brenda toyed with the food on her plate while the children told Mitch in detail about their day. Dan relayed the highlights of the earlier game and described the difference Judy's presence made to the second one.

"She stoled a base," Katie reported, waving her bear bottle excitedly. "Everybody clapped."

"This morning we decided on a design for my planter." Liz pushed her empty plate aside, her large hyacinth eyes lively with interest. "It's called a scroll band, and it has all these kinda curly things—" Liz made a spiral gesture with her fork. "—and leaves that twist and turn. Can I get Judy's book and show you?"

"Sure." Mitch nodded, his eyes soft as he watched his daughter hurry out of the room. Liz, he thought, seemed to be rapidly losing her reservations about Judy.

Waiting for Katie to demand that she be allowed to accompany her sister, Judy was surprised when the child seemed vaguely preoccupied, her bear bottle clutched in one hand while she jabbed a small bite of potato with her fork over and over again. Then she noticed that Katie's eyes would wander to the top shelf of the hutch and her new cup.

With Mitch and Brenda in conversation, Judy closed her hand over Katie's to stop her from perforating her potato. "Don't play with it, Katie," she corrected softly. She noted that the ham was gone, along with half of her small salad. "A couple of bites of potato and you can have dessert," she bargained.

"How many's a couple?"

"I'll settle for two."

Katie contemplated the bites of potato on her plate, as though eating two of them constituted an ordeal. But with a heavy sigh, she speared the first.

"Dessert?" Judy looked up from Katie's plate to see Mitch looking at her, his hazel eyes interested.

"Ice cream," she said. "With caramel sauce. The kids voted."

Mitch nodded. "I can live with that."

"One could also die with that." Brenda shuddered in horror. "Do you know how many calories you've eaten tonight?"

Brenda was asking the question of Judy, preparing her, Judy was sure, for a lecture on nutrition. But before she could reply, a small, firm voice said from the doorway, "Judy works out with Jane Fonda every morning." Liz's guileless eyes passed ever so lightly over Brenda's impressive measurements. "She can eat more calories than you can."

Mitch met Judy's eyes, his widening slightly in acknowledgment of his daughter's defense of her. Brenda uttered a gasp of indignation.

"Ice cream for you, Miss Madison?" Judy asked, her expression carefully controlled.

Brenda looked at her suspiciously and replied with a pointed glance at Liz. "A small scoop, please. No sauce."

"Right. Mr. Kramer?"

"Two scoops," he said, taking another quick sip of his drink. "Lots of sauce."

As Judy turned away to the kitchen, she caught Liz's grinning glance and winked. A victory, she thought, very pleased with herself and Liz.

When she returned with a tray of parfait glasses, Liz was sitting in her father's lap, the old rosemaling pattern

book spread out on the table. She had found the pages of
borders and pointed to the scroll band.

"Isn't it pretty? Judy's going to do it in pink and lavender for me. Those aren't tra-di-tion-al rosemaling
colors—" the word was new to her, and Liz spoke it
carefully "—but it'll match my room. She's gonna do the
same pattern, only smaller, around Katie's flowerpot. In
blue and yellow. That's more traditional." This time she
said the word with confidence.

Mitch hugged her. "That's going to be beautiful. And
you already are."

Liz giggled. "Oh, Daddy," she said, as she scrambled
off his knee. "I'm going to put the book right back in
Judy's room. We have to be very careful with it."

Judy saw Brenda turn away from Mitch and Liz. She
concentrated on her ice cream, a frown between her eyes
as though there were pain there.

After dessert Dan excused himself to go back to the
ball field, and Liz and Katie helped Judy clear the table
and load the dishwasher. Mitch and Brenda lingered at
the table.

As Judy wandered in and out, gathering plates and
putting food away, she heard Brenda ask, her eyes cast
down toward beautifully manicured fingernails, "So
how's . . . Lee?" The question had an exaggeratedly casual tone, as though the interest it expressed was not casual at all.

Mitch waited a moment before he replied. "Why don't
you stop by the site and see for yourself?"

Judy carried a tray of glasses into the kitchen. When
she returned to the dining room with a pot of coffee and
cups, the conversation had heated.

"Why should he come to see you?" Mitch was asking. "You told him to leave."

"Because he doesn't care!"

"Well, if he doesn't, why do you?"

Brenda sprang to her feet, her wide blue eyes becoming wider. As her face contorted, Judy thought in amazement that it seemed even more beautiful. "You're always on his side!" she shouted and stormed away, the front door slamming behind her.

"Her purse!" Judy said in dismay, reaching to the hutch where Brenda had left it.

"She'll stop at the porch," Mitch said calmly, pouring coffee into the two cups. He shook his head with a roll of his eyes. "Our discussions about Lee are always punctuated with her outbursts. Thanks for the coffee." He took a cup in each hand and wandered out, letting the screen door slam behind him.

Darkness had fallen when Mitch returned to the kitchen. The light over the table was on, and for an instant his heart jolted when he saw the three heads close together, bent over a project.

During those years that were such an important part of his life, that had been a familiar sight—Mandy's head bent over cookies or a storybook or a piece of needlework, and a child's head on each side of her. First it had been Dan and Liz, then when Dan had grown and left his mother's side for his father's and his peers', it had been Liz and Katie. But for such a painfully short time.

For a moment he thought that the scene was like one of those children's puzzles that showed a picture with something out of place and challenged the player to determine what was wrong. It wasn't until the head rose and eyes focused on him that he realized what was different—dark hair, dark eyes.

"Is everything all right?" Judy asked.

He stared at her, still trapped in the curious step back in time of a moment ago. Was everything all right? He wasn't sure. Judy was sitting where Mandy had always been, and, though the sight had startled him, he realized that it didn't offend him. He liked seeing Judy with his children. It was when she got close to him that he became frightened.

Then Liz looked up at him, and he felt secure again. His role as father had saved him more than once.·

"Come and see, Daddy," she coaxed. "Judy's putting the pattern on."

Mitch went to stand behind Judy, his nostrils catching a whiff of that herbal, citrus fragrance that seemed always to surround her. He remembered that Mandy had smelled of roses. He admired Judy's ability to work with a child crowding in on each side of her. He knew what a challenge that was to one's patience and coordination.

She had tracing paper on the side of Liz's planter. On the paper was a heavily outlined drawing of the scroll border Liz had showed him earlier, and Judy was tracing the last curl of the design with a lead pencil.

"There's chalk on the back of the paper," Liz explained to him. "And when she goes over the design with the pencil, it puts it on the planter."

The planter was no longer the red-orange clay of yesterday, but had been painted purple. Mitch smiled. If Liz had her way, the entire world would be purple.

"There." Judy removed the paper, revealing a faint tracing in white chalk of several S and C curves, some reversed, some intertwined. Mitch was surprised by the intricacy of the design.

"That looks very complicated," he said, taking the chair beside her and pulling Katie out of her way as Judy blew delicately on the chalk. "Don't let Liz overwork you."

Judy held the planter away from her, tilting her head to the side as she studied the transferred pattern. Mitch's attention was distracted from the design as the overhead light reflected in Judy's hair. Mandy's hair, he thought, had been like gold in an alchemist's caldron—rippling and burnished. Strangely he could picture it in his mind's eye, but not her face.

"Rosemaling designs are all fairly complicated. It's the nature of the form," she said, putting the planter down to turn and smile at him. "It's a rather robust style of painting. The colors are rich and strong, the lines graceful and full. I often think if Botticelli with his lush, plump nudes had been Norwegian instead of Italian, rosemaling... would have appealed to him."

Judy finished her commentary a little lamely as she realized that Mitch was watching her, but not really listening to her. His eyes were on her hair. She ran a hand over it, sure it must be standing up; she did have a tendency to pull on it when concentrating.

"How did a woman who is part Norwegian end up with hair the color of a starry night—" he paused thoughtfully, narrowing his gaze as Katie leaned sleepily back against him "—with all that movement and sparkle."

Unnerved by his attention, Judy handed the planter, pencil and chalk to Liz and made a production of wadding up the newpaper she had put over the table to protect it. "You forgot my dark-haired Irish and Italian ancestors. Not a blond one in the lot."

Mitch watched her self-conscious movements and wondered what in the hell was wrong with him. She was his employee; he was sure she didn't want him staring at her like some character out of a Brontë novel.

"Can't we paint just a little bit tonight?" Liz was pleading.

When Judy looked as though she were about to relent, he stood with Katie slung over his hip and gently pulled Liz's hand from Judy's shoulder. "Judy's had a long day, Liz. Let her have some time to herself. It's about time for you to hit the hay anyway."

Reluctantly Liz nodded. "Okay. But it's gonna be so pretty. I can hardly wait."

"We'll work on it first thing in the morning, I promise." Judy hesitated before hugging Liz, not sure the gesture would be welcome yet. But Liz squeezed her hard in return. Katie reached out of Mitch's arms to her. As Judy leaned into the child's embrace, her head came close to Mitch's shoulder, and she smelled his tantalizing masculine scent. "See you in the morning, Katie."

"Are we gonna do our robics?"

"You bet."

Satisfied, Katie fell back against Mitch's shoulder.

"Night, Judy." Liz called over her shoulder as Mitch led her away.

In the girls' room, he settled Katie in her bed. Liz climbed in her own and leaned on her elbow, staring at the flower box on her bedside table. "Judy's neat, isn't she?"

Mitch closed the window halfway and drew the curtains, their lavender figures cavorting on a field of pink flowers. He picked up a scruffy brown bear wearing a T-shirt Katie had outgrown and sat in the white wicker rocking chair it had occupied, holding it in his lap.

"Yes, she's neat," he agreed. "I like her, too."

"Maybe she'd paint something for you." Liz smiled at him, always anxious to share whatever she had. "She said she'd do the sign over the front door if you didn't think she was being pre...pre..." Liz frowned over the word. "It sounds like presomething, but it's not."

Mitch studied his daughter with fascination, wondering if all children were as bright and eager to learn new things as his children were. "Presumptuous?" he suggested.

"That's it." Liz leaned back into her pillows and dangled a foot out from under the sheet and light blanket. "What is that?"

"It means...taking liberties."

"Taking liberties." Liz repeated his words, and when he didn't see the light dawn in her eyes, he groped for another explanation.

"It means she might repaint the sign, thinking she's doing me a favor, but I might like it the way it is and not want it painted. So she hasn't done me a favor, she's been presumptuous."

Elizabeth nodded. "I get it. Would she be if she did?"

Mitch tried to unravel the question by identifying the pronouns. "Judy?"

"Yeah. Would you think she was pre-sumptuous?"

"No." He smiled. "I'd think she was pre-cisely what the sign needed."

Liz smiled at his wordplay, then added more seriously, "And maybe us, too."

"We're what the sign needed?"

"No. *Judy's* what *we* need."

"Yes. A good nanny."

"Mmm." Liz turned onto her side again, frowning at her father. "She can't cook all the stuff Aunt Glenna fixes, but she's lots of fun to have around. You know what?"

"What?"

"I didn't think I was gonna like her. And sometimes I wasn't very friendly." Rolling onto her stomach, her chin in her hands, Liz looked confused. "But she was nice to me anyway. And did stuff for me. I thought only moms were like that."

Mitch rocked idly in the chair. "Well, nannies kind of do a mom's job—taking care of kids when a mom's not around."

Liz fixed him with that steady gaze that meant she was phrasing a heavy question. Still rocking, Mitch braced himself.

"Do you ever wish Mom would come back?"

"Yes." No matter how much the honesty hurt, he knew it was better for him and for her. "But she can't, Liz."

"I know." Liz sighed, having long ago accepted that. Then she frowned at Mitch in concern. "But you'll want to have a wife again sometime, won't you?" She looked him over critically and said with grave indulgence, "You're not *that* old."

Relieved that the discussion was not becoming metaphysical, he accepted that backhanded compliment with good grace. "Thank you, Elizabeth."

"Are you gonna marry Brenda?"

Wondering if he had dropped his guard too soon, Mitch shook his head. "No, I'm not."

Liz nodded sagely. "Good. I don't think she likes kids. But you should marry somebody. Dads are supposed to have moms to go to bed with."

Telling himself that he could handle this without panicking, Mitch stood, replaced the bear and sat on the edge of Liz's bed. "You have to have somebody really special for that," he said. He was surprised to find emotions turning inside him, swells of longing, eddies of confusion that had been haunting him for several days. "You have to love someone for that, Lizzie."

"What makes you love someone?"

He had definitely dropped his guard too soon, he thought, looking into her attentive expression. "Oh, kindness, softness, laughter..."

Liz concentrated. "Softness. You mean like...cuddly?"

He laughed. "That's nice, too. But I mean softness inside. Someone who doesn't talk mean and isn't always angry and smiles a lot."

Liz nodded. "Like Judy."

Mitch thought about that. Soft described Mandy—loving, sweet, amenable. But Judy? He considered the capable, controlled way she tackled everything—those she knew she could handle and those she attacked with more heart than skill—the way she looked at him when they were confused by each other, all dark eyes and parted lips. And it suddenly occurred to him that softness could have more than one form.

"Yes," he said. "I guess she is."

"But you can't marry her 'cause she's going to England."

"Right. And she might not even like me."

"Oh, I think she does." Liz's eyes widened. "I heard her tell her friend on the phone that—" she deepened her voice in imitation of Judy "—the kids are wonderful, and their father is gorgeous."

Mitch arched an eyebrow. "Really?"

"That means she thinks you're cute, doesn't it?"

Mitch got to his feet, pulled her blankets up and leaned down to kiss her good-night. "Lizzie, you shouldn't eavesdrop on a private conversation."

Settling down under the covers, Liz looked up at him. "She wasn't trying to be quiet or anything. Katie and I were right at the table, having lunch. She said you were 'mysterious,' too. What's that?"

"Um, hard to figure out."

Liz grinned, as though she could read her father inside and out. "You're not mysterious, you're just tricky."

Interested now in this dissection of his personality, he looked down on his daughter. "Oh?"

"Yeah," she said. "You just always *act* like nothing bothers you. Like when Mom died and I broke the picture and we talked about it. I cried and cried, but you didn't—until you went to bed."

When he looked startled, she confided earnestly, "I heard you. And when you're mad at Dan or me or Katie 'cause we've done something bad, you never get mad. You just act like you really *would* be if we ever did it again. You're tricky, Daddy. And I think you're soft, too. G'night."

Wondering if he should be considering sending Liz to Oxford with Judy, Mitch turned out the light and left the room.

Chapter Six

Judy sat up in bed, not certain what had awakened her. A shout? A crash? At the moment there wasn't a sound in the house but the alarmed pounding of her heart. Pulling a pink cotton robe over her nightshirt, she hurried across the hall to the girls' bedroom. Liz was fast asleep, but the covers on Katie's bed were thrown back to reveal the absence of its occupant.

Quickly checking the bathroom first and finding it also devoid of Katie, Judy ran down the stairs to the living room. Standing in the dark for a moment, she listened and heard nothing, but felt the indefinable presence of someone else in the room. Thinking belatedly that checking an unfamiliar noise in the dark in the middle of the night was not the wisest course of action, Judy held her breath and flipped on the light.

Finding a masked burglar in the dining room would have been no more frightening than the scene on which her eyes focused. Katie, in pajamas covered with a Big Bird design, stood on the first shelf of the hutch. The narrow space allowed little room for even her small feet to move, and she clutched the topmost shelf in one white-knuckled hand. Four fingers of her free hand were hooked in the handle of her mug, and her elbow clutched her bear-shaped bottle.

"Hi!" she said cheerfully, peering over her shoulder as Judy ran to her. In front of the hutch, Judy found the folding step stool collapsed on the floor. Its crash was probably what had awakened her.

Kicking the stool aside, she grasped the child firmly by the waist and swung her to the floor. "It's the middle of the night, Katie," she whispered, relieved to have the child out of danger. "What were you doing?"

"I wanted a drink," Katie replied as though a midnight climb of an eight-foot hutch were nothing unusual. She held up the bright cup. "In this."

Judy pointed to the bottle tucked under Katie's arm. "But to drink out of the cup, you have to—"

"I know." Katie cut her off, handing over the bottle.

For a moment Judy stood quietly, startled by the success that was a milestone in the child's development.

"Can I have Pepsi in it?" Katie asked with a conspiratorial grin.

"Well, sure." Judy took her hand and led her into the kitchen. "Half a cup."

Katie held the cup carefully with both hands while Judy poured, a crackling foam rising to the top of the cup.

"That's the way Daddy likes it," the child giggled. "With a head on it."

Judy laughed and leaned down to kiss the top of her head. "Take it to the table so you don't spill, okay?"

As Judy turned to pour a small glass for herself, she found Mitch standing there in a pair of jeans and nothing else. His chest was smooth and muscular, the color of expensive brandy. He exuded an aura different from his usual daytime laid-back efficiency and relaxed friendliness. His thick hair was slightly mussed, his eyes dark and lazy as they wandered over Judy's bare legs and feet and cotton robe. Barefoot himself, he walked silently into the kitchen.

"What are we drinking?" he asked.

"Ah... Pepsi," Judy answered, feeling her pulse sputter. He was broad and beautifully built. She had suspected that, but seeing it for herself was more disabling than the suspicion. To cover her swift and sudden loss of equanimity, she gave him a big smile and a glass of Pepsi thick with foam. "With a head on it just like you like it."

He accepted it from her and grinned, considering her for a moment before joining his daughter. "With little girls in the house, one has no secrets. Couldn't sleep, Katie?"

Katie emerged from her cup with a foam mustache and an 'Ah!' of satisfaction. "I was firsty."

"I see that. Good?"

She nodded, then paused, as if waiting for him to notice the cup. When he said nothing, she held it up. "I'm drinking in this."

"Yes."

"Bear is over there." She pointed behind her to the counter. "Tomorrow Judy can put him in the dishwasher."

He nodded gravely. "To get the Germans out."

"Yeah. I'm gonna have my milk in this." She peered into the bottom of the cup and giggled. "I can see the kitty with the parasol." She downed the rest of the drink and beckoned Judy. "Come see."

Judy looked over Katie's shoulder and dutifully admired the elegantly attired kitten.

"Maybe we should keep it on the rack," Mitch suggested, pointing to a wooden accordion rack that hung on the wall over the counter, its pegs laden with a collection of mugs. "So she isn't tempted to climb up after it again. I'm too old for that kind of scare in the middle of the night."

Judy looked at him in surprise. "I was hoping you hadn't seen that."

"The crashing stool woke me, too, but by the time I could get myself together to investigate, you were already on the scene. You do move quickly," he said in admiration.

Judy shrugged off the praise. "When you spend your whole life with young children, you have to." She rinsed Katie's cup out and set it upside down on the counter to dry. "I'd better get Katie back to bed."

He was looking at her as though seeing her in another setting. His hazel eyes were pensive, his manner distracted as he watched her tug Katie off her chair.

"Or did you need something before we go?" Judy asked.

Did he need something? Mitch hadn't thought so. He'd adjusted to being a widower, a single parent. Perhaps it was just that life had taken on a new—what was it? A freshness?—since she'd been here. And strangely, the addition of something new in his life made him remember the things he missed, the things he had thought he'd learned to live without, the softness. It was probably because she thought he was gorgeous. Praise was appealing, especially when one was approaching the hill and resisting going over.

"No," he said finally, getting to his feet and leaning down to scoop Katie up. "I don't need anything. Good night, baby. And next time you want something in the middle of the night, you should get Judy or me first, okay?''

"Okay." Katie hugged her father.

Judy reached up to take the child from him, but he set Katie on her feet. Then he patted Judy's back in a purely platonic way. "She's too heavy for you to carry up the stairs."

The issue became academic as Katie took off at a run the moment her feet touched the carpet. Mitch and Judy were left facing each other in the pool of light near the dining table, he curiously sober, she with a wary brightness in her eyes.

How could a woman be so beautiful in a simple cotton robe in the middle of the night, he wondered.

How could a hand touched to your back, Judy asked herself, make something tingle in the pit of your stomach?

"Good night, Judy," Mitch said finally. "I'll get the light."

Judy nodded, wishing she had a reason to stay up with him, wishing she didn't need one. "Good night, Mitch."

It wasn't until Judy reached the top of the stairs that she realized she'd called her employer by his first name.

When Mitch heard Judy close the girls' door and then her own, he turned off the light but stayed where he was for a long moment, listening to the silence. His pulse was fast. He was beginning to do more than notice Judy. He hadn't quite developed a need for her, but his awareness was sharpening. He was becoming interested in her. He realized that with a feeling of panic.

Suddenly filled with restless energy, he went to the window in the living room and brushed the drapes aside roughly. Watching the moonlight on the quiet street, he thought about what an ordeal it was to get to know a woman. Understanding her once you knew her could be even more exasperating. He had loved Mandy eagerly because she had given him her heart and her soul unconditionally. Her generosity had opened up the young man he had been and changed him forever.

He had no love left to give a woman; Mandy had it all.

So what was happening to him? Was he reacting like Dan did to a well-filled leotard? He laughed grimly to himself as he let the drapery fall. He went out onto the porch, knowing there was no way he was going to sleep, at least not for a while.

Stretching out on the swing, he propped his head on a pillow and breathed in the cool, salty night air. He longed for Mandy and the sanity and simplicity of their relationship with a desperation that hurt. But when he closed his eyes, the image that rose out of his mind was Judy.

ROLLING UP THE SLEEVES of his chambray shirt, Mitch walked through the quiet kitchen, heading for the den where he thought Judy would be working out with the girls. But he found the room empty.

Frowning, he went back to the kitchen, wondering if Judy had slept late because of last night's disturbance. If so, he'd better see what Liz and Katie were up to. He was relatively certain they hadn't slept in.

Then the sounds of feminine laughter and conversation from the back of the house caught his attention. He found Judy and the girls sitting on newspapers spread on the deck. Liz's flower box was on an old towel on Judy's lap. Liz sat on her right, the work close enough to her nose to get paint on it, and Katie sat on her left, sipping something from her mug. Mitch was pleased to see that even in the light of day, Katie saw no need to return to her bottle.

He remained silent as he walked up behind Judy, not wanting to startle her or disturb her concentration as she drew her brush along a full curve, leaving a path of white and pink and lavender in its wake.

But Katie spotted him and, with delight, sprang to her feet. "Hi, Daddy!" In her haste she bumped Judy's arm and the curve took on an erratic lunge.

"Look at what you did!" Liz immediately accused.

"Katie," he scolded softly, getting down on one knee to take her in his arms. "You have to be careful when Judy's working."

Judy, sitting Indian style, turned to smile at Mitch and pat Katie's leg with a paint-smeared hand. "It's all right," she said, running a cloth along the smear. "My mother always said a mistake is nothing more than paint on a rag. See?" The error was removed as though it had never been.

"Whew!" Liz looked at Judy in relief and was surprised when Judy, Mitch and Katie began to laugh. "What?"

"You've got paint on your cheek," Judy explained, dabbing at it with a clean corner of her rag. "There."

"I think that means you were a little too close, Liz," Mitch said. "When that brush went wild you became part of the design."

The child smiled ruefully. "I can't help it. She makes everything so pretty."

Judy smiled at Mitch. "I understand that you wouldn't consider it pre-sumptuous of me to touch up your sign over the front door." She said Liz's new word with the same careful inflection the child used.

"That's right. Paint whatever you want," he said, getting to his feet. Then he added with a grin, "Just leave my truck alone. It'd be hard to explain to my crew." He leaned down to kiss the tops of the girls' heads. "I'm off to work. What's for dinner?"

"Spaghetti and ham have exhausted my repertoire." She sloshed her brush in a jar of turpentine and wiped it off, then squinted up at him. "But I see Glenna has a few standard cookbooks, so I'm going to try baked chicken."

He nodded and started to turn away. "Shall I plan on Miss Madison?" she asked.

He rolled his eyes. "She's not speaking to me at the moment, at least not civilly. I doubt that we'll be blessed with her company."

"Don't you have to work at night anymore, Daddy?" Liz asked, her expression innocent. "You never used to be able to come home for dinner."

"I've . . . changed my schedule," he said, swearing he could detect guile behind the innocence. "I'm working in the office here instead of in the trailer."

Liz nodded. "That's nice. See ya."

"Yeah," he replied, feeling as though his mind had been read by an eight-year-old. "See ya." He blew a kiss at Katie, then walked into the house.

While Judy worked, Katie wandered off the porch to ride her tricycle up and down the path. Liz leaned back on her hands, watching Judy's careful strokes.

"When are you going to England?" she asked.

"When the summer's over and your aunt comes back from her vacation."

"That's where the pilgrims came from."

"That's right."

"All the way across the ocean."

"Yes."

There was a moment's silence while Judy leaned back to assess her work. Then Liz asked, her tone laced with subtle concern, "That's so far away. Won't you be lonesome? I mean, you won't know anybody there."

Judy dropped her brush in the turpentine and wiped her hands on a rag, smiling at Liz. "A friend is coming with me. We'll have so much to do and see, there won't be time to be lonesome."

Liz studied her quizzically. "When we go to Aunt Jackie's, I miss Daddy, even though there's lots for us to do. I have fun, but I miss him and wish he was there, too."

"I don't have a family, Liz." Judy wiped off paint tubes and capped them. "I won't have anyone to miss, or who will miss me."

Liz's soft blue eyes widened. "There's nobody to love you?"

For a moment Judy couldn't answer. Her solitude was something she'd adjusted to long ago, but Liz's distress somehow brought home to her the vastness of the world and her lonely insignificance in it.

"It's all right," she replied finally, wondering for the first time in a long time if it really was. "My friend will be with me."

"A lady?"

Closing her paint box, Judy looked at the child closely, wondering what had prompted that question. "No. A man. His name is Dale."

"Are you gonna marry him?"

Judy laughed, gathering up her gear. "No, Liz. He's just a good friend."

Liz helped her pick up the scattered newspaper. "Daddy says you have to have softness to get married. And laughter." She paused, thinking. "And kindness. That's the other thing."

Judy nodded, thinking that did sound like a winning combination. "Your father's very smart."

"And gorgeous?"

Startled, Judy looked at Liz and saw that her expression was definitely impish. A feeling of dismay began to take hold of her. "You heard me say that?"

"Uh-huh."

She swallowed and asked calmly. "Did you tell your dad?"

Liz nodded, apparently pleased with herself.

"Oh, God," Judy murmured, hanging her head. Then she looked at Liz and tried to ask without urgency, "What did he say?"

Liz shrugged, standing with her armful of paper. "Just that I shouldn't eavesdrop." And she headed for the house.

As Judy followed with her paint box and brushes, she wondered if Mitch had been annoyed, amused or was already calling Summer Nannies to have her replaced.

SHE FOUND OUT just how he felt the following Friday night when he took her and the girls to Seaside, while Dan and his friends went to a movie. A favorite coastal attraction for young and old, Seaside's main street, full of arcades, gift shops and fast-food stands, was alive with laughing crowds of teenagers, vacationing families and strolling couples.

Lights brightened the corridor of activity as Liz and Katie walked along hand in hand, and Mitch and Judy followed behind, several paces apart.

"Daddy, look." Liz pulled Katie to a stop at the window of a men's clothing store. She pointed to a bright floral shirt on a smiling mannequin. "I'll bet you'd look *gorgeous* in that."

With a hand to her mouth to cover a giggle, Liz glanced at the adults and moved on, towing Katie with her.

Even with her eyes closed in mortification, Judy felt Mitch's glance. But when she looked at him as they fell in step once more behind the girls, he looked back at her in questioning innocence.

Judy sighed. "I know you know," she said.

He smiled broadly then, a chuckle escaping him. "I didn't know you knew I knew."

Playing the game, Judy said, "I've known you knew for a week now."

Mitch's chuckle became a laugh as he moved closer to her to make room for a crowd of singing teenagers walking by arm in arm. "I wasn't going to mention it for fear you'd tell me you hadn't meant it or that Liz had misunderstood. I've been pretty impressed with myself since she told me."

He appeared so amused that some of the embarrassment left her. "Well, I apologize. My friend Dana had called to see how I was doing. I'm afraid that wasn't a very professional remark."

The teenagers had passed, but Mitch didn't trouble to put space between himself and Judy again. He looked down at her, a spark of seriousness crowding the humor in his eyes. "I think that was what I liked about it."

Sensing dangerous ground, a little alarmed by the look in his eyes, Judy remained silent.

"Your remark about my being mysterious did puzzle me, though," he said.

With a small groan, Judy dropped her head back and slanted him a scolding glance. "It would have been chivalrous of you to let that one pass."

He shrugged. "I couldn't. You now have me thoroughly intrigued with myself. Mysterious?"

Accepting that she was going to have to explain, Judy began to try, but was interrupted by the girls pleading to ride the Tilt-a-Whirl. While Mitch bought tickets, Judy had time to think. With Liz and Katie safely tucked in a bubble-roofed car, Mitch joined Judy at the railing that separated the watching crowd from the ride.

As the music began and the ride started to move, Judy smiled up at him. "Well, you're open and candid, and all in all, very democratic for an employer, but..." She paused, wondering if she'd be overstepping if she went on.

"Go on," he encouraged.

"Well, you're very quiet about your wife." Judy waited, wondering how he would react. As the children spun by, screaming giddily, she waved.

"That's because sometimes it would be like talking in front of her," he replied after a moment. "She's still that much with me at times."

"How nice to have loved someone so much."

As Judy looked up at him, he turned and leaned his elbows on the railing. "We had a good life together. I think I've adjusted to being without her, and yet, I guess, in some ways I haven't."

"I suppose by guarding your feeling for her, you can keep her closer," Judy guessed. She had done that when her mother died—thought about her constantly, replaying her favorite times with her over and over in her mind, not sharing them, except with Mike, because that somehow softened the intensity of her feelings. And with her mother gone, the feelings were all she had left. "It sort of minimizes the loss, doesn't it?"

Mitch looked down into Judy's dark, thoughtful eyes and nodded, then looked away. "Yes, it does. Sometimes I hold on to her so hard, I feel as though the clock has stopped. I'm not sure if that's good or bad."

Judy waved again as the girls made another pass. "I imagine one day you'll want to move on," she said. "Into another relationship. I imagine she would want that for you."

Mitch continued to watch the crowds passing on the street. Mandy probably would. She had always wanted what was best for him. And whether he was ready or not, he was beginning to feel that he'd had enough of loneliness, enough of emotional solitude, even enough of mostly male and juvenile companionship. He needed a woman in his life.

With that realization, Mitch turned to Judy to find her watching him with a contemplative smile.

"What?" he asked.

Judy studied the lingering faraway look in his eyes and laughed softly. "And you think you're not mysterious." She turned as the crowd spewed out of the gate laughing and staggering, and she caught the girls as they ran to her with their pink cheeks and bright eyes.

"I'm firsty!" Katie complained.

"Can we have cotton candy?" Liz pleaded.

They stopped at a beachside stand to satisfy the girls' requests and continued their stroll.

"Tell me about the man you're going to England with," Mitch said, keeping his eye on the girls, who had stopped at an arcade to watch the spirited play at a video game.

Nibbling on a chunk of caramel corn, Judy laughed at the very thought of Dale. "He's a good friend," she explained. "A veritable maniac and great company. He's getting his degree in languages."

"You're going to live together?" The question was casually spoken, but Judy thought she detected the subtle undercurrent of disapproval.

A mild annoyance rose in her, but she decided that Mitch's patience, when she asked about his wife, deserved the same tolerance in return.

"Yes," she replied, moving closer to him as a group of brawny, noisy young men in shorts and T-shirts crowded the sidewalk. "Just like I'm living with you."

She was pushed against him as she spoke, and he put an arm around her to fend off further jostling. His eyes looked into hers, then went over her face with slow deliberation.

Her breath caught at his closeness. She felt the strength in the arm around her, the warmth and solidity of his chest, the broad back against which her hand was splayed. Suddenly the crowd disappeared, sound evaporated, and there was nothing but his longing, golden eyes.

Then something came between them, something she'd seen in his eyes earlier when they'd talked about Mandy. Mitch's bristly lashes fell.

As she tried to draw air without gulping, he sighed and smiled wryly, releasing her. "Like you're living with me? England's got to be more exciting than that."

"Nannies are supposed to be dull," she said lightly, trying to dampen the charged atmosphere. "Haven't you read the classic Gothics?"

"The implication wasn't that *you* were dull." The girls moved on, and Mitch and Judy followed. "And, anyway, doesn't the nanny always turn into a goddess when she takes the pins out of her hair and discovers the master's tortured past?"

She laughed, feeling the tension ease. "My hair's too short for pins, and you're happy with your past. So I guess we just remain the dull nanny and the gorgeous, mysterious master."

"Those are the right ingredients," he pointed out.

"Yes, but the wrong story line. I'm going to Oxford, and you're happy with things the way they are."

It surprised Mitch that his instinct was to refute that statement. He had come very close to kissing her; that surprised him, too. But he hadn't kissed a woman in a long time. He wasn't sure what had stopped him—guilt or nervousness.

Picking up Katie as she came to him with raised arms and heavy eyelids, Mitch decided that Judy was probably right. They might be the right characters in the right roles, but the whole thing was plotted wrong. And better left alone.

Chapter Seven

"Could you help me for an hour or so?" Mitch asked.

The girls were in bed, and Judy had been about to go to her room, when he emerged from the kitchen with a tray containing a pitcher of lemonade, two glasses and a plate of cookies.

"Help you with what?" she asked, following him out to the screened-in porch. Since that night in Seaside a week ago, their relationship had been more guardedly friendly than professional.

The night smelled of summer and the ocean, and she felt her body react to the magic of it, as though her senses sharpened yet slowed to take it all in.

Mitch put the tray down on a small wicker coffee table and pointed to the chintz upholstered swing. "Sit down. I'll be right back."

Before she had settled into a corner of the swing, her legs tucked under her, he was back with a clipboard and pen.

"My crew and I always have a Fourth of July picnic farther down the coast where there's a cove." He poured lemonade into the glasses and handed her one. "Glenna usually plans and shops for the food, but she's probably on a gondola in some Venetian canal about now." He offered her the cookie plate. "So it's up to us."

"How many people?"

"Twelve in my crew. Wives and girlfriends and about fifteen children."

"Good grief."

"Yeah. Brenda offered to handle it, but if she does, she'll leave out the onions, the horseradish, the cherry peppers and the volleyball net. And the guys will crucify me the following Monday morning."

Judy shook her head in mock sympathy. "Tsk tsk."

"You may scoff," he said, nibbling on a chocolate-covered graham cracker, "but her husband's out for my hide already."

Judy froze with half a cookie in her mouth. Then she chewed and swallowed, frowning at Mitch. "Liz told me Brenda was divorced."

"Not exactly. She's married to my foreman. They've been separated for six months. She's trying to use me to make him jealous, but it doesn't seem to be working."

"You'd let her do that?"

"Yes, sort of." He stretched his legs out, crossing his ankles. "They're both my friends. I can't just push her away when she comes to see me. She tries to be coy, but the conversation always comes around to Lee, anyway. She spends time with me to find out about him."

"Does he still care about her?"

"I'm sure of it."

"Then what's the problem?"

Mitch shrugged. "Two tough-minded people. He wants her home raising babies, she wants to have a shop. I think in reaction to the way he'd like to...confine her, she's flaunting her freedom in his face with her seductive clothes and making sure he knows she spends time with me."

"Why does he want to confine her?"

"He's basically an old-fashioned type. And I suppose it's an instinctive reaction to loving a woman who looks like that."

Judy put her glass down on the table. "Does having a family have to preclude her having a shop?"

"I don't know the fine points of the argument," Mitch said, leaning his head against the back of the swing. "Just that the longer they're apart, the further apart they become. I'd like to put them in a locked room and let them fight it out."

Judy shook her head. "That doesn't sound like it would work."

"It does." Mitch smiled, staring at the ceiling. "One time Mandy and I were arguing over whether or not to leave Portland to come to Manzanita so that I could start my own business." It surprised him for only a moment that he was discussing his marriage with Judy, then he went on. "I was foreman with a big construction firm there, and we were comfortable. Dan was in school, and Liz was just a baby. Mandy thought it was a risk we shouldn't take."

He looked at her, and with a smile that held no criticism, he added, "She wasn't very adventurous. Loving, loyal and very dear, but not adventurous." He turned back to stare at the ceiling once more, his expression sobering. "I needed the change, and I wanted to prove to myself that I could do it. We had enough in the bank that it wouldn't have been too big a risk, but it was taking a chance all the same. We'd been fighting about it for days when it became time to attend the wedding of some friends of ours in Eugene. We left the kids with my parents as planned and took off. For the first hour we didn't speak to each other, then the next hour we shouted at each other. Then we began to try to make sense, and each of us began to see the other's side. We finally decided to give it a year. If I became successful, it would have been worth the move. If I didn't, we wouldn't have done anything that couldn't be reversed. We could always move back to Portland, and I could get another job. But we'd never have reached an amicable decision if we hadn't been closed up together long enough to get through the anger and the frustration that you always seem to have to go through before you get to serious talking.''

Knowing he'd shared something with her he didn't often discuss, Judy wasn't sure what to say. Bringing one of the children into the discussion seemed safest. "Liz showed me the picture she has of her," she said quietly. "She was beautiful. And Liz looks just like her."

"Doesn't she?" There was wistfulness in his voice. "She's like Mandy in a lot of ways—gentle and generous and always up. But she's more determined, more of a fighter."

Judy laughed softly. "But you just told me that Mandy fought with you for days and shouted at you most of the way to Eugene."

"Actually that time stands out in my mind as about the only time we fought seriously. We disagreed occasionally, but she usually came around to my way of thinking." He turned to her again and echoed her laughter. "I suppose that sounds chauvinistic, and maybe I was. Mandy lost her mother when she was very small and was raised by her father and two older brothers. I think she found it natural to let me be in control."

He laughed once more, his voice rich with humor. "I think that's what was hardest for me when I found myself alone with the kids. Mandy understood what I wanted and saw that the kids conformed. Then, all of a sudden, I was faced with three very independent, free-thinking, free speaking kids, who were as much at a loss as I was, but anxious to argue with me over everything."

He sat up and picked up his drink. After a long swallow, he settled into the corner of the swing, facing Judy. His eyes shone in the encroaching darkness. "That was when I realized that I had loved my kids, had supported them as best I could, protected them, defended them... but I had still shortchanged them. I had put myself between them and the world, but I'd never really given them of myself. I'd spent a lot of time at work and depended on Mandy to deal with their problems." He finished the contents of his glass and put it on the table. When he spoke again, his voice had a mild rasp in it. "I don't think I truly became a father until Mandy died."

That admission swelled Judy's respect for him, and before she could stop herself, she reached out to pat the arm he'd stretched out on the back of the swing. "Well, once you caught on, you did remarkably well. I don't think there are three happier, more well-adjusted kids anywhere."

"Really?" He didn't move a muscle, but Judy felt the warmth of him under her hand, the power at rest. Darkness had fallen, and the shadows seemed to pulse around them, bringing them closer, though neither of them stirred.

"Really," she whispered.

Then Mitch turned his arm, his hand cupping her elbow. Sensation raced along her upper arm to her heart, causing it to falter in its beating.

"You're doing a wonderful job for us," he said softly.

It no longer seemed like a job, but she suspected it would be dangerous to mention that. "I . . . enjoy being here."

Mitch no longer felt able to analyze or understand what drove him, where Judy was concerned. He knew only that he was going to kiss her. It occurred to him that, though he'd just spent a long time talking about Mandy, his mind and his senses were filled with Judy. He leaned forward, closing the small gap between them, and planted a brief kiss on her lips. She tasted of lemon and sugar.

Blood seemed to rush everywhere inside Judy, not from passion, but from tenderness. It occurred to some still-operating part of her mind how spare a commodity tenderness was in the average person's life. There was kindness and caring and concern, but that touch of tenderness that made one feel precious beyond price was rarely encountered.

Then she leaned forward and kissed him with the same sweetness he'd shown her, the same brief but tender touch.

Yes, Mitch thought, putting his hand to the back of her head to prolong the moment. She is soft. His heartbeat quickened, and his blood stirred, and he knew the man inside him had come to life again.

Pulling back, afraid something vital in her system would short-circuit, Judy reached to the table to pick up his clipboard.

"Write this down," she said, handing it to him.

After an instant's pause, Mitch reached behind him to flip the light switch. Dim but sanity-restoring light replaced the soft darkness.

"Hot dogs, hamburgers, buns—both kinds," she recited. "Beans, potato salad, jello salad, pickles . . ."

"CHERRY PEPPERS!" A tall, burly, platinum-haired young man looked over the buffet table and swatted the back of the smaller, darker man beside him. They'd been introduced to Judy as Bob Norgaard and Mick Taylor. "All right! Horseradish! Salsa and chips! Maybe we won't have to fire the boss after all."

"See what I mean?" Mitch, turning hamburgers on the barbecue, grinned down at Judy, who was placing open buns around the rim. "They're an ungrateful, unforgiving lot." He made the comment loud enough to be heard, and the two checking out the buffet table, turned to look at him, then at each other.

"Looks like he's gonna have to be the first one in the water," Bob said.

He ignored the threat. "Oh, yeah? And who's going to cook?"

"You're a great builder and not a bad boss," Mick said, shaking his head. "But any one of us can turn out better burgers than you do." They began to close in on Mitch.

A young man, probably still in his teens but already built like a linebacker, separated himself from a circle of men drinking beer farther down the beach.

He studied the standoff and grinned. "What's the problem?"

"The boss called us ungrateful and unforgiving," Bob replied, advancing on Mitch.

"The hell he did," the boy exclaimed. Then he turned to the group he'd just left. "Hey, guys!" They looked up as a group. "The boss just insulted us!"

Mitch groaned and strengthened his grip on the spatula. He pushed Judy aside. "Stay out of the way," he warned, an unholy light agleam in his eye. "This is going to get ugly. Dan!"

Dan approached from the other direction with Kenny and Dusty as the beer-drinking group joined Bob and Mick and began to form a menacing circle around Mitch. He assumed an easy crouch, spatula at the ready. Dan stopped between his father and the tightening circle.

"Yeah?" he asked.

"I need you," Mitch said.

Dan took a cursory look at the determined, burly group. "You're outnumbered," he pointed out.

Mitch tossed and caught the spatula, challenging Bob, who was coming in closer than the others. "It doesn't matter," he said quietly, "if your heart is pure."

"But, Dad," Dan said gravely, "that leaves you out."

Mitch dropped his guard to turn to his son. "Do you want to be the first one to get the broadside of this spat?"

And that was all they needed. The circle closed in, and a struggling, laughingly cursing Mitch was lifted on six pairs of hands and carried to the water. The rest of his crew, setting up the volleyball net a safe distance from the food, joined them at the waterline, shouting and cheering. Wives and girlfriends laughed and held the staring children back.

"That's the price one pays," Janet, Bob's wife, said, "for being loved by a bunch of rowdy kids at heart." Shaking her head at their antics, she retrieved the spatula from the sand and rinsed it in a tub of sudsy water under the buffet table.

Judy laughed, shading her eyes as a cheer louder than the previous ones accompanied a big splash.

"They find an excuse to do this to him every year," Janet said, checking the burgers for doneness, "and he still gives them generous Christmas bonuses. I'd fire the lot of them."

Judy noticed a light-featured man standing apart from the group, which was now knee-deep in the water. He, too, was tall and muscular in a white T-shirt and jeans, but he definitely did not join in the spirit of the yearly free-for-all. Judy turned to ask Janet who he was and became aware of Brenda, in white shorts and a yellow sweatshirt studded with stars. She was standing with her back to the buffet table, staring at the man Judy had noticed.

"Now there's the one who should have been thrown in the water," Janet said, angling her chin toward Brenda. "Letting a great guy like that get away."

Judy turned back to study the big man with the grim expression. So that was Brenda's husband. "She doesn't look very happy about it, either," she noted.

"Too proud to admit it."

"Pride's a terrible burden."

Janet nodded. "Pride just gets in the way. When you get down to it, love is what you should protect, not pride."

The crowd was now moving out of the water and back up the beach toward the food. A drenched Mitch was getting affectionate slaps on the back, a towel dropped on his head, a beer forced into his hand. He snapped the towel at Dan, who got too close with a taunting remark. The boy ran off with his friends, laughing.

With Janet assuming charge of the barbecue, Judy moved toward Mitch, who sprinted away from the group as it dispersed at the buffet table.

"Do you want me to run home and get you a change of clothes?" she asked, taking the end of the towel he held in his hand and catching the water running off his face. She dabbed at his chin then up the side of his face, drying the water streaming from his hair.

Judy looked up from her ministrations to see his eyes, still full of laughter and devilment, going over her face in careful concentration. He smiled, and she felt as though he had kissed her.

Rubbing the towel in his hair, he draped it around his neck and pointed to the parking lot. "I brought a change of clothes. They always find an excuse to throw me in. Save me a couple of burgers."

The parking lot stood at the top of a high graded bank that led down to the beach. Standing atop the bank in the sea grass that was still and golden in the warm afternoon was Lee Madison. He was looking down at Mitch, with his hands at his sides in a way Judy mistrusted.

"Back in a minute," Mitch said.

But before he could move away, Judy caught his arm and indicated the top of the bank with a slight tilt of her head. "Should you go up there?"

Mitch looked at Lee, then looked back at her with a grin. "If I want my clothes, I should."

She rolled her eyes impatiently. "You know what I mean. He looks like he's . . . waiting for you."

"Want to come and protect me?" he suggested.

Sighing, Judy let go of his arm. "Go ahead. You deserve to get beaten up."

As she turned away, he hooked a finger in the hood of her sweatshirt, stopping her. She turned to him with mild impatience.

"I'm flattered by your concern," he said softly. "But I think he went up to get a case of soft drinks out of his van."

She shrugged. "I just hate to see you trounced twice in the space of fifteen minutes. Call me if you need me. My Tae Kwon-Do isn't bad."

His eyes went to the shape of her breasts under the sweatshirt and the trim length of her legs beneath her shorts. "There doesn't seem to be an inch of you that isn't bad."

Whatever had remained of their businesslike relationship seemed to have fled today, replaced by an exploratory flirtation. It concerned Judy at the same time that it excited her. Trying to divert his attention from her, she waved a hand in the direction of his wet clothes. "You're going to get pneumonia," she warned.

He reached out to pinch her chin. "Always the nanny. I'll be right back." And then he was loping up the hill, the long muscles in his legs bunching as he leaped from rock to rock.

Judy stared after him, feeling such affection for him that it truly became a concern. Unless Lee Madison kills him, of course, she thought dryly as she turned back to the picnic. In which case her problem would be solved.

After lunch a serious game of poker began on a blanket under a red- and yellow-striped umbrella. A pregnant woman settled down to read in a makeshift lean-to, having collected around her all the napping babies. The older children helped the younger ones build sand castles and play in shallow waters with Janet's father in attendance.

The more energetic gathered for a game of volleyball.

"So how'll we divvy up?" Mick asked.

"How about husbands against wives?" The suggestion came from Mick's wife, a redhead with two ponytails. It was met instantly with shouts of ridicule.

"Be serious, Bobbi," Mick scoffed. "We'd cream you."

Bobbi turned to the women gathering around her. "Are we going to let them get away with that?"

Bold threats and promises were flung across the net to the men, and the game was on—wives and girlfriends against the husbands and boyfriends.

The women were behind by six points when Judy decided that if they were going to recover they would have to play at the net. The men drove the ball too powerfully for the women's back lines to return. These plays invariably ended in a point for the male side.

When Judy finally rotated to the net, she found Brenda at center net. She went to her while the men were gloating and calling insults across the sandy court.

"We're going to have to kill the ball right here to even up this game," she said quietly.

Brenda looked at her in surprise and smiled wryly. "I suppose you were also St. Clement's School for Girls' volleyball varsity."

Judy couldn't help smiling. "I was. I also coached fifth grade volleyball."

Brenda laughed, her blue eyes warming, her manner going from goddess to giggler. "I can't kill the ball worth a damn, but I can set it up for you if you can do it."

"All right. We'll teach them to scoff."

Judy ran back to her position and braced for the serve, finding a very familiar pair of eyes leveled on her through the net. Mitch was directly opposite her in white shorts and T-shirt, healthy and unharmed by Lee, who was positioned in the center.

"Watch this, Kramer," Judy said as the ball left the server's hand. It sailed low over the opposite end of the net and fell without challenge.

Mitch peered at Judy through the net. "Brilliant play, Cassidy," he said.

She made a face at him and concentrated on the serve. It came straight at the second row, where Bobbi stopped it, and Brenda sent it toward Judy in a high, slow arc. Judy waited until it was inches above the net, leaped with all the agility she'd had at sixteen and slammed it to the sand between Mitch and Lee.

For several seconds the two men stared at each other, then turned simultaneously to stare at Judy. Cheers rose from the women, and Brenda gave Judy a thumbs-up sign before getting into position again.

"Did you see that, Kramer?" Judy whispered.

"If I'd seen it," he returned archly, "I'd have stopped it."

She smiled. "Better luck next time."

The next play had Brenda going down on her knees to retrieve a low ball and sending a forceful return to the back line with both fists. It ended when one of the men fouled out the ball. Judy saw Lee, hands on his hips, study his wife through the net. Brenda gave him a lift of her eyebrows, then looked at Judy with the gleam of battle in her eye.

The next several vollies were fierce. The men worked Judy and Brenda mercilessly, trying to catch them off guard and wear them down. But what they lacked in strength, they made up for in stamina and the determination of the underdog.

The women were ahead by a point when Lee slammed the ball over the net. Brenda moved to intercept it, but misjudged and stopped the ball with her face rather than her hands. She went down with both hands over a bleeding nose.

Lee was under the net and kneeling beside Brenda even before Judy could reach her. Leaning her against his arm, he pulled her hands away from her face.

"Mitch!" he bellowed.

"Right here." Kneeling at her other side, Mitch gently ran a thumb along the line of her nose. Judy reached around him with a handkerchief to dab at the blood and make the injury easier to assess.

"What do you think?" Lee asked.

"Doesn't feel broken." Mitch touched Brenda's nose once more, and she caught his wrist, pushing it aside.

"It isn't," she said, trying to sit up. Then she groaned and put a hand to her head. "I think I'm going to die, but I'm pretty sure my nose isn't broken."

"Come on." Lee lifted her in his arms and stood. "You can lie down for a while in the back of the van."

Her arms wrapped around his neck, Brenda studied him suspiciously for a moment, then dropped her head to his shoulder, apparently too dizzy to argue.

"Want me to help you get her up the bank?" Mitch asked.

Lee shook his head. "I'll manage."

"Here." Janet handed Brenda some ice wrapped in a tea towel.

Brenda smiled weakly. "Thanks, Janet."

As Lee trudged away with his wife, the assembled party exchanged grinning looks. Mitch's gesture of crossed fingers expressed everyone's thought.

Then he turned his attention to Judy. "And you!" He jabbed a finger at her shoulder. "Where did you learn to play like that?"

She shrugged, barely holding back the laughter. "I coach volleyball, remember?"

"What!" the men complained.

"And we're a point ahead!" Bobbi said, giving Mitch a shove toward his side of the net. She took over Brenda's spot. "You guys get back there and try to save your-selves. I'll set up for you, Judy."

"We might as well give up," Mick Taylor said in exaggerated despair. "Bobbi can't play worth a damn, but if we win, you know we'll all be sleeping on the sofa."

"If you don't shut up and serve," Bobbi shouted, "you'll all be sleeping in the hospital!"

Amid threats and laughter, the game began again.

By evening most of the couples with young children had left. Those remaining gathered around a camp fire, telling jokes and stories about one another. Laughter and a mellow mood filled the cool night air.

"Girls okay?" Mitch handed Judy a cup of coffee as she joined the circle and sat beside him.

"They're fine." She looked several yards beyond the circle to where Liz, Katie and the remaining children lay in sleeping bags. "I just wanted to make sure their bags were zipped up. It's getting chilly."

"Here." He shook out the blanket they had brought and put it around himself and Judy, pulling her close so that he could close the ends together. "Better?"

Yes, it was better. Being that close to him was better than anything she had ever felt. And for now it didn't matter that they both had reasons to think this course was dangerous. It was enough that the night was fragrant, that everyone around the circle was in someone else's arms and that this group's sometimes gentle, sometimes rude, but always sincere camaraderie cast a glow over everything. Judy leaned on Mitch's shoulder and turned her back on caution.

"Lee and Brenda never came back," Janet said, staring into the fire. "I hope she's okay."

"She's fine," Bob assured her with a laugh. "She was yelling at Lee and stomping off to her station wagon when I went up to get the kids' sleeping bags."

"Damn!" Bobbi said feelingly. "I thought this afternoon was a perfect chance for them to work it out."

Mick, who sat behind his wife, his arms around her, leaned down to look into her face. "After he broke her nose with a volleyball?"

She reached up and rapped a slender fist on his head. "It wasn't broken, and they were alone in his van to talk things over."

"They don't understand talking," Bob said. "They just understand yelling. And I hate to break this to you, boss, but did you remember that they were in charge of deciding on and finding our donation for the auction? I doubt that either one of them gives a rip about that right now."

"Thanks, Bob," Mitch said evenly. "Considerate of you to volunteer."

"Now, wait a minute...."

"What auction?" Judy asked.

"All the businesses in Manzanita get together at the end of the summer," Janet explained, taking a rock from her husband's hand as he threatened to hit Mitch with it, "and hold an auction of goods or services to raise money for the hospital. The auxiliary's always looking for toys for the children's ward, or books and games and video movies to help the patients pass the time. Or sometimes the money helps the hospital purchase special equipment that their regular budget can't afford."

"We like to support the venture," Mitch said, "because they've patched up everybody in the crew at one time or another."

"Seems to me Lee said something about making a trunk for the auction," Mick put in. "I don't know if he's done it or not, but somebody should check with him before we make other plans."

"Considerate of you to volunteer," Bob said, laughing with great satisfaction. Mick returned the laugh with a great lack of sincerity and made a throat-cutting gesture with his hand.

"What kind of a trunk?" Bobbi wanted to know.

"One of those large, foot-of-the-bed kind of things. You know what fine work Lee does."

"Great," Mitch said. "Maybe we don't have a problem after all."

The coffeepot did one more turn around the camp fire, then Janet sighed. "Much as I hate to break this up, we'd better get the kids home." She reached out to pat Mitch's knee. "Thanks, Mitch. It was wonderful, as always."

"Sure." Mitch got to his feet and offered a hand to Judy, then wrapped the blanket around her.

Mitch doused and covered the fire while Bob and Mick carried their sleeping children up the bank, Janet leading the way with a lantern.

"Well, Brenda and Lee seem to be a lost cause," Bobbi said with an air of resignation while she waited with Judy. "What about you and Mitch?"

Judy laughed, gesturing self-consciously toward Mitch. "I'm just the nanny."

"Somehow I don't think he thinks of you that way," Bobbi said, fingering the blanket Judy still clutched around her shoulders. "If I were you, I wouldn't let him escape." Bobbi said goodbye when Mick returned to help her up to the car.

Judy waited with a gently snoring Katie while Mitch carried Liz to the car. Then she led the way with the lantern and the blanket while he carried Katie.

"So what do you think of my friends?" he asked as they drove home through the darkness. Nothing was visible but roadside shadows and the glittering swath the moon cut on the ocean.

Judy turned to smile at him. He referred to them not as his employees but his friends. She thought it said a lot about the man. And suddenly all the concerns that had died in the firelight on the beach came to bristling life.

"They're wonderful," she said. "You're a lucky man."

"I am, aren't I?" There was a smile in his voice as he glanced in her direction. "Do you have to sit way over there?"

"Yes."

"Why?"

"Because you're concentrating on your driving."

"No, I'm concentrating on you being way over there. If you came closer, I could concentrate on my driving."

Judy let the silence stretch for a moment before deciding it was time to remind him of the obstacles in his path. "I'm going to Oxford, remember?"

"So you've told me. I think it's great."

"Nothing is going to prevent my doing that."

"Good for you. I like a determined woman."

"I thought," she reminded gently, "that you liked a woman who was gentle and generous and came around to your way of thinking."

He nodded, staring at the road. "I loved a woman like that, yes." He gave her another quick glance, then settled back in his seat as they emerged from the woods and the road straightened. "But I think I could learn to love other things in a woman—things I might have once thought . . . inconvenient. Maybe we never stop growing up."

Judy studied his profile, backlit by a street light, as they stopped at an intersection, and she scooted over to sit beside him.

"My life would be a lot simpler if you could try to be less likable," she said, resting her elbow on the back of the seat and her hand on his shoulder. "A little less nobility, a little less consideration and I might be able to convince myself that I really don't want to know you any better."

He lowered his head modestly.

Judy rested her chin on the hand on his shoulder. Sighing, she approached the question carefully. "I'm not sure this is a good idea, anyway, but . . . you . . . I mean, do you think you could . . . love again?"

Mitch felt her breath against his chin and smiled, suddenly at peace with the knowledge that he was coming to care for her. "For a long time, I didn't think I could. It felt as though all my love was tied up in Mandy and always would be. But—" he slanted her a smile that was so gentle she almost felt it "—I'm beginning to understand that I can't keep giving love where it can't grow anymore. She was everything to me, will always be an integral part of me, but I guess I'm ready to go forward. You said I would be one day."

Cautions crowded Judy's mind, but she couldn't bring herself to voice them. He felt free after a long imprisonment of grief, and she didn't want to confine him with warnings and portents of doom.

Resting her head against his shoulder, she closed her eyes and let herself enjoy the warmth of the rough fingertips that caressed her cheek.

Chapter Eight

"All right! Here's a Honda VF500 Interceptor," Dan read from the classifieds while Judy worked on the KRAMERS sign that usually hung over the front door. Liz and Katie were across the street, disassembling a doll carriage with Jamie and Linda Morgan. "'Never been down, extremely clean, eighteen hundred dollars.'" Dan looked up from the paper, his dark eyes bright. "What a steal!"

It was a crystal clear evening, and Dan and Judy worked at a card table set up on the deck. She raised her head to look at the boy, and the smells of linseed oil, paints and turpentine that had filled her nostrils for the past hour were replaced by the fragrance of pungent pine and the exotic perfumes of a coastal night.

"A steal?" Judy grinned across the table at Dan. "You sound as though you had eighteen hundred dollars."

"That's dirt cheap for an Interceptor." He gave her a grimace of exasperation. "Of course Dad would have me on foot till I'm thirty. He probably—" The ring of the telephone through the sliding glass doors to the kitchen interrupted his complaint. He got to his feet, assuming a look of suavity and sophistication. "That's probably Chelsea, finally coming to her senses. Oh, the burden of this perfect body." Slapping a hand to his reasonably broad but still thin chest, he coughed and ran in to answer the phone.

He was back in a moment, his eyes large, the laughter gone from them.

"Dad's in the hospital," he said, his voice reflecting a concern he was obviously trying not to show. "Lee wants to talk to you."

Automatically dropping her brush in the jar of turpentine, Judy ran to the phone, her heart pumping, her throat going dry. "Hello?"

"Miss Cassidy, this is Lee Madison."

"Yes." Her voice sounded high and panicky, and she made a conscious effort to take an even breath. "What's happened?"

"He's okay," Lee said quickly. "But his right leg is broken. The doctor says it's a simple fracture and shouldn't develop into any kind of a problem, but he'll be out of commission for a while. They'll be finished with him in a few minutes. I called Brenda, and she's coming with her station wagon. We'll bring him home."

After a swift surge of relief that the injury was nothing life threatening, Judy felt her heartbeat settle down to normal. "Is there anything I can do?"

"Just get his bed ready."

"Right."

Dan, pale and tense, asked the minute she hung up the phone, "Well?"

"A simple broken leg," she said, expelling a sigh of relief at the same moment that Dan did. "Not that a broken leg is that simple, but at least it's nothing worse."

"Yeah. Are we going to go get him?"

"Lee and Brenda are bringing him home. We've got to get his bed ready." Judy started toward Mitch's room. "Would you go get the girls?"

"Sure," he replied, and left.

Judy went into Mitch's room. It was blue and pale yellow with long drapes, which she pulled aside for a view of the street. She put fresh sheets on the bed, and a pitcher of water and a glass on the bedside table. When the girls came in, she was hanging up clothes. Judy assured them that although their father would look tired and different with a cast on his leg, he would eventually be fine.

"Is he gonna have crutches?" Liz asked.

"Yes, I'm sure he will."

"And he won't have to go to work?"

"Not for a while."

Katie looked at Liz, her eyes alight with the possibilities. "He can play dolls with us, and go to the beach, and—"

"He's gonna be sick!" Liz said impatiently. "He won't feel like playing. We'll have to be quiet and not bother him." She looked at Judy for corroboration. "Right?"

"At least the first couple of days." She sat on the foot of the bed and pulled the girls down beside her. "He'll probably be very uncomfortable and he can't go to work, so you can cheer him up by telling him what's going on in the neighborhood and stuff like that."

"It's hard to think of him with something broken," Dan said soberly from the doorway. "He throws those pieces of lumber around like they were matchsticks. I guess I always thought he was stronger than they were."

Judy thought about the man who was raising three happy, well-adjusted children while coping with the death of the one woman who had been his whole life, and she smiled at Dan. "He is, but he's also breakable bone just like the rest of us."

The sound of a slowing car invaded the room, and everyone turned to the window to see a station wagon pull up in front of the house.

"There they are," Dan said, and he hurried for the front door, with the girls at his heels. Judy caught up with them in time to prevent their sabotaging Lee and Brenda's cautious efforts to get Mitch out of the back of the wagon.

"Brenda, you've got to lift and pull," Lee said impatiently.

Mitch's left arm was around her shoulder, and Brenda glared across his chest at Lee. "Well, he's not exactly a featherweight, you know."

His other arm around Lee's shoulder, Mitch looked up at Judy and shook his head in good-natured exasperation. He was pale, but very much himself, Judy noted in relief.

"Why don't you let me try to—" he began.

"Will you shut up," Lee interrupted. "You're not supposed to put any weight on it for a couple of days. All we need is for you to fall out of the wagon."

Mitch closed his eyes, obviously summoning patience. Brenda drew a deep breath, as though that would give her greater strength.

"I'll take that side," Dan said, assuming command of a rapidly deteriorating situation with a manner so impressively mature that the adults involved were surprised into silence. "Why don't you guide his leg, Brenda, until we get him out."

Dan moved into Brenda's position under Mitch's arm. Eye to eye with his father, he smiled. "Gone klutzy on us,

Dad? You ought to be more careful. Bones get brittle at your age."

"Give me a couple of days," Mitch threatened, "and I'll show you how brittle they can be at *your* age."

"Don't lose your sense of humor, Dad."

Mitch smiled placidly. "I'm not. I could find it very amusing to beat on you. Now could we work on getting me out of here?"

Dan grinned at Lee. "Testy, isn't he?"

For the first time since Judy had known Lee, he smiled. "Give him a break. He's in pain. Ready?"

"Ready."

In a matter of minutes, Mitch was deposited with care on the bed in his room, Brenda gingerly letting his leg down, Liz and Katie immediately climbing up on either side of him to offer comfort. Judy fluffed some pillows behind him, and Lee, with a strong arm around Mitch's middle, pulled him into position. The two looked at each other one long moment, then Lee straightened and asked briskly, "Comfortable?"

"Yeah," Mitch replied, his tone also curt. "Thanks for staying with me."

Lee lifted a casual shoulder. "It's hard to abandon someone dumb enough to fall out of the back of a truck."

Unable to see the undercurrent of caring entwined in the criticism, Liz frowned at Lee. "My dad isn't dumb," she corrected with every evidence of making an issue of the question if the man so wished.

Lee gave her a brief, bright smile. "Sorry, Lizzie." Then he looked at Mitch, the smile gone. "If you need anything, call."

Brenda leaned down to give Mitch a hug.

Judy followed Lee and Brenda to the door. "Thank you so much. Are you sure I can't fix you something to eat or get you a drink?"

"No, thanks." Brenda smiled, and Judy thought how beautiful she was when she wasn't affecting sophistication. "We'll get something on the way home." Then she looked up at Lee with a frown. "Where's your van anyway?"

"At the site," he replied. "I went in the ambulance with Mitch. You can just take me there."

Brenda asked, a suggestion of disappointment in her voice, "Aren't you hungry?"

Lee seemed to be concentrating on her eyes, reading hard. "Are you?"

Judy saw the impatience in Brenda's blue eyes and said a silent prayer that Brenda wouldn't blow it. "I'm starving," she said finally.

"All right," Lee conceded, his quiet but hard-edged voice softening just a little. "We'll eat before we get my van. Miss Cassidy?"

"Judy. Yes?"

"Call."

"I promise."

Judy returned to the bedroom to find Liz pouring Mitch a glass of water and Katie straddling his waist, rubbing eight tiny fingertips across his forehead.

"She's rubbing away my headache," Mitch explained as Judy approached the bed.

Liz tried to push Katie out of the way to offer Mitch the water, and the child resisted, shoving her sister's arm. Water splashed onto Mitch's face and soaked his grimy chambray shirt.

"Okay, girls." Judy took the water glass from Liz and replaced it on the bedside table, then lifted Katie from Mitch's waist.

"He gots a headache!" Katie complained.

"I know. Liz, please get a towel from the bathroom." Judy sat on the edge of the bed with Katie while Liz ran off obediently. "Sweetie, I have some pills the doctor sent home with your dad to help his headache. What he needs to do right now is sleep, and so do you. Okay?"

Katie looked from Judy to her father. Mitch held out his arms.

"Come on. Kiss me good-night. You can tuck me in for a change."

Pleased at being able to make an important contribution to her father's recovery, Katie crawled into his hug and proceeded to tuck him in, in a very businesslike fashion. Though Judy had carefully made the bed, Katie tucked the blankets in at the bottom and checked the hospital corners. Then she went up the side to his chin, where she tucked the blankets in tight enough to strangle.

Mitch coughed dramatically, and Katie giggled.

"Here." Liz handed Judy the towel, watching her little sister loosen some of the tucking around her father's shoulder. "But he's all wet," she said.

Judy nodded, pulling Liz aside. "I know, but she needs to feel like she's doing something to help. If you can help me by getting her off to bed, I'll get him dried off and settled for the night. Then I'll come up and tuck you two in, in a little while."

Liz nodded, squaring her shoulders. "She means well." She said it with such serious indulgence that Judy had to hug her.

"Of course she does."

"Good night, Daddy." Liz leaned over her father to kiss him good-night, then took her sister firmly by the hand. "Come on, Katie. Tell Judy if you need us, Daddy."

"I will." Mitch winked at Liz. "Thanks, Lizzie."

She winked back. "Sure."

The moment the girls were out the door, Judy pulled the covers back and helped Mitch to a sitting position, smiling with him as she handed him the towel. "Nothing like a good drowning for a man with a broken leg."

While Mitch dabbed at his face, Judy unbuttoned his shirt, tugging at the sleeves to remove it. As he flung an arm out to oblige her, she was faced with that smooth expanse of chest and the rippled muscle above his belt buckle.

She eased him back against the pillows, gasping as he winced when the movement caused him pain.

"I'm sorry," she whispered.

"Not your fault," he assured her. "Everything seems to hurt."

"Just tell me where you keep your pajamas, and I'll leave you to get some sleep."

"I don't use them," he said with a glance filled with pain but tinged with humor. "Maybe you'd better get Dan."

She shouted, and the boy appeared instantly. "Yeah?"

"Would you help your dad out of what's left of his jeans, please?" She turned to smile at Mitch. "Would a cup of coffee help?"

He nodded. "Sounds great."

"Watch his leg," Judy cautioned Dan.

Dan walked into the bedroom, rubbing his hands together. He stood over his father and motioned toward the cast with a wicked laugh. "Perhaps we could come to some sort of agreement about my bike."

Judy closed the door as Mitch put an arm across his eyes and groaned.

After putting on a fresh pot of coffee, Judy ran upstairs to check on the girls and was relieved to find them both asleep. She turned off lights, secured blankets and hurried back downstairs to clean up the work she'd left on the card table on the deck when the call had come from Lee.

She took a moment to wonder how Lee and Brenda were doing, sharing a meal for the first time in their six-month separation. It was easy to see that feelings were still strong between them, but the resentments were visible, too.

Deciding that it was more important tonight that she be near the invalid than near the children, Judy made up the living room sofa for herself, putting the few things she would need—alarm clock, Mitch's medication—on the coffee table. Then she poured a cup of coffee and went to check on the progress in Mitch's room.

She found the bedroom door open and Mitch propped up on his pillows, the blankets pulled up to his waist. He wore a crisp white T-shirt. Dan was sitting on the edge of the bed.

"Well, don't worry about that stuff," the boy was saying. "I can handle it. And that stuff you were going to do on the roof, we can do next summer. I mean, nothing's leaking. And you always said your crew works better without you 'cause when you're not there, they're working instead of hassling you all the time."

Mitch nodded philosophically. "That's true."

"And Judy takes care of everything around here, so all you have to do is lie there and figure out how to buy my Honda Interceptor. Oh, hi, Judy."

"Dan," Mitch pleaded.

"Okay, I'm going. I have to go to work early tomorrow, but I'll check with you before I leave."

"Thanks, son."

"Sure."

Dan left the room, and Judy put the mug in Mitch's hand and looked around, trying to see if everything was in order and if there was anything else he would need. When she felt a tug on her hand, she looked down at Mitch in surprise.

"Sit with me for a minute," he said, tugging until she sat on the edge of the bed by his waist. He took a deep sip of coffee and closed his eyes, savoring it.

"God, that's good." Then he looked at her. He seemed worried. "Will you be all right?"

Judy arched her eyebrow. "You're the one with the broken leg."

"I'm the one in bed," he countered. "You're the one watching three kids, cooking and cleaning, and now adding a little nursing to your chores."

Wondering how many men would have worried about their broken leg being an inconvenience to someone else, Judy leaned toward him earnestly. "If you could give up eating, it would help. Then I wouldn't have to walk all that way from the kitchen with your food. What do you say? Are you up to a three- or four-day fast until you can hobble around?"

Mitch rolled his eyes and took another sip of coffee. "I think you're spending too much time with my son."

"Isn't that why you hired me?" she asked innocently.

"You were supposed to influence them," he pointed out. "They were not supposed to influence you."

"Ah," she said as though that were a revelation. "You should have explained more carefully." Then focusing on his pallor and the pain lingering in his eyes, she stopped teasing. "Do you feel like eating anything?"

His eyes widened in surprise. "You just put me on a four-day fast."

She waved a hand carelessly. "Tonight you look a little peaked. We'll waive the fast."

"Thanks." He smiled and put the coffee mug on the nightstand. "Actually my stomach's a little unsettled. And I think that painkiller they gave me before I left the hospital is about to take effect."

"Well, let me help you get settled." Judy got to her feet and cradled his head in one hand. "One pillow or two?" she asked.

"One," he replied, sinking into it wearily after she had plumped it.

He gave her one last, lazy look before closing his eyes. "Thanks, Judy," he mumbled.

Before she could tell him it was no trouble, he had fallen asleep.

THE FIRST THING Judy heard when she awoke was a pithy, heartfelt oath. Staring into the darkness, her heart beating fast, she reached a hand out and encountered a nubby fabric. After a moment of confusion, she remembered she was sleeping on the sofa and threw the blankets back. She grabbed her cotton robe and headed toward Mitch's room.

She found the bedside lamp on, though it lay on its side. Mitch was trying to pull himself up on his good leg and not being very successful.

"What are you doing?" she demanded in a whisper as she walked into the room.

He looked at her grimly. "I'm trying to get to the bathroom. You would be wise not to stop me."

Smiling, she righted the lamp and reached down to hook an arm securely around his waist. "How about if I give you a hand?"

He put his arm around her shoulder. "I don't want you to get hurt."

Judy looked into his concerned dark eyes and saw that the pain was back. She smiled and tightened her grip on him. "Then my advice would be, don't fall on me. Got a hold of the table?"

"Yeah."

"Okay. Here we go." She lifted, Mitch pulled himself up, and then they were both standing, he with his plaster-wrapped leg sticking out. She leaned forward to reach the crutches Dan had propped against the wall and handed him one. "I'll get you as far as the bathroom sink. Ready?"

He was pale, and the pain was now in his voice, as well as his eyes. "Ready."

After a couple of awkward steps, they coordinated their movements, and Judy got him to the sink with relative ease. "There. I'm going for your medication, but don't try to go back to bed until I can help you."

"I wouldn't think of it," he said wearily.

Judy closed the door behind him and picked up the water jug. In the kitchen, she rinsed it and filled it with fresh water. By the time she had retrieved the pills and put them and the jug on the bedside table, he was standing in the bathroom doorway, leaning on one crutch, one hand holding the doorway molding.

Judy looked resolutely away from the long, muscular leg that extended below a pair of white cotton briefs.

"Maybe I should draw up a will," Mitch suggested, the teasing note in his tone blunted by the pain there.

Judy got under his arm and wrapped hers around his waist. "You'll live, Mitch," she replied, bracing herself as she took much of his weight. "You just won't be very comfortable for a few days."

Judy eased him onto the bed and let him sit a moment while she took the crutch and propped it against the wall.

"Drink this." She handed him a tablet and a glass of water.

He complied, then handed back the glass. "I'm sorry I woke you."

"No problem," she said, and eased him back.

Settling into the blissful softness of the pillow, Mitch looked up at Judy, thinking that he hadn't been handled with such . . . softness in a long time.

She smiled. "Need anything else?"

There was that question again, but now he knew the answer. He'd keep it to himself, however, until he felt better able to handle her arguments, because he felt sure she would have some.

He winked at her. "I'm going to be fine," he said, and closed his eyes.

Chapter Nine

His damned leg hurt like hell, and he was looking at two weeks completely off the job and another four after that before he could do any more on the site than supervise. He'd never been one to stand around and watch. He trusted his crew implicitly, but when a man's name was on his business, he owed it to himself and to his family to be there when business was conducted. His plans for the summer were shot to hell, and he was hungry.

Mitch glared at the open doorway as footsteps approached his room. Judy walked in, a blue cotton shirt open over her leotard. He watched her shapely legs, clad in some light, black fabric, as she walked gracefully to his bed with a tray.

"Good morning," she said cheerfully, putting the tray on the nightstand. Then she cradled his head, propped up his pillows and held them against the headboard. "Can you scoot yourself up?"

He complied and was rewarded with a tray placed across his knees. On it was a cup of coffee, a plate filled with bacon and eggs and toast, and a pot of jam. His mouth watered. "This is just what I wanted," he said in wonder, looking up to Judy.

"I thought it would be," she said, smiling down at him. "I know you didn't have any dinner last night. If you want more, holler." And she left, the roundness of her hips beneath her shirt tantalizing him as she walked away.

Mitch tucked into his breakfast, still in pain, still worried about his business. But something—or someone—had alleviated the pall of bleakness under which he had awakened.

When Judy returned to pick up his tray, Janet Norgaard trailed along behind her. She carried a magazine in a brown wrapper, and a square tin.

"A gift from Bob," she said, handing him the magazine. She smiled at Judy. "It's the current *Playboy*, so you might monitor his pulse. These are cookies from me and the kids." Placing the tin on the bedside table, she asked solicitously, "How do you feel?"

He shrugged. "Passable, I guess."

"Why don't you let me take the girls for the weekend?" she suggested. "They're darlings, but it's hard to keep young ones quiet, and you need your rest for the next few days. It'll lighten Judy's load. What do you say?"

She pointed a thumb over her shoulder toward the commotion in the living room. Apparently she'd brought her children along. "As you can hear, the kids are in agreement."

He was used to having his children around and clamoring for attention at life's worst moments, but there'd be little he could do for them for a while. The burden would be on Judy. "Thanks, Janet," he said, pulling her down for a hug. "You're too good for that shiftless husband of yours, you know."

Janet patted her hair. "I know. But it was marry Bob or follow Warren Beatty from set to set. I finally said, 'Look, Warren, I need security.'"

"I'm sure he was crushed."

"Oh, he was! He's been trying for years to console himself." She patted his head as though he were one of the kids. "Judy and I'll help the kids get a few things together, and I'll bring them back Monday."

The women disappeared, and the raucous childish laughter moved upstairs. Mitch fell back against the pillows and closed his eyes. How could the simple acts of having eaten and spoken to Janet exhaust him? Was he getting that old?

He roused himself out of a doze a while later to be kissed goodbye by a gaggle of little girls, two of them his own, the rest Bob and Janet's. He waved in response to the shouts of "Bye, Daddy" and "Bye, Uncle Mitch," then found himself wrapped in a blissful silence. He fell instantly asleep.

When he awoke, Judy was standing over him, holding a glass of lemonade.

"How do you feel?" she asked.

Rest seemed to have lessened the pain in his leg, and he became aware that it had been more than twenty-four hours since he'd had a bath. The emergency room had bathed his leg before setting it, but he now longed for a hot, leisurely soak. Knowing that was impossible, he grumbled moodily, "I feel filthy."

Judy put a hand out to flick a hank of dusty hair back from his forehead. "How about a bath?"

His hazel gaze widened slightly. She felt herself drawn into it but resisted.

"Please define 'bath,'" he said. "In detail."

"I will bring you a basin of warm water, a washcloth and a towel." She grinned, aware of destroying his fantasies. "I'll give you some privacy, and you will take a 'bath.'"

Mitch shook his head at her. "You can take a beautiful, tantalizing, stimulating word like—" he paused to give the word an almost erotic sound "—bath, which brings to mind warm water lapping along a languid body." He paused again to close his eyes and add reverently, "Or maybe two languid bodies, and reduce it to—" he frowned censoriously "—a basin of water and privacy. And you don't even look remorseful."

Standing firm against his charming pout, Judy folded her arms. "Do you want the basin or not?"

He sighed heavily. "Sure." Then he added as an afterthought, "Please."

Judy cleared off his bedside table, moved it within easy reach and covered it with a towel. She brought a half-full basin of warm water, a washcloth, soap and a towel. With a heartless wave she closed the door behind her, giving him the privacy she had promised and which he would have willingly foregone.

Judy wandered around aimlessly for a few minutes, trying to decide if she should take out her paints, when the telephone rang.

"Hi, Jude, it's Dan. Is Dad awake? Dusty's mom called and invited me to spend the weekend with them. They're going to Kah-Nee-Ta, and I don't have to work tomorrow. Can you manage Dad while I'm gone? I mean, he's kinda heavy if you have to move him around."

Good question, she thought. Although his weight was the least of her problems.

"Sure. Hold on."

After she shouted Dan's request through Mitch's bedroom door, there was a brief silence.

"Will you be all right?" he asked Judy.

"Of course. Pick up your bedside phone. He's on the line."

Shortly after that, Bob Norgaard called.

"How's he doing?"

"He looks considerably better than last night, and he's in pretty good spirits," Judy replied. "Janet came for the girls this morning. That was nice of you two."

"No problem. Think he could take the crew stopping by tonight after work?"

"I'm sure he'd like that."

"About seven?"

"Fine."

"Anything we can bring you?"

Touched by his thoughtfulness, Judy wondered if other people's families could be as thoughtful as Mitch's friends were. "No, thank you. But I appreciate your asking."

She walked to Mitch's bedroom and entered after being assured he was decent. She told him about Bob's call.

"The whole crew's coming over?" he asked.

"He didn't say." She emptied the basin in the bathroom and returned to face him, her hands on her hips. "Feel better?"

"Much," he replied, then ran a hand through his hair. "My hair feels filthy, though. Not much I can do about that, I guess."

"Well, maybe I can help you there." Judy considered the height of the bed off the floor and the distance from the bathroom to the bed, and decided that though there was bound to be a moderate amount of sloshing and splashing, a shampoo could be accomplished.

He looked at her doubtfully. "How?"

"With the basin. We'll just lean your head over the side of the bed, I'll suffer a few trips back and forth to the bathroom for fresh water, and you'll feel as though you've been coifed by Jose Eber himself."

"Who?"

"Never mind. Sound good?"

"Wouldn't that be a lot of trouble for you?"

Judy shrugged away his concern. "With the children gone, there's not that much for me to do."

He closed his eyes and offered nobly, "Then, by all means. Have your way with me."

Judy rolled her eyes. "Lie still, and I'll put some towels down." She went into the bathroom and opened the medicine cabinet, scanning the shelves. "Shampoo?" she asked.

"Under the sink."

She was back in a minute to place a towel on the floor near the side of the bed. She pointed to the spot on the mattress's edge just above the towel. "Can you move around to put your shoulders right here and hang your head over?"

With a little assistance from Judy, Mitch moved into position. She eased a towel under his shoulders and put another across his chest for good measure.

"I feel as though I'm going to be beheaded in a Turkish bath," he said.

"You offered to let me have my way with you," she reminded.

"Should have known better," he said, raising his voice as she went into the bathroom and ran warm water in the basin. "It's never wise to let a woman have her way."

"More of your chauvinist philosophy?" Mitch heard the teasing in Judy's voice along with the slosh of water, a small grunt, then a thud as the basin landed heavily on the towel.

Mitch closed his eyes and smiled. "I suppose we should suspend this argument until I've been safely shampooed. I wouldn't want to offend you while I'm in such a vulnerable position."

"Wise decision," Judy applauded. "Now just relax and enjoy this."

The next moment, he felt warm water running over his scalp. Sensation followed the water, raising goose bumps on his skin. He suspended thought and movement to enjoy the unexpected delight.

"Too warm?" Judy asked.

"Ah, no," he said, having a little trouble focusing on the question.

Judy applied more water. She paused to dab water out of his eyes and his ears with the edge of the towel that was draped across his chest. He felt a small stream of something cold, and Judy began to shampoo vigorously.

He sighed, and Judy asked in concern, "Too rough?"

He smiled to himself, thinking how sweet a sometimes-vigorous touch could be. "No. It's fine."

He heard the splat of suds falling on the water as Judy squeezed the shampoo out of his hair. "Back in a minute," she said.

When she returned she poured more warm water on his hair. He felt her kneeling near his shoulder, and when she reached under his head to rinse the hair there, he felt her breasts bump against his chest. He remained still, unwilling to shatter the blissful moment.

Judy applied more shampoo, and he enjoyed the luxury of going through the entire process over again—the rough massage, the movement of water over his scalp, the delicious feel of her fingers combing his hair, the tug of her fingers as she squeezed the water out.

"Now, don't move yet," she instructed.

Not certain he could stir himself to move ever, Mitch was pleased to comply. Expecting her to blot his hair with a towel, all his senses came alert when she placed her fingertips at his temples and moved them in a pattern of small circles along his hairline down to his ears. By the time she had completed that little maneuver a second time, he felt as though every bone in his body had been rendered useless.

"Where'd you learn to do that?" he groaned.

"The woman who cuts my hair does that after a shampoo," she explained, the sound of her voice diminishing as she went back to the bathroom with the basin. "Doesn't it feel great?"

Another groan was his only reply.

Then she was back again, putting a towel over his head, her hands under his back pushing him up, helping him move back to the pillows. She worked the towel vigorously over his hair.

When she had finished, he felt the wet ends of his hair all around his face. Never one to put a lot of stock in his appearance, except to be sure that he was clean, he found himself wondering what he must look like. He chanced a glance at Judy, expecting her to tease. But she was looking at the things on his dresser. She pulled a comb out of the whale-shaped holdall Glenna had given him one birthday to keep keys and wallet and all sorts of things he needed for a workday morning.

Judy came toward him, holding up the comb. "This what you use?"

He nodded. She handed him the comb and turned away, looking at him over her shoulder and promising to be back in a minute.

And she was—with a blow dryer.

As she got on her hands and knees to plug the appliance in, he considered protesting. He had always thought men who had their hair blow-dried were foppish. But if Judy intended to perform the service for him, he knew he didn't have the fortitude to object. He would simply enjoy it and worry about how to explain it when his crew visited later.

Judy knelt on the bed, facing him. She sat back on her heels with the comb in one hand, blow dryer in the other.

"A left side part, right?" she asked.

He put a hand up to it. "My left. Yes."

She pushed a button, and the dryer started with the high-pitched whine of a landing jet. She ran her fingers through his hair, sweeping back and forth with the hot air issuing from the dryer. It felt blissfully delicious. Maybe men who appeared in public with blow-dried hair were having it done by women rather than doing it themselves and deserved his envy rather than his scorn.

Then she combed his hair back repeatedly, working the drier over and over it.

He was occasionally distracted from the hedonistic pleasure by the rapt expression on Judy's face as she worked on his hair. At one point she frowned, turned the drier off and sat with both hands on her knees. She lifted the comb and flicked a hank of hair on his forehead with it.

"You have a lock of hair right in the front," she said disgustedly, "obviously placed by a saboteur."

He nodded resignedly. "A cowlick. My father had the same thing. In every other way I resemble my mother.

She always said he was out to undermine everything she ever did.''

Judy took a moment to chuckle, then frowned again as she studied the stubborn lock. "What do you do with it?''

He shrugged. "I ignore it.''

About to suggest that perhaps the discreet application of a curling iron would solve the problem, Judy took another look at him and decided that the cowlick could be ignored. He looked gorgeous. The hair turning in the opposite direction lent a rakish, artlessly masculine air to his appearance.

She surfaced from her study of him to find his hazel eyes on her. They were almost gold in the bright afternoon light streaming in from the window behind his bed. And all that gold was focused on her, seeing into her, she was sure, knowing how she felt.

"Well.'' She got to her feet and put a hand to the back of his head. Finding it still damp, she turned on the dryer again and worked on it until it was dry.

She turned off the machine, causing a sudden, heavy silence. "Now, I'll leave you in peace,'' she said brightly, twining the cord in figure eights from the handle to the nozzle and back again.

Taking the dryer from her, Mitch put it on the bedside table and pulled her down to sit beside him. "Not on your life,'' he said.

"Now, don't start, Mitch,'' she warned quietly, her eyes large and dark. His indisposition had provided a welcome suspension of their developing relationship. But his eyes, at least, suddenly looked remarkably fit.

"It's there, Judy,'' he insisted. "I'm not *starting* anything. And, anyway, I think it's time we stopped dancing around it. I'm going to kiss you again.''

"And what," she asked gravely, "if I don't want to kiss you?"

He studied her a moment. After a small shake of his head, he released her wrist. "I'd say you're not going with your true feelings, but I wouldn't insist."

Judy studied him in consternation. She half wanted him to insist so that she could blame the kiss on his forcefulness rather than her own desire for it. She admitted aggressively, "Well, you'd be right."

It took Mitch a moment to grasp that she was capitulating. "You mean you want to kiss me?" he asked.

She smiled despite her better judgment. "That makes it sound as though I want to do all the work, without involving you."

"Oh, never fear," he said feelingly. "I'm not one to stand by." He held her arms and studied her face.

He saw wide dark eyes and thick lashes fluttering. Her skin was pink and glowing, her lips parting in nervousness or anticipation, he wasn't sure which. He ran his fingers into the glossy darkness of her hair and pulled her closer. Her eyes found his one last time before their lips met, and he saw only eagerness there.

He moved his mouth on hers with gentle exploration, and she responded with lips that were warm and mobile. He nibbled on her bottom lip, the line of her jaw, her earlobe and then, ever so gently, grazed her cheekbone with his teeth as he went back to her mouth. Her hands moved to his hair, and a sigh escaped him. He pulled slightly away from her, his eyes running quickly over her face as he smiled.

It was a curious comma to a kiss, an unusual hesitation that she understood perfectly. This experiment had all the earmarks of unqualified success. Things turning out to be what they seem was such a rarity in life that it deserved a moment's accolade. She had to smile back and give herself over to accomplishment of the deed.

Mitch pulled her up so that she lay across his chest. Then his mouth opened over hers, and his arms trapped her in his powerful embrace.

Warmth invaded her, and she became aware of her pulse keeping pace with the growing demands of her body. As Mitch's tongue traced the outline of her lips, Judy could feel her blood surge. She had trouble breathing, and she had vague thoughts of coming up for air. But the chest she lay on was so sturdy and warm, the arms that held her so possessive, the lips that seared hers so tender in their forcefulness that breath seemed less necessary to life than Mitch's embrace.

Judy kissed him back with an ardor to match his own, her lips mercilessly teasing his mouth, his ears and a spot at his throat she found enticing.

They finally pulled apart, both breathing hard, eyes trapped in each other's. Mitch righted Judy until she sat on the edge of the bed.

"You know what I think?" he asked.

Judy's voice was just above a whisper. "What?"

"I don't think it matters a damn what either of us had planned come September." Judy didn't have to ask why; she knew what he implied. But he felt the need to say it anyway. "This isn't going to stop here. I suspected it. Now I'm sure of it."

Judy stood, trying to discourage what he was thinking, afraid to think it herself. "Listen to me," she said firmly. "It was a truly remarkable kiss." She drew a breath, waiting for his complete attention. He had a tendency to study her features while they were talking, and she got the impression he didn't always hear everything she said.

Realizing that she was waiting for him, Mitch pulled his eyes away from her mouth and tried to look attentive. "Yes."

"Be sensible," she implored. "That kind of chemistry is dangerous. It can only cause problems."

Mitch bent his good leg under the blanket and rested his wrist on it. "You mean it won't stop at a kiss. It could become...important."

She didn't hesitate. "Yes."

"Judy." He held her hands and stared at them while he thought. "What are you afraid will happen?"

Judy shook her head, annoyed that he insisted on extracting from her what she didn't want to say. So she said it on a little burst of anger. "This is going to become physical, and then...I will have to walk away in September. I *have* to go in September, Mitch."

Mitch freed one of her hands and smoothed her hair, flicking an errant strand in place. His eyes were caring and grave. "What if I promise that when September comes, I won't do anything to try to stop you? Trust me, that I understand how important Oxford is to you."

Warily Judy studied him, trying to decide if what he promised would make it any easier. It would, of course, on one level, yet caring about him would make it difficult to leave him even if he didn't try to stop her.

He reached out to cup the side of her face in his hand. His dark hair caught the sun filtering through the drawn curtains, and the light seemed to glow in his eyes as well. "You've been walking around on the edge of my life for too long, now," he said quietly. "I want you to come in."

Holding his hand to her face, Judy closed her eyes and wondered if any other man in the world had this perfectly balanced combination of gentleness and strength.

Putting his hand down beside him, she stood and gathered up her blow dryer and the towels. "You should rest."

He smiled at her winningly, abruptly changing tack. "Will you bring a couple of sandwiches and come and sit with me? We'll watch soap operas or *Donahue* or something."

"Your crew's coming to visit after work. I should bake something."

"They'll just want beer, and there's plenty in the refrigerator. Don't you want to see *All My Children*?" he asked, giving her a cunning glance. "Liz tells me, when you ladies are going to be out for the afternoon that you tape it. So I know you watch it."

Judy rolled her eyes. "All right, all right. You're going to behave yourself?"

He raised his right hand. "My solemn promise."

Judy walked away, muttering to herself, wondering why she didn't believe him.

Chapter Ten

On Mitch's instructions, Judy had stopped thinking of the object on which she sat as a bed.

"It's as though we were sharing a sofa," he said blithely, nibbling on a potato chip as he scoured the television channels with the remote control. "I've never felt the need for a chair in here, so the logical place for you to sit is on the bed. Right here, on the other side of the sandwiches and potato chips. Hey, a *Perry Mason* rerun. What do you think?"

They had spent the past four hours nibbling constantly and watching television. After the sandwiches and potato chips, there were ice cream, cookies and more potato chips. They saw Perry Mason save the day, Oprah Winfrey arbitrate a discussion on open marriage, and several soap operas, including *All My Children*. Judy answered all Mitch's questions about who was married to or living with whom, who had been married to whom, who was being blackmailed by whom and why.

Now Dan Rather was reporting the news. There was chaos in the Middle East, riots in Japan, a trial over the Chernobyl incident in Russia. But Judy wasn't listening. She was thinking what an enjoyable afternoon it had been, and what a fool she'd be to turn her back on this man without making an effort to see what could develop between them. It would be something good, she was sure of that, and if he promised not to try to stop her from leaving in September, what could be the harm? Each would have experienced something special and would be able to move on in his or her own direction, enriched. That was logical. Dangerous, but logical.

A commotion outside the window brought Judy to her knees on the mattress. Pushing the curtains aside, she saw six men in jeans, ragged shirts and steel-toed boots, laughing and jostling their way to the front door.

"Your cheer-up committee is here," Judy warned, leaping off the bed and heading for the living room as the doorbell began to peel.

Mitch smiled, fluffing the pillow beside him. "Straighten that side of the bed," he called quietly, intercepting her exit, "or you'll be in for a lot of ribbing."

Without comment Judy did as he asked and turned away to get the front door, refusing to meet his eyes.

During the visit, she sought refuge on the deck, putting the finishing touches on the KRAMERS sign. Loud conversation and laughter came from Mitch's room.

"Hi."

Judy jumped at the quiet but unexpected sound, her brush falling into the paint on her palette. Wide-eyed, she looked up at the intruder with a hand to her heart. "Brenda!" she said with a breath of relief. "You startled me."

"Sorry. I thought you could use a little help with dinner if you've been nursing the invalid all day." Brenda took the chair opposite her at the card table and tapped the top of a covered bowl. "Pasta salad."

"Thank you." Genuinely pleased, Judy smiled warmly. "That was thoughtful."

Brenda shook her head dismissingly. "When I had a miscarriage right after Lee and I got married, Mandy cooked for us for a couple of days. What're you doing?"

"Just touching up the sign that goes over the front door."

Frowning, Brenda turned her head to try to see the sign right side up. "Looks a lot classier than it did before. What're all those special little..." She indicated the flourishes with which Judy had detailed the corners.

Judy explained about the art of rosemaling, and though the sign was not really representational of it, she had borrowed rosemaling designs to spruce it up.

Brenda took Judy's book of designs from the far end of the table and leafed through it while Judy worked.

"Is...ah...is Lee here?" she asked with studied casualness.

"Yes." Judy replied without looking up from the sign, trying to match Brenda's nonchalance. "How did dinner go last night?"

Brenda looked up in surprise at Judy's question.

Judy studied her, the brush poised like a pencil in her fingers. "You must know that Mitch and all the crew are hoping you'll get back together. So do I. I don't know either of you that well, but it's easy to see that you're still in love."

Brenda slumped in her chair, the last barrier between them disappearing. "I used to think so, too. I'm not so sure anymore."

"Then last night *didn't* go well?"

"On a superficial level, well enough. We were civil, we talked around all the things that matter to us. We didn't fight, anyway." Brenda's eyes grew dark and empty. "I had hoped he'd call me today. But he didn't."

"Why didn't you call him?" Judy suggested.

Brenda leaned her chin on her hand with an expression of self-disgust. "Because if he'd sounded impatient or anxious to end the conversation, I don't think I could have taken it. I'm a terrible wimp where he's concerned."

"Why don't you invite him to your place for dinner and tell him up front that you want to discuss your problems and try to find a solution?"

"I'm not sure there is one."

Judy smiled. "I'll tell you what I tell my students. There's an answer to everything. You just have to study."

Brenda expelled a breath that fluttered her bangs. Judy thought now much she was coming to like her.

"Lee wants a baby," Brenda said.

Judy nodded. "And you want a shop. But does having one mean you can't have the other?"

Tears brimmed in Brenda's eyes. They pooled in her bottom lids and spilled over. She wiped them away quickly, impatiently, then folded her hands on the table.

Judy reached out to cover her hands sympathetically. "I'm sorry. I didn't mean to pry."

"It's all right." Brenda shook her head. "In a small town and as part of a tight group of friends, everyone knows your business, and I'm used to that. Or, at least, they think they know your business." Drawing a deep breath, Brenda gave Judy a hesitant smile. "After the miscarriage, I was almost afraid to try to get pregnant again. I'd been a spoiled only child with every advantage and all the coddling and support a child could ask for. Then Lee came along and did the same thing for me. Loved me and cared for me and adored me. Then we lost the baby." She shook her head with remembered pain. "That was the first important thing in my life that didn't go my way. It was the first thing I'd ever gone after that

I didn't get. And on top of all that psychological stuff, there's the real grief of knowing that there had been a life inside me and that it died.''

Tears came again, but this time there were too many to wipe away. Brenda dropped her head on her folded arms and cried. Judy ran into the house for Kleenex and two cups of coffee. When she returned to the deck, Brenda was rummaging through her purse for a hanky.

''Here.'' Judy put the box and the coffee in front of her and sipped at her own cup. ''Don't feel like you have to go on if you'd rather not.''

Brenda dabbed at her eyes, blew her nose and drew a deep breath. ''I've never talked to anyone about all this. Do you mind?''

''Of course not.''

''Well . . .'' Brenda began, then stopped and frowned, obviously searching for an explanation. ''I know many women have gone through the same thing and not taken it so hard. But I knew Lee was disappointed. I was looking for something in his workshop one day and found a—'' she paused to draw a steadying breath ''—a cradle he'd been working on. To surprise me, I guess. I felt so *responsible*. Like there was something I should have been able to do or say. Anyway, for a year and a half I didn't want to try again for fear of having the same thing happen. I didn't think Lee or I could take it a second time. Then when Lee dragged me to the doctor and the doctor told me that there was no reason I shouldn't be able to carry a healthy baby to term if we tried again, I agreed to try.''

She shook her head in a kind of frantic rejection of what she was about to say. ''Nothing happened. The first time, we'd been married only three months when I got pregnant. Then, because we wanted it so badly, it wouldn't happen. And the more it wouldn't happen, the less I wanted to try. I know it wasn't fair." Brenda closed her eyes for a long moment, and when she opened them, they were filled with misery. "I just pushed Lee away. This is all my fault. I blamed myself, and he tried to reason me out of it, and that only made me angrier because his understanding somehow only made me more to blame. We fought all the time."

Judy sighed and dropped her brush into the turpentine, leaning back in her chair. "It certainly is a tangle, but the important question is still do you want him back?"

Brenda didn't have to think. "Yes." Then she frowned grimly. "But I don't think he wants me. I thought he'd be angry when I started seeing Mitch, but he wasn't. The day of the beach party, when he carried me to the van, I thought I'd have a chance to talk to him. But it ended with him scolding me for putting him at odds with his best friend. He wasn't jealous, just disappointed in me. We parted, shouting at each other. I don't think he cares anymore."

"I don't believe that. Try to talk to him. Explain to him all the things you explained to me. Without getting angry."

"What if I got him back and still couldn't get pregnant?"

"I'm no expert." Judy leaned forward, crossing her arms on the table and grinning at Brenda. "But if you did it before, chances are you can do it again. And if you get all the problems talked out, you can both relax, and I'll just bet it'll happen."

Brenda sniffed, looking touchingly hopeful. "Think so?"

"Yes, I do."

Brenda studied her a moment before nodding, as though having made a private decision. Then she, too, folded her arms on the table, and she leaned toward Judy. "So how're you doing with the boss?"

Startled by their sudden role reversal, Judy began to busy herself with closing up her paints. "He's just that—my boss."

"Come on," Brenda scolded gently. "I've been honest with you."

Judy stopped fussing with tubes and screw tops and gave Brenda a wry look. "I'm leaving in September for a year in England. I can't let anything happen."

Brenda looked confused. "Why not?"

"After that," she went on, "I owe three years to the school district that's sending me on sabbatical. It's in Washington."

Brenda considered that information with a frown. "But didn't you just tell me that there's an answer to everything?" she said after a moment. "Or at least a compromise?"

Judy opened her mouth to explain that her case was an exception, then closed it, changing her mind. "Me and my big mouth," she acknowledged dryly. "How about more coffee?"

"Please."

"Look at this!" Brenda said excitely when Judy returned with the carafe of coffee. She was pointing to the illustration of a trunk in Judy's book of rosemaling patterns.

"Yeah," Judy nodded, sitting opposite her again. "It's a bridal trunk, sometimes called a dowry trunk. Why?"

"It's just like the trunk Lee made for the auction. He didn't have room for it in his apartment, so he's storing it in our...my garage. If you put the...rosemaling on it, it would be just what Kramer Construction's contribution to the auction would need to make it one of the highest bid items of the evening." Then she frowned. "How long would that take to paint?"

"Not more than a week if I had long blocks of free time. But are you sure Lee would want that done to the trunk? The night of the picnic, everyone was talking about what perfect work he does. Maybe he wouldn't want it painted on."

"Oh, he's not like that." Brenda dismissed that possibility with a wave of her hand. "He's quite a modest man, actually. Confident, but modest. Like Mitch. I think that's why they've been such good friends."

Bob Norgaard appeared on the deck. "We're leaving, Judy."

Brenda immediately grabbed his arm, pulling him to the table to study the bridal trunk in Judy's book. Soon the other visitors, a quiet Lee included, were on the deck, passing the book around, agreeing that decorating Lee's trunk with rosemaling was an excellent idea. Lee seemed as enthusiastic as the rest of them.

"Are you sure?" Judy insisted. "I'll have to paint over it with enamel. I mean, if you chose the wood for grain or—"

"I did, of course," he said, studying the illustration while Brenda unobtrusively studied him. "But if I did a good job, it'll look like a fine piece of work, even under your paint. In fact, my work and your paint should complement each other. But has anybody asked Mitch about this?"

A moment later Mitch looked up from his *Playboy* magazine as the six friends he thought he'd just said good-night to reappeared en masse, with Brenda and Judy following along behind.

The *Playboy* was tossed out of his reach despite his objections, a book pressed into his hands, and the project explained before he could speak.

"So what do you think?" Brenda demanded.

Mitch looked for Judy in the crowd. She was leaning against the foot post of his bed, and he took a moment to admire her, ignoring the rest of the intruders. "Can you do it in time? Or more important, do you want to do it?"

She smiled, bitten by the group's contagious enthusiasm. "I'd love to do it."

Lee nodded. "I'll bring the trunk over tomorrow. Come on, guys. We'd better clear out so he can have some dinner."

As the group called their goodbyes once again, Lee turned to look at Brenda. The angular lines of his jaw softened almost imperceptibly. "Bob and I rode down to the site together this morning. Want to give me a ride home?"

"Depends." Brenda folded her arms. "Is there dinner in it for me?"

The slightest smile played at Lee's lips. "I took you to dinner last night."

"That was Chinese. Tonight I'm in the mood for Italian."

"And I suppose you won't settle for pizza."

She shook her head. "I was thinking of calzone at Emmanuel's."

He nodded after a brief moment's thought. "That does sound good. You're on."

"Good." Brenda turned away from him to give Judy a hug. "Thanks for the coffee and...everything else." She winked. "See ya."

"What was that all about?" Mitch wanted to know when the noisy group had left and Judy returned with a tray containing Brenda's pasta salad, garlic toast and iced tea.

"We talked on the deck while you guys were telling dirty stories," Judy explained, taking her plate and resuming her place on the other side of him.

He slanted her a frowning glance. "Were you eavesdropping?"

"No. But when men laugh that loudly, they've either won money on a game or they're telling dirty stories."

"Quite the little philosopher," he teased, then poked one of the colorful noodles on his plate with the tip of his fork. "What is this?"

"Pasta salad. Brenda made it."

"It's green and yellow and—" he looked at her for reassurance that he wasn't losing his mind "—and red."

Judy rolled her eyes at him. "Where have you been? It's pasta made with vegetables, popular with everyone. It's good for you. Eat it."

Mitch took a tentative taste of the curly noodle, apparently decided it was palatable and helped himself to a more substantial bite.

Sitting cross-legged, Judy turned so that she could face him. "Brenda told me about the miscarriage. It seems that that's a lot of their problem." She related much of what Brenda had told her. "I guess she just appreciated having another woman to talk to."

"From a bad start, you two are getting pretty chummy."

"I like her," Judy said, daring him to find fault with that. "And she loves him and wants very much to get him back and make their marriage work. You have to admire that in anybody."

They had almost finished dinner when Mitch carefully tore the last piece of garlic toast in two. "And what do you recommend for us?"

"Well, there's ice cream for dessert, and for your viewing pleasure—" she consulted the television guide at the foot of the bed "—I'd recommend *The Golden Girls* at nine."

Holding back a smile, Judy looked up at Mitch to see how he'd taken her deliberate evasion. Holding a red rotini on the tip of his fork, he asked with understated calm, "How'd you like a noodle in your ear?"

"You're an invalid," she reminded laughingly, "and I'm stronger than I look. I'd think twice about threatening me."

"You—" The ring of the telephone cut off his retort, and he made a teasing gesture at her with the fork as she got on all fours to answer the bedside telephone.

"Judy?" A vaguely familiar feminine voice asked. At Judy's affirmative reply, she went on, "This is Glenna Kramer. Have I got pictures of England for you!"

"Oh, that's wonderful!" Judy covered the mouthpiece and whispered to Mitch, "It's Glenna."

Glenna went on excitedly to describe the endless list of sights to see and the wonderful shopping. Judy listened greedily and asked questions.

"Do you mind?" Mitch teased quietly, wrestling for the phone. "She is *my* sister, after all."

Judy yanked the phone out of his grasp. "But she's researching for me," she said with a righteous tilt of her chin. "It'll be your turn in a minute. Have a little patience."

"Sounds like you two are getting along all right," Glenna observed, curiosity rife in her remark. "I'm bringing you back tons of reading material. Put him on. He'll only pout."

"Bye, Glenna. See you when you get home." Judy handed the phone over, making a face at Mitch as she left the room.

She had started the dishwasher and gotten bowls down for ice cream when she heard movement at the kitchen doorway. She looked up to see Mitch standing there, leaning on his crutches. He looked as though the trip from the bedroom had been an effort.

"Geez." He leaned against the doorway, bracing himself with one crutch. "I didn't realize how far it was from the bedroom. What's taking you so long?"

She frowned at him as she took the carton of ice cream out of the freezer and carried it to the counter. "You were talking to your sister. I was trying to provide you with some peace and privacy. One scoop or two?"

"Two," he replied. "Lots of sauce. And don't try to act noble. You gave me privacy *after* you got all the news first." He stopped teasing, his expression softening. "Sounds as though she's having a great time. She's spent so much time caring for this one and that one in our family, that it's great to see her developing a sense of adventure."

"Where is she now?" Judy asked. "I forgot to ask."

"Germany. She's taking a boat down the Rhine tomorrow."

Judy groaned. "Doesn't that sound romantic?" She picked up both bowls and found Mitch blocking her path. "Move it, buster," she demanded with a grin.

Laboriously he moved back into the hallway to let her pass. "You know, you're a little sassy for an employee."

"You could always fire me," Judy suggested over her shoulder as she turned into the bedroom. "But who'd do your hair?"

"Good point. What are you going to need for the trunk project?"

After putting the ice cream on the bedside table, Judy relieved him of his crutches and automatically put her arm around him on his cast side to help ease him onto the bed.

"Some enamel and a few more tubes of oils, depending on what colors you want used." She put one knee on the bed and bore part of his weight as he sank down. When she tried to move away, he refused to free her. She offered no resistance when he reached up and pulled her head down. The kiss did not have the morning's passion, but it did have a certain knowledge that made it that much more dangerous. He knows me, she thought in alarm. He understands how important he's becoming to me. Yet she felt no desire to pull away. Instead she leaned into him and let the kiss take her.

When they finally drew apart, he continued to hold her arm as he searched her eyes for... she wasn't sure what.

"The ice cream's melting," she pointed out quietly.

He smiled with a sweetness that was uniquely him. "The question is, are you?"

Chapter Eleven

"I'm going to go crazy," Mitch warned. Drawing a peeler down the length of a knobby potato, he glanced at Judy from his position on the sun porch swing. "Even in the army, I didn't have to peel potatos."

"Poor baby." Judy sat cross-legged on a plastic tarp that covered the round braided rug near the swing. She shook her head in feigned sympathy as she concentrated on her task. She guided her brush along the outer edge of a long swirl on the humped top of the trunk Lee had built, then leaned back to study it critically. Satisfied with the effect, she grinned up at Mitch. "That's the way the mop flops. Getting down to the basics is good for you, reminds you what's important in life."

There was a plop as he dropped the potato into the pan of water at his feet. "How important are peeled potatoes?"

"Have you ever eaten mashed potatoes with the peel left on?"

With an exasperated groan, Mitch frowned at Judy and reached out with a wince to rub the casted leg he had propped on the coffee table. After three weeks of confinement, he was feeling frustrated and restless and just a little sorry for himself. With the awkward cast, he was useless at the site, and sitting at home reminded him of all the jobs he'd wanted to do around the house during the summer and couldn't.

Recognizing the look, Judy dropped her brush into the turpentine. "Want another lemonade?"

"No, thank you." He went back to his chore with an air of martyrdom. The woman was beautiful, intelligent and motivated, he thought grimly, but she could certainly learn a little about rendering sympathy.

Mandy would have fussed over him from morning till night. Once he'd had the walking cast put on, Judy had pretty much left him to his own devices and used her free time to work on the trunk. Casting a moody glance at her head bent over the task of cleaning her brushes, he wasn't sure if the neglect he felt was because she wasn't pampering him the way Mandy would have, or because he found himself continually seeking her company, while she seemed content with absorbing herself in her project.

"Well, dinner will be ready in about forty-five minutes." Standing, Judy pushed the trunk out of the middle of the porch and packed up her paints and brushes. "How are you doing?"

Walking past him with her supplies, she looked at the pot of water he had filled with potatoes. Her eyes widened. "So you can belabor the injustice of your fate and peel potatoes at the same time. That's the sign of a true executive."

He was offended for just a moment, then he saw the light of mischief in her eyes and sighed. "You've missed your calling. You should have been a warden."

She laughed and left the room, shouting back, "Teacher and warden are sometimes synonymous."

Before he could get to his feet, Liz appeared. Her face and limbs were so black she looked as though she'd been tarred and not waited for the feathering.

"Aunt Jackie's on the phone," she said excitedly, the whites of her eyes highlighted by her griminess.

"How'd you get so dirty?" he asked.

"Katie and I cleaned the fireplace," she replied, then went on with what she obviously thought was more important than her appearance. "Aunt Jackie says that Uncle Bill has to make a business trip to Portland, so he could pick us up now and take us to Bend for our two weeks, since you've got a broken leg. You can rest and don't have to drive us over next week."

Mitch struggled to his feet. While half of his mind was wondering if his daughter would ever be clean again, the other half was thinking that Jackie's idea was an answer to his prayer.

"UNCLE BILL'S COMING FOR US in three days?" Liz asked, her hyacinth eyes wide as she looked up from her dinner.

To make Liz and Katie presentable for the table, Judy was half an hour late with dinner. Mitch was pleased that Judy had praised them for their industry rather than scolding them for getting dirty, and dirtying almost everything in the vicinity of the fireplace.

Dan cut a piece of Salisbury steak. "What if I can't get off work early? My vacation's scheduled for the next week."

"I'll call Mr. Johnson first thing in the morning," Mitch promised. "I don't think he'll refuse to let you go."

"Can Judy come?" Katie asked.

"No," Mitch replied casually. "Your aunt and uncle want to spend time with you kids."

"Well, what's she gonna do here?" Liz asked, eyes on her plate.

"Wait for you to come back."

"So she's gonna stay with you for two weeks?" Dan gave his father a look so knowing that Mitch replied with a mildly aggressive tilt of his eyebrow, "Yes."

Understanding Mitch's tone, Dan shrugged. He stabbed a spear of broccoli and looked at his father with wide-eyed innocence. "Just asking. Guess who called today. Besides Aunt Jackie."

"Who?"

Dan looked casual. "Chelsea. She invited me to her house for dinner tonight."

"Oh?"

"Yeah. Seems you were right." He shook his head, his amazement genuine. "She likes me!"

Mitch frowned. "She obviously needs counseling."

Dan smiled broadly, looking from his father to Judy. "Isn't love great?"

"Mmm," Mitch replied. He turned back to his dinner, then chanced another look across the table. Dan and Liz, usually at odds about everything, were sharing a conspiratorial wink. Mitch turned to Judy. She was trying so hard to look anywhere but at the children that she had to have seen that exchange.

Good, he thought. Neither of his children ever missed a trick, and for once, it might be to his advantage. He wasn't averse to Judy's seeing their delight at what they thought was a developing relationship. It was one more point on his side. Judy might steel herself to walk away from him, but could she turn away from those adoring young faces?

While the girls pleaded for new shorts for the trip and Dan bargained to be allowed to take money out of his savings account for a new pair of jeans, Judy entertained the greedy thought that she would have Mitch to herself for two whole weeks.

"YOU'RE SURE they've got everything?"

From the sidewalk in front of the house, Mitch and Judy watched Bill Graham, Mitch's brother-in-law, fit the children's luggage into the back of his station wagon. With Dan's assistance and the girls' supervision, he then stuffed in the requisite blankets, toys and presents purchased for their cousins.

"I have no idea if they have everything," Judy admitted candidly. "I had control of things until I found the goldfish bowl in Katie's tote, and my aerobics tape and some of my makeup with Liz's things. Then I lost ground trying to set things to rights."

As they spoke, Katie raced past them into the house, calling back, "Forgot sumpfin," in response to their questioning looks.

Dan came back to shake hands with his father. "You gonna be okay, Dad?" he asked, chancing a quick, straight-faced look at Judy. "Go easy on him, Judy. He's older than he looks."

"I'd like to say I'm going to miss you, Dan," Mitch said, carefully grinding the hand he held.

"Ouch! Ow!" Dan yanked his hand away to flex it gingerly. "See?" he said to Judy. "No sense of humor."

"I'll watch myself," Judy promised solemnly.

"Bye, Dad." Dan put his arms around his father, hugged him quickly, then pulled away as Katie ran past him, her precious tea-party cup held aloft.

Dan shook his head, watching her hand it to their uncle who, patiently and without complaint, found a safe place for it. "She's as dependent on that thing as she was on the bottle," Dan said.

Mitch laughed. "But it won't look quite so bad at the prom. Be careful, son."

"I know. Be helpful, stay out of trouble, don't wander off on my own, don't take a horse out alone and keep my eye on Liz and Katie. I've got it, Dad. See ya."

The girls ran toward them, and after several hugs and a final trip to the bathroom for Katie, Bill drove away. The children stuck their heads and hands out of the car and shouted and waved.

"It's going to be so quiet," Judy said thoughtfully as she and Mitch walked up to the house. She cast him a playful side-glance. "Maybe I should take the two weeks off. You'll be paying me for nothing."

He stopped at the foot of the porch steps and looked down at her with an expression that combined tolerance with mild impatience. She knew he often didn't know what to make of her; she knew, too, that a man who could be tolerant of what he didn't understand was a rare find.

He ran his hands down her arms, catching her elbows to raise her hands to his waist. "I'd like us to take advantage of these two weeks," he said, his hazel eyes softening as they moved over her face. "I'd like us to get to know each other without having the children between us."

She opened her mouth, a warning on her lips. But he stopped her with a shake of his head. "I know all the cautions. When my children are involved, I have to be careful. But this is just me—" he smiled disarmingly "—and you make me feel as though I've come alive after a long time in limbo. What do you say we lock up the house and take a trip?"

Her eyes widened in surprise. "Seriously?"

"Yes."

"Where?"

He put an arm around her shoulders and started awkwardly up the steps, stopping at each one to swing out the inflexible casted leg. Judy put an arm around his waist to provide balance, but the moment she felt the lean sturdiness of him against her, she found it difficult to remember that the gesture had a practical purpose. "I was thinking we'd drive to Portland and spend the night at Jantzen Beach, where they have several great restaurants and dancing."

"Dancing?" Judy teased as he laboriously cleared the top step.

"Sure," he replied, pushing the screen door open for her. "I can stand in one place and sway to the music. Then we'll spend a couple of days driving along the Columbia River Gorge. Have you ever done that?"

She shook her head, her thoughts running away with her, her heartbeat quickening. "Never."

"Good." He looked into her eyes, his expression possessive. "I'd like to show you one of the most beautiful sights in this country. And it goes on for miles, one eye-filling, heart-stopping scene after the other." He sighed, a small smile stealing across his face as though something he'd waited for a long time was finally coming to pass. "I'll give Lee a call, and if he thinks he's got everything under control, we can leave in the morning."

Lost in his eyes, blind to the danger, Judy agreed.

"OF COURSE, YOU NEGLECTED to mention that I'd have to do the driving," Judy teased. The wind from the open window was making a tangle of her short hair as she guided the station wagon along the tree-lined highway.

Sitting behind her, his leg propped up on the back seat, Mitch leaned forward to give her hair a tug. "I also hadn't counted on having to sit in another seat."

Judy shrugged. "That's what you get for being six-foot-one and wearing an inflexible cast."

"I could have sat in the front with my foot in your lap," he suggested.

"The cast is on the other leg. You'd have had to stick it out the window."

"God, woman," he grumbled good-naturedly, "have you no sympathy?"

"I'm sorry." With doubtful contrition she smiled at him in the mirror. "It's just that I love that injured look you get when I refuse to spoil you. You will live through this broken leg, Mitch."

"Oh? And how many legs have you broken?"

She caught his eye again in the mirror. "Both, actually. One when I was seven in a fall off a bike, and the other just two years ago when I took my classroom roller-skating."

Mitch laughed before he could stop himself. But Judy's frowning reflection in the rearview mirror made him stop and ask solicitously, if unsteadily, "What happened?"

"The boys were playing crack the whip," she explained. "You know. That game where the skater in the middle simply pivots, and each skater down the line has to skate harder and faster as the whip lengthens. Well, they thought it would be a great trick to add Miss Cassidy to the end of the line." She signaled to pass a slow camper and completed the maneuver before continuing the story.

"I kept up as best I could, with everyone now watching us. But the boys, being boys, were determined to outskate me, and they did."

Mitch, envisioning her shapely legs in tights and a skating skirt, prompted, "And then?"

Judy laughed as she remembered. "Well, I lost control and went zinging across the floor on my bottom at such speed that my skates went right through the plasterboard wall of the manager's office." She laughed harder as Mitch joined her. "Imagine the manager's surprise when eight madly spinning wheels attached to two feet broke through the floor molding in front of his desk. At least he was kind enough to call an ambulance. See? There's no reason for you to act superior about your injury."

"And I suppose you stoically carried on, hobbling to school in sleet and snow."

"It was April," she corrected, "and I took a taxi. Actually I did feel a little sorry for myself, too. That was one of the times when living alone wasn't all it's supposed to be."

"What about the other times?" he asked interestedly. "When you're feeling strong and healthy and in control? Do you like living alone?"

Judy considered that a moment, leaning her elbow on the open window and tilting her head sideways. "I get a lot accomplished because I'm alone, and that's important to me. But my mother and my brother and I had such a good time together. I miss that closeness very much. After I graduated from college and got out on my own, I'd sometimes spend a weekend or a holiday at my mother's. I always had a hard time readjusting to my quiet apartment after that. There's probably no greater blessing than sharing space with people who love you and understand what you're trying to do."

Mitch smiled at her in the mirror. "Or even someone who doesn't understand you but loves you anyway."

"I don't know. I think I'd have to be understood to be happy."

"Is it possible for any man to really understand a woman?"

Finding him in the mirror, Judy gave him a scolding look. "Aren't we just beginning to realize that men and women aren't really that different?"

Mitch smiled and leaned back into the corner of the station wagon's middle seat. "Forgive me," he said. "But, having lived with three women, four counting you, that isn't my finding at all. When I was first married, I thought I understood women. But maybe it was just because Mandy understood me so well and catered to doing and being what I wanted, that I congratulated *myself* on loving and understanding the right woman. When Dan was born, he and I related to each other from the very beginning."

Mitch paused to chuckle. "Then Liz and Katie came along, and my orderly catalogue of information on living with women went down the drain. They are smart, stubborn, sweet, tactically brilliant, guileless and yet surgically accurate in their analyses of people and situations they consider worthy of inspection. Their juvenile eyes see things I miss completely, and yet they're able to make generous allowances for lapses in me that I would find unforgivable were I in their positions. They can make me feel all-powerful or smaller than the meanest lowlife, with just a look. God."

Laughing softly again, he ran a hand through his hair as Judy glanced away from the road and up at his reflection. "And then, if you want to get really complex, there's you."

"I'm not complicated," she denied.

"You mean there's something simple in devoting your life to children but not wanting to get married, in being attracted to me while continuing to push me away, in being lonely yet persisting in living alone?" His voice quieted. "In chasing a dream so single-mindedly that you risk missing all the real life along the way?"

For a long moment Judy drove without replying. Then spotting a Rest Stop sign, she made the turn and pulled into a parking space. The only other car there was an old Volkswagen bug at the opposite end of the lot.

She turned off the motor, and silence pulsed around them. Then she turned to Mitch. "Children have enriched my life a great deal," she said, "even though at this point in time they can't be my own. And when the time comes, I will deal with the loneliness."

She sighed and, looking into Mitch's deep eyes, smiled. "This summer, I don't feel as though I've missed a thing that life has to offer. And would I be here with you if I were continuing to push you away?"

Mitch looked back into her even gaze and asked, a pulse ticking in his throat, "Why did you come, Judy?"

"You invited me."

"But why did you come?"

She reached a hand out to him, and he took it, thinking there were depths to her complexity he hadn't even imagined. "Because you asked to get to know me and invited me to get to know you. Because I've never had an offer I was more anxious to pursue."

Mitch studied the honesty in her eyes. He brought her hand to his lips and kissed it, holding it against his cheek for a moment before letting it go. With that gesture, he relegated Mandy and his loving memories of her to his past. He was going forward, and he suspected it was going to require all his wits and energy to do so.

"I don't think you'll regret having come," he said.

"No," she agreed. "Neither do I."

After a few moments spent poring over the map, Judy drove back onto the highway, following the route Mitch had marked. Within half an hour they were checking into the Red Lion Hotel at Jantzen Beach—a sprawling, elegant complex of restaurants, shops and meeting facilities.

Mitch signed for adjoining rooms, turned their luggage over to a bellman and led Judy to the coffee shop.

"I wonder what the kids are doing now?" Judy asked as she perused the menu.

"Pestering the horses," Mitch replied. "But until we get home again, they're a forbidden subject."

Judy scolded him with her eyes over the top of the menu. "They're my job."

"You're on vacation," he reminded her, closing his menu and putting it aside. "And they're in very capable hands. Think about yourself. Or me, if you must have a diversion. The seafood salad here is excellent. Dan tells me seafood is an aphrodisiac."

Judy looked into his bland expression and laughed. "How does he know?"

Mitch shook his head. "I was afraid to ask. But I'm all for testing theories."

JUDY FOUND that standing in a dark corner with Mitch and swaying to the music held more romance for her than any intricate dance she had ever shared with a man. Wrapped in his arms, her arms around his neck, Judy moved to the mellow strains of a show tune on the dining room's dance floor. The beat she moved to had less to do with the music and more to do with some rhythmic undercurrent she felt rather than heard.

I want this, she thought with a fervor she found startling. Mitch's arms around me, a place where we can be together without thinking of his children or my own future. A time when I am not required to be anything but simply a woman falling in love with a special man.

"What?" Mitch whispered into her ear.

She pulled slightly away, looking into his eyes. "Did I say something?"

"No. But you shrank against me, as though you were afraid of something."

Dismissing her momentary fear, she smiled at him. "Some romantic you are. I was nuzzling."

"Well, then." He pulled her back into his arms. "Do go on."

Mitch didn't know why she chose to evade the question, but the concern he had felt in her when she pressed against him had showed in her eyes when she looked up at him. She had dismissed it quickly, but it had been there. He knew she was afraid to let herself care for him; she had already admitted as much. Yet she had come with him. It startled him to realize that she felt his caring for her could hurt her in some way. He would have to prove to her that she was wrong.

It occurred to him that Mandy had always trusted him to know what was right for her, and her confidence in him had always fortified his faith in himself. But Judy had priorities that didn't involve him. She believed in her own ability to do what was right for herself. He found it difficult to deal with the fact that her strength served to make him question his own.

How had this happened to him, he wondered, holding
Judy even closer. How had he fallen in love with a
woman who wanted different things out of life than he
did?

There. He felt his spine relax, and a breath he'd been
holding left him in a rush. He loved her. And he wanted
her to love him. And stay with him.

Judy pulled back to smile into his eyes. "Are you
shrinking into me or nuzzling?"

He shook his head and planted a kiss on her forehead.
"Neither. Come on upstairs, and I'll tell you about it."

"Upstairs?"

He saw a doubt in her eyes, then her lashes fell and
rose, and it was gone. He knew what she thought, but
before he made love to her, he wanted that doubt not
merely pushed aside, but absent.

"To the balcony off your room. I want to show you
Portland's skyline."

Judy opened and closed her mouth, at a loss. That had
not been at all what she'd expected.

Five flights up, she smelled the cool and mysterious
wind off the river that separated Oregon and Washington. It combined the curious mixture of scents generated
by a busy city and its surrounding forests. The tang of
pine blunted the odors of exhausts and industry, and the
perfume of wildflowers lent a sense of unreality to the
light-spangled skyscrapers that dotted the horizon.

"Oh." Judy sighed her approval of the view as Mitch
wrapped his arms around her from behind. She leaned
her head back against his shoulder. "Do you ever miss
this in Manzanita?"

"No," he replied easily. "This was a busy, exciting
place to be when I was young, but I don't need that anymore. I like Manzanita's quieter pace and being my own

boss." He laughed softly, his breath fluttering the curls near her ear. "At least at work. But for those who have to be in a metropolitan center, this is the best there is."

"Do I detect a note of prejudice?"

"Possibly. Because Portland has done the impossible. It has saved and restored its old buildings, and built new ones with street-level activity space—shops, galleries, restaurants—to make downtown more human. Many of the skyscrapers have mirrored facades that reflect our beautiful surroundings back at us."

The wind whipped up, and Mitch tightened his grip on Judy. "But the most amazing thing to me is that the city realizes that its backbone is still commerce. And it seems to have been able to combine beauty and business without having to sacrifice either one."

His arm shot past her to point at a cluster of lights to the northeast. "See that light, higher than all the others? That's the Donald Jepson Tower."

"An office building?"

"Yep. I worked on that just before I packed up Mandy and the kids and moved to Manzanita."

She turned in his arms, feeling a chill at the thought of him working hundreds of feet off the ground. "Wasn't it frightening?"

"Sometimes," he admitted, "when the wind came up. And sometimes it was exhilarating. But usually it was just a job."

Before Judy could censor the thought, she asked, "Wasn't Mandy frightened for you? Didn't she ever ask you to do something else?"

"Yes, I think she was frightened sometimes," Mitch answered, a little surprised by the question. "But she never asked me to quit. It was what I did. She accepted that."

"She was a generous lady," Judy said, turning back to the starry night and the fairy-tale view. Folding her arms, she leaned against him with an aggressive bump. "I'd have made you quit." He said nothing, and she added with a sigh, "Well, I'd have at least asked you. Loudly."

"It was my job," he insisted quietly. "As devoted as you are to yours, you should understand that."

She turned to him, her arms still folded. "My work doesn't put me in danger and frighten those who love me."

"No." His voice was quiet but even. "But it's about to put you out of reach of those who want to love you."

With the fragrant wind around them and the lights of Portland behind them, they stared each other down. Judy finally dropped her eyes, and Mitch shifted his weight.

"I wonder why we care so much," she asked.

Mitch pulled her to him, running his fingers through the soft curls at her temples to frame her face in his hands. He knew why he cared, but he still saw doubts in her eyes. "Oh, because we see something in each other that's been missing in our lives for too long."

Slipping her arms inside his open jacket, Judy wrapped them around his waist. "We're so different," she complained, but he noted with a smile that she did it while tightening her hold on him.

"That doesn't seem to matter."

"It will in the end."

"If we don't let it end, it will never matter."

With a sigh Judy dropped her head to his chest. "That doesn't make the sense I'm sure you'd like me to believe it does, but I like it."

She liked it, he knew, but she was still afraid of it. He held out his wrist. "Two a.m.," he said. "You'd better go to bed. We don't have a long way to drive tomorrow, but I would like to get there in one piece.''

Leaning back to look at him, Judy pinched his ribs. ''Careful. There aren't many men who have nannies who can double as chauffeurs. I could look elsewhere for employment, you know.''

Mitch parted the curtains and ushered Judy back into her room. The door that connected it with his stood open.

''That's a strong threat,'' he laughed. ''I wouldn't want to have to answer to the kids for having lost you to another household.'' He took a step backward toward his room. ''Get some sleep. I'll see you at breakfast.''

Judy stared at the door between them long after he had closed it. She had never known a man she so enjoyed being with, except perhaps Dale, but with Dale, enjoyment had been the extent of her feelings. With Mitch she felt amused, alert, alive.

She made herself face the truth—that she was falling in love and that Mitch was a little afraid of her self-sufficiency. She became concerned by the fact that she seemed to be losing it.

We should be spending this night in each other's arms, she thought with a weary sigh. We should be loving each other as we've wanted to do for weeks. But then, nothing was quite the way it should be. The route to her quest had always been so clear, but now feelings were scribbled all over it, and the x that marked the spot was beginning to blur.

Chapter Twelve

Mitch showered and dressed, ticking off in his mind the things he should take care of before he and Judy were on the road again. Hearing little noise beyond the adjoining door, he approached it with a frown, hoping Judy hadn't chosen to sleep late. He was starving.

She responded instantly to his knock, wearing khaki shorts and a crisp white short-sleeved shirt. The curly sides of her short hair were swept back with combs and nothing adorned her face but a trace of pink at her lips and freckles across her nose and cheeks. Longing stalled Mitch's heart.

"Good morning," she said cheerfully. "I've got my bags in the car, and I had the desk make reservations for us at that bed and breakfast in the gorge where you wanted to stop today. The bellman will pick up your bags while we're having breakfast. And we should get gas before we leave town."

Mitch followed her into the empty elevator, feeling a mild annoyance that she'd been able to see to all their needs without his assistance, rather than enjoying the rare luxury of having to worry about nothing.

"I just couldn't see you hobbling out to the parking lot with our luggage," she said, her tone suddenly subdued, "when I was able to take care of it."

Mitch turned to her, frowning over her ability to read his mind. "I appreciate it."

"No, you don't," she challenged. "You're irritated by it. Admit it."

"I'm not irritated, I'm just not used to being . . . cared for."

"You know, it's interesting," Judy said, hooking her arm in his as the doors parted and they walked across the carpet to the dining room, "that, on the one hand, you love to be spoiled and fussed over, and on the other hand, you resent my assuming control of our circumstances. Even if it makes more sense for me to handle it than for you to try and do it in a cast."

Stopping just inside the dining room, Mitch looked down at her and said firmly, "I said I was not irritated."

"I know." She smiled as the hostess beckoned them to follow and added in a whisper over her shoulder, "But you lied."

"THAT'S THE WAY I AM." Thirty miles out of Portland, the matter was still under discussion. "I'm used to handling things. You wouldn't want to leave your children with an incompetent, would you?" Judy asked, keeping her eyes on the road.

"Of course not." Mitch took a handful of Cajun-flavored potato chips from the bag they were passing back and forth. Even though he'd just had breakfast, he couldn't resist the luxury of indulging his periodic cravings for junk food without having to justify himself to Lizzie.

"Then isn't your attitude childish?"

"Yes."

Judy looked for Mitch's eyes in the rearview mirror. "What?"

"I said yes," he repeated patiently. "My attitude is childish. But I'm also used to handling things. With you driving and my leg broken, I feel a little unnecessary."

"You're not unnecessary," Judy said gravely. "You've got all the money."

The bag of potato chips bounced off the back of her head and landed on the seat beside her while she laughed.

"Okay, I apologize," she said, dipping into the bag. "In my zeal to take care of things so you could just relax and not worry about anything, I overstepped. I promise not to take over, if you promise not to get upset when it's easier for me to do something than it is for you."

"Why are you concerned about my relaxing?" he asked. "I've done nothing but sit for almost three weeks."

"That's true, but I know there's a lot going on in your mind. You're worried about your business, about all the things you were going to do to the house during the summer, about your friendship with Lee." She gestured with a potato chip. "What preys on your mind can be more exhausting than physical labor. And I think you should take advantage of this opportunity to sort of...renew yourself."

Mitch reached a hand forward to stroke behind her ear. She tilted her head, rubbing it against his hand. "I want you to enjoy it, too."

"I will. I am." Judy pointed to a highway sign. "Corbett. Is this our turnoff?"

While Mitch directed her onto the old gorge highway, he was thinking that he might never get his mind right again. First irritated with her assumption of control, he was now touched that she had done it to free him of concern. She joked about refusing to spoil him, then put herself out to help him.

While Mandy had catered to him in many ways, there were certain tasks she had considered outside her province, no matter how busy he was. But Judy apparently felt no such limitations. He felt like a man lost in the wrong century.

They stopped at Multnomah Falls to watch the 620-foot cascade of water, then again at Crown Point where the magnificent view of the Columbia River Gorge left Judy speechless for a long time.

"I didn't even bring a camera," Judy lamented.

Mitch put an arm around her shoulders. "It doesn't matter. You'll remember it."

Leaning her head on his shoulder, she spoke softly. "I've never seen anything more beautiful." She twined her arms around his neck and smiled. "The beauty of nature usually makes one feel small, but curiously, I don't feel that way today."

She looked up into his eyes, and he saw that the fear that always lay behind her affection for him was gone. He stared into the dark depths of her eyes, drinking in what he saw there.

She swept one hand in the direction of the blue and green grandeur before them. "I feel part of it, as though I have a giant in me and I can do anything, be anything."

He smiled down at her, enjoying her fanciful imaginings, believing them. "And what do you want to be?"

She brought her hand back to stroke her knuckles down his cheek. Her eyes grew solemn. He expected to hear career plans, dreams for her future once she was armed with her master's degree.

Instead she said, "The woman you love, the woman who loves you."

Mitch felt the late-morning breeze stir the hair on his forehead, sweep across his bare forearms. The fragrance of pine and rhododendron filled his nostrils, and if he turned his head, he would behold one of the wonders of creation. But all he could see was Judy, and as he drew in a gulp of air to steady himself, he found it filled with her light herbal scent. The sensuous stroking of her knuckles across his cheekbones overwhelmed him, and his ears rang with the words she had just spoken. *The woman you love. The woman who loves you.*

She *had* said it; he saw the power of it in her eyes. "You are," he said, crushing her to him. "I think you have been for some time. I do love you, Judy."

Judy lost herself in his arms, considering nothing, concerned about nothing but the warmth and the strength in him, the kindness and the caring with which he had so generously offered friendship. Feelings had blossomed into something more complicated and demanding, and she found such freedom in finally acknowledging it.

"I'm so happy to be here with you," she said, leaning back to look at him. "Loving you."

He shook his head before pulling her to him again. "Do you have any idea how I feel, hearing you say that?"

"I can see it in your eyes."

Mitch held her away from him, cupping the back of her head in his hand, and lowered his mouth to hers.

Judy reached up to meet his lips, her passion as bright as his, her need for him as desperate. But she kissed him with a tenderness that dissolved his growing urgency and made him take time and care.

His lips traced the contour of her face, then stirred unbearable sensations at her ears before moving back to her mouth and finally drawing away.

Mitch glanced at the other sightseers who were staring determinedly in other directions. "I think it would be wise of us to leave," he said.

Judy nodded. "I agree."

They returned to their car and drove to the Gorge Vista Bed and Breakfast. The inn was a Queen Anne-style house with cupolas and gables, built on a knoll in the heavily wooded forest above the gorge. The sign on the lawn boasted that it had been built in 1889. A porch swept out in a half circle on the west side, while patios extended on the other three. Painted white and gray, it was an architectural masterpiece.

"It's almost as wonderful as the gorge!" Judy exclaimed as she and Mitch went arm in arm up the front steps.

A motherly white-haired woman behind the desk read upside down from the register as Mitch signed in. "Well, the Kramers!" she said, as though she knew them well and had been awaiting their return. "I'm Dorothy Powell."

Mitch and Judy looked at each other and grinned, but didn't correct her.

"You're just in time for lunch. Come into the dining room and meet everyone."

At the moment the last thing on Mitch's mind was lunch. But feeling the strength of his passion, and knowing how he wanted to have Judy—gently, lingeringly—Mitch understood that a distraction would help him to slow down. Meeting the sparkle of amused frustration in Judy's eyes with a wink of promise, he put a hand to her back and pushed her gently to follow their hostess.

"Lunch at a bed and breakfast?" Judy asked as the woman led them past a stairway and toward the rear of the house.

"Oh, pooh!" the woman said. "I'm only supposed to provide breakfast, but my sister is such a wonderful cook, and we've always got plenty. You can contribute to the kitchen fund if you'd like to, but it isn't required. Sis and I are both grannies whose kids are scattered all over the place, and we just love having people around."

In the dining room, a glassed-in porch looking over a rose garden, Mitch and Judy were introduced to a honeymooning couple, a businessman on his way to Portland from Boise and a retired couple from New York who had traveled cross-country in their camper.

Pearl, Dorothy's sister, of similar proportions and temperament, brought out game hens on a platter complete with dressing, potatoes, squash and rolls.

Judy looked in amazement at Mitch, who was seated across from her at the large table. But he was already in conversation with Mr. Goodwin, the businessman, and they were passing platters while Dorothy and Pearl rushed around filling coffee cups and bringing other treasures from Pearl's kitchen.

"In New York," Gina Ferrero, a lavender-haired woman with false eyelashes and a smile that never quieted, confided to Judy, "you'd pay three times as much for this kind of food and accomodations, and you wouldn't get half the service. Vito and I are coming back next year. Aren't we, Vito?"

Small and spare, as quiet as his wife was chatty, Vito responded to an elbow in his ribs. "Yes, we are, chicken."

While the honeymooners sat isolated in their adoration of each other at the far end of the table, Judy learned Gina and Vito's life history, starting with Uncle Marco, who had doubtful connections and disappeared mysteriously during the St. Patrick's Day parade, never to be heard from again, and ending with little Regina, their eight-year-old granddaughter who was studying dance under a well-known ballet teacher.

Her lunch finished, her hands knotted in her lap, Judy fought an urge to reach across the table and capture Mitch's hands.

Only half listening to Goodwin's detailed explanation of what an arid seller's market the northwest part of the country had become, Mitch looked up at Judy and found her concentrating on his hands as they toyed with his coffee cup. When he stilled their movement, she looked into his eyes, and he saw the same impatience there that he felt, the same need to finally explore what had haunted them for so long.

Mitch pushed his chair back, carefully balancing his heavily burdened leg as he stood. "If you'll all excuse us," he said with a gracious smile around the table, "we'd like to unpack and get some rest."

"Of course." Dorothy, who was refilling Mr. Goodwin's coffee cup, put the pot in the center of the table and led the way out. "If you'd like to dine with us, dinner's at seven. Or if you prefer, there's a wonderful French restaurant about ten miles east, right on the gorge road."

Dorothy went upstairs, down a small corridor and threw open the door at the far end, stepping back to let them pass. Judy went past the brass bed and bentwood rocker to open French doors, and there she beheld a magnificent view of the gorge. Lace curtains blew in at the open windows, moved by a breeze that was fragrant with the perfumes of summer.

"Mrs. Powell, this is perfect." Judy spun around to see Mitch at the foot of the brass bed, watching her with a gleam in his eye and a smile pulling at his lip. Then she remembered that she had neglected telling him that when she'd had their reservations made that morning, they were for just one room.

"Everyone calls me Dorothy." Then she withdrew, saying, "Enjoy your rest."

When the door clicked closed, Judy crossed the few feet that separated her from Mitch and wound her arms around his neck. "Do I know how to make a reservation, or what?"

"I applaud your efficiency," he said, pulling her against him with a hand at the small of her back. But one eyebrow rose in surprise. "You made a reservation for one room this morning?"

"Yes. Even last night," she said, her eyes growing solemn, "I didn't want you to leave me."

"I didn't want to. But you were still afraid of this, last night."

She sighed and smiled. "I'm not afraid anymore. I love you, Mitch."

Mitch enveloped her in his arms. "Judy, I love you, too. So much."

Slowly, with the care of someone who has dreamed of the experience for a long time, Mitch held Judy away from him and unbuttoned her shirt, pulling it free of her shorts. Leaning down to slip it off her arms, he took the opportunity to taste her mouth.

Her lips never leaving his, she slipped her hands under his cotton sweater and worked it up his chest. They finally pulled apart to take it off.

He unfastened the two covered buttons that joined the wisp of lace at her breasts. Then his hands enclosed her with a gentle awe that touched her more deeply than any extravagant praise could have.

"Look at you," he whispered, fascinated by her beauty.

She laughed softly, a little embarrassed. "Just a woman."

"No," he scolded. He pulled her against him, felt her soft swelling against his solidity and marveled that he could feel this way. His every thought seemed to be for her. "A special woman. Mine."

He dispensed with her shorts and panties, then his slacks and briefs. Reaching down, he tossed the bedspread aside, and together they fell into the square of sunlight warming the middle of the bed.

For a long time they lay wrapped in each other's arms, he stroking her back in gentle circles, she running her fingertips along his spine. Then his hands began to move in longer strokes, his touch becoming possessive, betraying a growing urgency. Her fingers began to explore farther, eager to learn more of the beautiful mystery of his body.

Mitch covered Judy's body with kisses, and she repaid him in kind, pausing to breathe a string of *I love you*'s from his navel to his breastbone. Her breath shivered up his chest, threatening to burst it, and he pulled her astride him, his hands settling at her waist. As he shifted her, moving to slip inside her, he watched her tilt her head, her eyes closing. She expelled a sigh of satisfaction.

Then she began to move over him ever so easily, her body fragrant and warm, undulating like something

brought in on the breeze through the open window. He
was lost in sensations building inside him.

Taking him inside her, her fingers locked in his, Judy
let relief wash over her. She had wanted him, needed him,
for so long. But in a moment relief was replaced by the
tantalizing spiral of desire renewing itself, strengthen-
ing, tightening. Together they crested, perched for mad-
dening moments on the peak of fulfillment, then came
down on a mutual sigh.

The breeze quieted, the lacy curtains settled, and Mitch
and Judy curled together. He held her closely, and she
clung to him, accepting the indisputable fact that needing him had changed her, would continue to change her.
And then she slept.

As Mitch threaded his fingers through her hair, gently
so as not to wake her, he realized with some surprise that
he was a different man from the one who had loved
Mandy. That man had been loving, had tried to be kind
and considerate, but he understood now that he had
taken more than he had given, and he couldn't help a
small feeling of resentment that Mandy had let him do
that.

Judy had taught him that he had more to give than he
had ever imagined. His children had taught him that, too,
of course, but it was easy to give to children. Giving to a
woman who was smart and strong and capable required
a generosity he was just beginning to learn about. He had
to find things to give Judy that had nothing to do with
control or power, but were more substantive things, the
things of which daily life was made—sweetness, endur-
ance, surprise.

Mitch closed his eyes, marveling that he understood
that, feeling at peace that he could accept it. All he had

to do to make her love him was let her be Judy; all he had to do to love her was to be Mitch.

"HERE IT COMES," Judy whispered.

Standing behind her, watching the sky, Mitch felt her shiver and held her more tightly. "You've been saying that for the past ten minutes."

"I know, but it's really coming now. Look!"

They stood alone on the highest point they could find behind the Gorge Vista Bed and Breakfast and watched the sun rise over the Cascades. The streaks of light against the fading night had changed a dozen shades of pink and purple while they watched. Below them, the river began to rise out of the shadows and catch the first light from the sky.

"There!" The first inch of sun flamed the mountain peak, then came out of hiding to mark the morning. "That was spectacular!"

Judy turned in Mitch's arms, throwing hers around him with the ebullience that had marked her every waking moment since they had first made love five days ago. They should have moved on. The gorge stretched for many more miles, and there were many more beautiful spots from which to view it, but she had wanted to stay, and he'd been unable to refuse her. And he understood how she felt about this particular place. Life had shifted gears here. Love had been born here.

"You are spectacular," Mitch said, burrowing his nose into her hair. Feeling her shiver again, he pulled away and buttoned the rolled collar of the thick sweater she wore. "I'll bet you're thinking of pancakes and sausage and hot coffee."

She wasn't. She was thinking that nearly a week of their precious time together was already gone.

"What?" he asked, seeing the shadows moving in her eyes.

Feeling the sudden tension in him, Judy lowered her eyes, wanting to hold tight to the euphoria as long as possible. When she looked up at him again, she was smiling.

"I was thinking," she said, rubbing the red tip of her nose, "that if Vito gets up before we get back, there won't be anything left for us. I don't know where that little man puts all that food."

Mitch grinned. "I'm sure he needs fuel for the furnace to keep up with robust, enthusiastic Gina."

"When we're old," Judy said, pulling him back down the hill, "will you still call me chicken?"

"I don't call you chicken now," he pointed out, watching his step.

She stopped on the overgrown path and turned to him. The air was still, but for the soft sound of her voice and the call of a heron. "In the night, you call me your beloved."

"You are," he assured her. "You will always be."

Suddenly the air was filled with the clanging of the triangle that hung on Dorothy's porch, calling them to breakfast.

Judy's expression went from angelic to devilish. "If you don't get a move on, I'm going to leave you here. Where Pearl's pancakes are concerned, it's every man for himself."

MITCH AND JUDY WATCHED the sun rise over the gorge every morning, took leisurely walks on a trail through the woods and spent lazy afternoons on the crescent porch with Dorothy and Pearl and the other tenants.

Neither entertained a thought unrelated to that particular time and place, and neither spoke of the past or the future. For Judy it was a time stolen from a life that had been full of purpose and direction. This small space of unscheduled days was like a gift, and she unwrapped it slowly, savoring every precious revelation.

For Mitch, it was as though all the demands heaped on him in the past two years had been magically waved away, and he was free to do what he wanted to do, to reach for what he wanted to have. He had to consider no one, answer to no one, and he found the freedom intoxicating, if a little unsettling. He finally put his vague unease down to man's fear of perfection. Because that was just what these days on the gorge with Judy were—perfect.

By the middle of their second week at the inn, the honeymooners and the businessman were long gone. Pearl and Dorothy sat at the dining room table, discussing their accounts, and Mitch and Judy shared the porch and a fragrant, starlit evening with Gina and Vito.

They'd spent most of the time listening to Gina's tales about their grandchildren, Vito nodding agreement as she alternately praised them and voiced concern about the loving but free and easy way the current generation was being raise. Then she asked unexpectedly, "How long have you two been married?" The Ferreros sat side by side in brightly cushioned wicker chairs, while Mitch and Judy faced each other on an old-fashioned glider swing.

Judy's eyes widened in alarm, not because she feared admitting the truth, but because she had become fond of the couple. At this point, explaining that she and Mitch were not married might make them think they had perpetrated a deception, no matter how innocently it had begun. She wouldn't hurt their feelings for anything.

Mitch, smiling at her, the leg in a cast propped beside her, solved the problem with a sincerely spoken simple truth. "It feels as though we've been married forever."

Judy caressed him with her eyes, silently avowing that she felt the same.

"That's how it is when it's right." Gina squeezed Vito's hand. "Vito and I were married just after high school. We're going on forty-seven years together, and we're praying that we'll have twenty more. Right, Vito?"

"Right, chicken."

"We got our health, and we got each other, and a little bit of money to see this beautiful country in our camper. Can't ask for more than that. Right, Vito?"

"Right, chicken."

"And when it's time to go, we'll know we've done the best thing possible with our lives. We haven't written a book or been president or gone to the moon. But we've loved somebody."

Without waiting to be asked, Vito volunteered, "That's right, chicken."

Touched by the couple's devotion and alarmed by her own growing devotion to Mitch and his to her, Judy lost herself in the movement of the swing. Gina laughed at how sober they'd become and changed the subject. But Judy wondered what on earth she was doing here in the Columbia River Gorge with a man who had three children, when she would be off to England soon.

She remembered a reckless decision to love him, a purposeful pushing aside of all the precautions, because he had promised that he wouldn't interfere when it was time for her to go. But now, as she looked across the swing into the eyes watching her, she saw possession and tenacity there—and love. The worst of it was the love she felt for him responded. She didn't want to leave him—ever.

God, she thought as the sound of Mitch's laughter tugged at her heart, what have I done?

"I GET SEASICK, I tell you," Judy protested as Mitch, already standing in the flat-bottomed excursion boat, offered his hand up to help her in.

"This is a river, not the ocean," he said, smiling apologetically at the boat's captain, who was waiting patiently behind her to board the other passengers. "Trust me." With a deft yank, he pulled her aboard.

"If I humiliate myself by getting sick," she threatened as he settled her in a bench seat for two in the middle of the boat, "I will hold you personally responsible."

Unimpressed with her threat, Mitch put an arm around her shoulders. "Well, I hope if you enjoy the ride and have a wonderful time, you will also hold me personally responsible and reward me appropriately."

"Dorothy won't understand if I'm unable to eat dinner."

"But Vito will be delighted." At her glare, Mitch patted her hand. "It's a beautiful day, the river is calm, you will not get sick. Now, hush. The captain's talking."

For two hours the boat wound in and out of the small, green islands that dotted the river. Her fear of seasickness long forgotten, Judy stared up at the majestic cliffs that rose on either side of them, green and streaked with wildflowers. At several points, graceful ribbons of water fell from a great height into the river.

Judy drew a deep sigh and put a hand to her chest, as though soothing a pain. Mitch tightened the arm that circled her shoulders. "Is it so beautiful that it hurts?" he guessed.

Dropping her hand, Judy leaned back against him, her eyes greedily tracing and retracing a long spill of silver water. "That's it precisely. What causes that kind of pain, I wonder?"

"The knowledge that we're more finite than what gives us such pleasure?" Mitch speculated.

"I suppose so. And that somewhere in the next century, a couple will sit in some futuristic boat right on this very spot and admire the falls like we're doing. And we'll be gone and probably forgotten." Judy turned to face Mitch, her eyes wide and troubled. "Isn't that sad?"

"Not if we've enjoyed being here, it isn't," he said gently, rubbing her shoulder, feeling a change taking place in her. "We all get our chance to be happy, to enjoy all we've been given and to give a shot at making ourselves memorable, at least to those to whom a memory of us is important."

Judy nodded agreement, but he could see something else at work in her eyes. He couldn't tell if she was looking forward or back. She snuggled closer to him, and he waited.

"I lied about my father," she said.

They were wending their way back to the point of embarkation now, the boat moving swiftly in the water. A sweet-smelling wind pushed against them.

"In what way?"

Judy stared ahead of her. "I didn't have one. Mike and I are illegitimate."

Surprised but not shocked, Mitch rubbed the hand that she had rested on his knee. "Do you find that hard to deal with?"

"No." She lifted her face to the wind. "I was happy. So was Mike. But my mother..." She stopped, shaking her head and tightening her grip on his hand. "There was a logger," she went on. "He was a friend of my mother's. Mike and I liked him and fantasized that he would become our father. I know my mother loved him. One night I overheard him tell her that he liked us well enough, but he didn't think he'd be able to cope with a couple of kids day in and day out, especially since we were somebody else's."

Judy sighed and closed her eyes. "I went into the room where they were, and saw the look on my mother's face so clearly. The surprise, the hurt and the knowledge that there was nothing in her future with this man, that even the friendship was over."

Feeling as though she'd withdrawn into her memories, Mitch stroked her shoulder. "She never married?"

Judy shook her head. "No. At a time when a young woman choosing to keep her out-of-wedlock child was very much frowned upon, she chose to raise us and did it with pride. She worked hard. Everybody liked her. And because they liked her, they liked Mike and me. There was never any...stigma...attached to us."

"There shouldn't have been."

"I know, but there often is. Even today there sometimes is. I see it in the classroom. Kids repeat things they've heard their parents say about other children. I think Mike and I were spared that because our mother was so special."

Trying to analyze why she had chosen this particular time to tell him the truth, Mitch struggled with that recurring sense of uneasiness. "Judy," he asked gently, "why is that on your mind today?"

"When Gina was talking last night about how loving someone is the most important thing we do, I was thinking about how much I love you." The wind whipped her hair back from her face, and she looked into his eyes, every feature stark in its honesty. "But there are other commitments besides the one between a man and a woman."

Trying not to panic, Mitch was quiet for a moment. "Between a woman and her mother?" he asked finally.

She nodded, drawing a deep breath. "And between a woman and herself."

Fear did begin to grow in him then, and, because he disliked being afraid, he also became angry. Usually slow to anger, he was confused by the depth with which he felt it, the intensity with which it compounded.

By the time they disembarked from the excursion boat and Judy drove the few miles back to the inn, Mitch was silent, his anger so great it reminded him of the rage he'd felt at Mandy's death. He felt as powerless now as he had then to prevent the loss he was about to suffer. Could he really have come this far only to watch her walk away?

Judy pulled into the parking area in front of the beautifully fussy house and turned off the motor. Seeing the grim set of his features in the rearview mirror, she made no move to get out of the car. "I didn't mean to cast a pall over our vacation," she said quietly.

"No matter how subtly you tried to put it—" Mitch pushed his door open "—you were simply telling me that you'll be leaving me. That's liable to darken a man's horizon in a hell of a hurry."

Judy turned swiftly, reaching out to him, stopping his move to get out of the car. "Please, let's talk about it. Tell me what you're thinking."

He looked at her one long moment and slammed the door, folding his arms then unfolding them, raising his hands in a gesture of frustration. "I'm not thinking, I'm *feeling*. And I'm not sure you want to know what that is."

"I can see what it is," she said with a small smile to which he did not respond. She sobered. "You're angry."

"And you can remain so unimpassioned." His voice was quiet, but his eyes were dark and bleak. "You're insulated by all your noble reasons for leaving. Your mother worked so hard for you. You, yourself, have devoted every ounce of energy to achieve this goal. That leaves me playing the selfish bastard because I can't stand the thought of letting you go. I look like the chauvinist pig who has to have things my way."

"You promised not to interfere—" she began to remind him.

"That was before I loved you!" he shouted. "That was when I was simply fascinated by you, intrigued and bewitched. But now I'm in love, and that makes me different from what I was then." He shook his head at her before leaning it back against the upholstery. He stared gloomily at the roof of the station wagon. "I think that's what I find hardest to bear—the fact that you say you love me, and yet it hasn't changed you. Your priorities haven't shifted, and nothing, nothing is different. You can walk away from me without looking back, because going to Oxford is what you've always wanted to do. God!" He lifted his head to look at her, his brow furrowed, his eyes anguished. "I don't understand that!"

Judy stared at him, startled. He didn't understand her at all. All these warm, lazy weeks of talking and laughing and sharing with him the secrets she almost managed to keep from herself, and he didn't understand.

With deadly calm she said, "That's because you're accustomed to loving a woman who always came around to your way of thinking, you said so yourself. She might argue, but in the end, Mandy did what you wanted. Mitch . . ." Emotion threatened to block her throat, and she swallowed, taking a breath. "You knew in the beginning that I wasn't Mandy. I'm Judy, and I have debts to pay, things to do."

Debts to pay. Even in the depths of his frustrated anger, Mitch knew that was where the answer lay.

"Debts to pay," he repeated aloud, trying to calm his voice to match hers. "Are you going to Oxford for your mother or for you?"

"For both of us!" she replied earnestly. "Don't you see? Had my mother thought of herself first, of what it would be like emotionally and financially to raise two children by herself, you'd be talking to another woman right now, because Mike and I would have been aborted. I wouldn't exist." She paused to heave a deep sigh and went on quietly, "But I am. Life has a finer quality and seems to demand more of me because I might not have had it. I'm going to Oxford for her, as well as for me, because I was that important to her. And that makes me important to me."

He studied her levelly for a moment and shook his head. "And there just isn't room for me, is there?"

Judy reached over the seat to touch his shoulder. "Of course there is, just don't...don't make demands on me."

Mitch gestured in exasperation. "I am not a potted plant! I am a man who loves you. I refuse to live on the sidelines of your life until you're ready to put me in. I love you now. I want to fit in your life now."

"Now," she said as though it were something she had learned by rote, "I'm going to do a year at Oxford, and then I owe three years to my school district for having sent me. I explained that to you. How do you see yourself fitting into that?"

"All right," Mitch said, folding his arms and staring at her evenly as he considered the challenge. "If you do truly love me and want to be with me, you can have your year at Oxford, and I'll pay off the school district when you get back so that you can teach here."

Judy's eyes filled with tears as she understood both the selfishness and the generosity in his gesture. "I know your business is doing well, but half my salary would be a substantial chunk out of your profits. You need your capital to have something to start with when you win a bid, and to replace your old equipment. Lee told me you've finally gotten far enough ahead to look at another truck. Even General Motors can't afford to pay out money that doesn't promise a fair return."

"You're copping out," he accused quietly. "I consider you a good investment, and you know it."

"Now what kind of a lover would I be," she asked, whispering, "if I let you sacrifice your security for my dream?"

When he closed his eyes, at a loss for a reply, Judy said softly, "But it doesn't mean I don't love you."

He smiled mirthlessly. "What good is love that isn't acted on? People have to accept and give love to be whole. The world turns on it, Judy. As a teacher, you can pass on all the world's knowledge to the kids you encounter, but how will you ever understand and relate the drama and power under the facts if you've never made the decision to love the man who loves you?"

When Judy turned away from him to stare out the windshield, he added determinedly, "I suspect you don't understand the brave and noble Europeans at all, if you don't understand what drove them. In fact..." He paused, weighing his words against her predictable reaction to them. Concluding that he had everything on the line anyway, he spoke them. "I doubt that you really understand your mother."

She whirled in her seat at that, her eyes snapping. "Love for Mike and me drove her, not love for a man."

He pinned her there with his eyes. "And so you can never have a man because she couldn't? Is that what you think? It would be disloyal for you to be happy because she never was?"

Her lips trembled. "You're affixing psychological significance that doesn't exist to simple ambition."

"Ambition is never simple. Something propels it."

"A thirst for knowledge."

"In your case I think it's a hunger for the truth. It's some need to find who you are in this search into your people's past, something that will legitimize Judith Cassidy."

"My mother never made me feel like that," Judy denied.

"You've done it to yourself," Mitch said. "You saw her rejected by a man who couldn't love you and Mike, and in your child's mind, you became the villain. Because of you, the mother you loved was deprived of all the softness and warmth of life with a caring man. Judy—" Mitch's tone took on a note of pleading "—you're living your life in atonement for having cost your mother her chance at happiness."

She looked sad and empty, he thought, as though perhaps she believed him, but couldn't find the point in it. Then he realized that he hadn't made it. She turned to open her door, and he stretched out to stop her with a hand on her shoulder.

"She wouldn't have been happy with him, Judy. She was generous, and he was selfish. If she did love him before that night, she could never have loved him after. And as far as your roots are concerned, I don't know where they began, but they are so deeply wound in me that neither one of us will ever be free of the other, whether this quest takes you four years or forty. You're going to grow in me and I in you, no matter how you turn away from it."

For a moment the silence was deafening, then Judy turned to Mitch, her eyes brimming, but grudgingly respectful. "God, you're tenacious."

He drew a hand down his face and pushed his door open. "I'm a builder. Hanging on in a high wind is one of the things I do best."

Chapter Thirteen

The French doors were open to the warm August night, and Mitch, curled on his side in the soft bed, stared at the stars, hearing Judy's accusation repeat itself in his mind. He had to acknowledge that she was right: he was used to having things his way. He had tried to adjust to life with a woman who was as strong and capable as he was, but now that it came to a choice between what each of them wanted, he wasn't sure how far he could compromise.

He knew she was a good teacher, he could tell by the loving way she dealt with his children, and he wanted her to go as far as she could with her career. But he couldn't sit back and wait until she found room for him in her life. He closed his eyes, forcing himself to consider that the alternative was losing her.

"Mitch?" Judy's whisper in the dark sounded like a shout. The touch of her fingers on his shoulder was the first physical contact he'd had with her since the argument in the car hours ago.

"Yeah?" He rolled onto his back, turning his head on the pillow to look at her. She lay on her side of the bed, staring at the ceiling. Moonlight showed the moisture in her eyes.

"I want you to understand," she whispered.

"I'm trying," he replied softly, "but I can't."

"It just isn't the right time."

For a long moment he was silent, feeling for the first time in this prolonged argument that they'd touched upon something he understood better than she did.

"When you're single," he said, "there might be a right time and a wrong time to do things because you're the only one to consider. But when you share your life with someone else, time is all you have. Period. Suddenly so much begins to happen in it that the plan is no longer yours, only the performance. Babies come at the worst possible moment, the water heater dies when you're broke, and your credit cards are charged to the max. And you fall in love—" he paused to sigh "—when there are all kinds of things against you. Your real strength is not in organizing things to work perfectly and on a timetable, but coping with the way they happen. You shuffle this, put that aside for a while and try to move forward together. Sometimes you even go backward together. But together is the operative word."

"How can we go forward together," she said with patience and frustration, "when I have to go and you have to stay? Mitch, you're the one who said you understood. You're the one who said you wouldn't stop me when I had to go."

In a flash of bleak humor, Mitch thought it fortuitous for both of them that years of dealing with his son had taught him creative alternatives to screaming.

"Judy, are you even listening to me?" he demanded, trying to keep his voice just above a whisper. Around them the house made its night noises—refrigerator humming, grandfather clock striking the half hour. "I love you. There's got to be an answer to this. But you're talking as though we should just go to Crown Point and jump off.''

"Are you going to wait for me for four years?'' she demanded.

"No," he said.

"So much for a solution.''

He turned, propped himself on an elbow to look down at her. "You don't want a solution. You want an excuse to throw this relationship away because you think you have no right to be happy.''

"That's ridiculous!'' Judy tossed the covers aside, trying to scramble out of bed.

But Mitch pulled her back, holding her to the mattress. "Is it?'' he demanded. "Is it? Then find a compromise.''

"Your idea of a compromise," she said, her body tense under his hands, "is for me to do it your way. Why don't you drop everything and come to England with me?'' The moment the words were out of her mouth, Judy regretted them, knowing they were unfair.

"If I could ignore the needs of the men I employ," he said, his voice soft with anger, "I would drop the business. But it's a little harder to push three children aside to make sure I get what I want out of life.''

He fell back against his pillow, and Judy flung an arm across her eyes, tears rising up in her throat. "I'm sorry.''

"So am I," he said. "You're turning your back on a hell of a lot.''

"I've been headed in the other direction for a long time, Mitch.''

He heaved a long, ragged sigh. "Then I guess this is where we say goodbye.''

Judy lowered her arm, turning her head on the pillow to look at him. "There are still two weeks before Glenna comes home."

"I know." As he fixed his eyes on the ceiling, Judy stared at his strong profile and felt a wrenching in her chest that she knew would live with her for a long time. "I'll need you to stay until then, of course. But as far as you and I are concerned, as far as what we almost had, it's goodbye."

Unable to see a way around it, Judy drew a breath and closed her eyes. "Yes," she said. "Goodbye."

SIMULTANEOUSLY and without discussion, Mitch and Judy decided to leave the inn for home the next morning. The trip that had been made slowly under a sunny sky with laughter and warmth was now made in one cloudy afternoon filled with traffic and silence.

When they walked into Mitch's house carrying their luggage, they found other suitcases on the living room floor near the stairs.

"Glenna?" Judy asked Mitch.

He nodded, recognizing the set he had given his sister as a bon voyage gift. She was home two weeks early, and he felt a grave sense of loss for the remaining days he would have had alone with Judy, the last chance he might have had to save their relationship.

He felt instant remorse for those selfish feelings when Glenna stepped out of the kitchen to see who had arrived. She had been a friend to him all his life, and she loved his children as though they were her own. And he and Judy had already said goodbye anyway.

"Hi, love," he said, going to take her in his arms.

A little plumper than when she had left, her usually neatly styled, short brown hair in disarray, she went into his embrace with a bright smile that turned without warning into a sob. Her face contorted as she buried it in his shoulder. Surprised, he tried to pull her away, but she clung, sobbing.

Her eyes wide with surprise and concern, Judy gestured toward the kitchen. "I'll make some coffee."

Mitch led Glenna to the sofa. Pulling her down beside him, he held her while she cried, wondering what on earth could have caused tears in his usually unflappable sister. As well as he could remember, the last time he'd seen her cry had been two years ago at Mandy's funeral.

Her sobs finally quieting, she drew away from him, pulling a hanky out of an apron pocket. "I'm sorry," she sniffed.

When she didn't offer a reason for her outburst, he frowned at her. "What's wrong, Glenna?"

She heaved a deep sigh and gave him a feeble little laugh. "Well, I guess it's just, you know, the kitchen is kind of a letdown after St. Peter's and the Louvre and Buckingham Palace."

Leaning against the sofa back, Mitch folded his arms and looked into her unconvincingly jocular smile. "You haven't lied to me since Dad left Mom when I was seven and you told me he was on a business trip."

She rolled her now-dry eyes and gave him a sisterly pat on the knee. "I was nineteen, and I was justified. You were too young to understand about such things, and they patched it up two days later, anyway."

He nodded, accepting her explanation. "Now I'm thirty-eight. I can handle the truth. What's wrong?"

Glenna shook her head, waving her hanky dismissingly. "It's just a personal problem."

Mitch studied her silently for a moment, alarm awakening inside him. "Health?" he asked.

Patting his knee again, she shook her head. "Nothing like that. You can't help me with this, Mitch."

"Particularly if you don't tell me what it is."

"I can't right now." She looked at him with a firmness that ended the discussion. Wiping her eyes once more, she indicated the kitchen with an inclination of her head. "I called Jackie to tell her I was home, and she said she took the kids a couple of weeks early because you'd broken your leg." Now it was her turn to look firm. "Why didn't you mention it when I called?"

"Because you'd have probably rushed home, and I didn't want that."

"Hmm." She was obviously not pleased with his explanation. "How come the kids are with Bill and Jackie?" she asked, her tone barely louder than a whisper. "And Judy is here, alone." After a swift glance at the luggage resting next to hers, she frowned at him. "With you. And where have you been, anyway?"

"Vacationing in the gorge."

"The two of you?"

"Yes."

There was silence for a moment while she considered her next question. In her eyes, Mitch saw her mind at work on the possibilities. Then she smiled cautiously. "You and Judy? I thought you sounded chummy when I called."

Frustrated when he didn't elaborate, Glenna asked with interest, "Well, is it serious?"

Mitch thought about that. "At the moment it's more...confused than serious."

"Well, what kind of answer is that?" she demanded on a whisper.

"The only one you're going to get," he replied, frowning. "You know, for someone who can't talk about her problems, you're sure asking a lot of questions about mine.''

Judy started into the room with a tray bearing coffee and cookies, but at the sound of the raised voices she turned back into the kitchen.

"Come on in," Mitch called, halting her escape. "Maybe you can talk some sense into this woman."

Judy poured coffee for the three of them then sat on the other side of Mitch. She smiled at Glenna. "So you're in need of my worldly wisdom and sage advice?"

"No." Glenna reached across Mitch to pat Judy's hand. "Though it's awfully good to see you again. Actually I have a problem I'm solving on my own, but Mitch seems to think I need his help with it. I don't." She looked from Mitch to Judy and back to Mitch again. "I'm more concerned about the two of you. You were thinking, probably, that you were going to have a great few days together before the kids get back, and here I come home early, unannounced." She put her cup down decisively. "I think I'll visit my friend Betty for a couple of—"

"You will do no such thing." Mitch glared at his sister.

"I'll just—"

"No."

Glenna looked around him at Judy. "Someone crown him king while I was away?"

Judy sipped at her coffee and saw his warning expression before going back to her cup. "I think it was a case of self-appointment."

"There are some women," he informed them, assuming an air of abused dignity, "who would be pleased to have a man concerned about them."

Glenna patted his shoulder consolingly. "We just don't happen to be among their number."

"Right," he said in ironic agreement. "That's why you were sobbing."

Putting her empty cup on the coffee table, Glenna stood and leaned down to hug her brother. "I appreciate your concern, but I'll be just fine." She glanced from Judy to Mitch, both concern and affection in her expression. "I'm going upstairs to unpack. You two just...relax."

Judy began to stand. "I'll get my things out of your room."

"No, no." Glenna stopped her with a raised hand. "I'm just going to lie down for a while. We can do all that later."

Mitch nodded, giving his sister a weak smile. "Just take your small bag. I'll bring the other two up for you in a few minutes. Welcome home, sis."

"Thanks."

At the sound of the upstairs bedroom door closing, Judy placed their cups back on the tray. "I can sleep in the girls' room until they come home," she suggested. "Then I can move to the sofa or something."

"We've got a cot in the attic," Mitch said with the same casual tone she used. "It's fairly comfortable. And it won't be for that long."

The last remark was a cruel thrust, he knew, but he longed to see some chink in Judy's armor, some sign that this was hurting her as much as it was hurting him.

"That'll be fine,' she said, standing without looking at him. "I'll be working on the trunk on the sun porch if you need something. I'll take care of dinner."

"Don't plan on me," he said, getting to his feet. "I'm going to call Lee and ask him to take me to the site and

see what's going on. There's probably enough paperwork to keep me busy till midnight. See you later.''

"Yes."

As Mitch disappeared through the kitchen and into his
room, presumably to shower and change, Judy put their
cups in the dishwasher and went out to the sun porch.
Though she'd been gone more than a week, the smells of
paint and turpentine rose as she approached the trunk.
Getting down on her knees, she studied her half-formed
design of flowers and leaves and had a sudden, clear image of her mother and the long hours they had spent together on rosemaling.

While Judy imitated her mother's style, then developed enough skill to create her own, they talked about
school and life and men. Judy missed that closeness now
with an intensity she hadn't felt since her mother's death.
Tears pooled in her eyes as she touched the trunk. Curious, she thought, that she could have gained so much this
summer, and lost so much, as well.

She would not have missed knowing Dan and Lizzie
and Katie for anything, and loving Mitch had given life
a depth, an intensity, it had never had before. But all that
had changed her, she realized, feeling a trace of sadness
for the innocent she had been. She had been so sure she
could have everything she wanted out of life. Of course,
then she hadn't wanted Mitch.

Chapter Fourteen

Pulling the husk off an ear of corn, Judy made a mental note to remember to ask Mitch if he wanted her to fix something special for the children's homecoming tomorrow.

She could ask him now. He was only inches away from her, prying the cork out of a bottle of French Colombard, but their ability to communicate had been strained by three days of nearly total silence. Ironic, Judy thought, how one could find no words when there was so much to say.

Glenna's presence helped somewhat, though she exhibited mercurial moods. Judging by Mitch's alternately patient and exasperated handling of the woman, Judy guessed she wasn't always this way. Her uncharacteristic behavior had something to do with her trip to Europe.

The telephone rang, and Judy, only inches away from it, put a hand out to answer it.

"This is Wernher Schmidt," a deep, rich voice said in rolling, accented tones. "I wish to speak to Glenna Kramer, please."

Something to do with her trip to Europe, Judy thought, holding the receiver out to Glenna. Of course— a man. "For you," she said.

Glenna held a fistful of silverware to her aproned waist and stiffened visibly. "Who is it?"

Judy shrugged. "A man."

"Thick German accent?"

"Yes."

Glenna turned back to the table she was setting. "Tell him I'm not home."

"No," Mitch said quietly, reaching out to stop Judy from speaking into the phone. He turned to his sister, frowning. "Who is it?"

Glenna did not look up from the table. "Someone I met in Europe."

"Why don't you want to talk to him?"

"It's . . . personal."

"I'd like to know, anyway."

Glenna looked up into her brother's implacable expression. "It's personal," she repeated.

"Does he have anything to do with your crying all the time?" Mitch insisted.

Glenna slammed the remaining silverware on the table with force. "I will not speak to him!" she shouted. Her face crumpled, and she ran from the room.

"Give me that." Mitch snatched the receiver from Judy and pointed toward his departing sister. "See if you can do something for her, will you? Hello? This is Mitch Kramer, Glenna's brother."

Judy found Glenna lying across her bed, sobbing like a teenager in the throes of unrequited love. She sat on the edge of the bed and put a hand to the shaking shoulder. "Glenna."

Glenna looked up, and seeing Judy, pushed herself to a sitting position, clutching a lace-edged hanky to her nose. "I'm sorry. I'm *never* like this. You must think me an awful fool."

"Don't be silly. Of course I don't." Judy put an arm around Glenna's shoulders and asked gently, "Are you in love with Warner Schmidt?"

"Wernher," Glenna corrected, drawing a ragged breath. "I am in love with him. But I'm trying to get over it."

"Why do you have to?"

Glenna shrugged, her tenuous hold on control threatening to slip. But she drew another breath. "Because he wants me to go back to Germany and marry him."

"You didn't like Germany?"

Glenna forced a smile. "I did. It's a beautiful country."

Judy thought, trying to locate the problem. "And you said you love him."

"I do."

"Then if you love him and you love Germany, why can't you go back to marry him?"

She sniffed, her chin quivering dangerously. "I can't leave Mitch and the kids. What would they do without me?" Glenna darted her a quick, hopeful look. "Unless you've worked things out and you're staying?"

Judy looked into Glenna's eyes and wondered grimly how many people she had to step over to have what she wanted. "I have to go," she said quietly.

"Of course you do." Glenna patted her knee and put the hanky to her nose again. "We all have to do what we have to do. And I have to stay with Mitch and the kids."

"Glenna," Judy said firmly, "Mitch would be furious if he knew you were giving up your chance to be married because of him and the children."

"I wouldn't tell him," Glenna said with dignity, "and I know you won't, either. I haven't even told Wernher."

"Glenna—"

"We met on a train from Munich to Herrsching," Glenna continued, deaf to Judy's interruption. "He has two children and several grandchildren, so we had lots to talk about. He's a chef, you know. He has three restaurants in and around Munich." She spoke with a pride that made her smile. "Well, one thing led to another, and he invited me to join him for dinner at one of his restaurants." Her cheeks flushed, and she gave Judy a charmingly embarrassed side-glance. "I stayed in Germany entirely too long."

"And yet you were home two weeks early," Judy reminded.

"Yes." Glenna sighed. "It was easier than fighting him. He wanted me to stay and get married right then. So I came home."

"Glenna, this is wrong," Judy said earnestly.

"It's right for me." Glenna spoke with determination and, finally, composure. "Mitch and the kids have been through so much. Mitch has never uttered one word of complaint, he just jumped right in and did what he had to do. Sometimes he stretches himself pretty thin to be mother and father and keep a firm hand on the business and that wild crew. It would be hard for any other person coming in off the street to understand that and do for him accordingly." She smiled fondly at Judy. "You, of course, were different. I saw that right away. Maybe it's all your experience with children. I knew the kids would love you. And I saw the devilment in your eyes, coupled with kindness, and I knew Mitch would like you." She studied Judy closely, her tone apologetic. "I didn't know he'd fall in love with you, and you having to leave soon. I'm sorry."

"Don't be." Judy forced a bracing tone of voice. "I've had a wonderful summer. Now, about your reason for coming home and not wanting to talk to Wernher—I have to tell Mitch something. He sent me up here to find out what he can do to help you. He's really upset that you're so unhappy."

"Just tell him . . . tell him that Wernher toyed with my affections when I was in Europe and broke my heart." Glenna grinned impishly. "That sounds sufficiently staid and old-maidish, like me. And that's why I won't speak to him on the phone."

Judy looked doubtful. "I don't know if Mitch will swallow that."

"If you make it convincing, he will." Knotting the hanky she held, Glenna frowned at its lacy edge. "Once Wernher understands that I won't take his calls, he'll give up, and we won't have to worry about it anymore."

Remembering the rich timbre of that voice, Judy withheld agreement.

"You and Mitch go ahead with dinner," Glenna said. "I'll warm something in the microwave later. I think I'll have a nap."

"WERNHER SCHMIDT TOYED with Glenna's affections," Judy said, sitting across the table from Mitch. Carefully she cut a piece of succulent T-bone, avoiding his eyes. "Then he broke her heart. That's why she won't take his calls and wants nothing more to do with him."

When her explanation met with silence, Judy looked up from her steak to find Mitch with the salt shaker poised over his ear of corn. "And I'm supposed to believe that?" he asked.

"Can't you?" she asked hopefully. "It would help Glenna a lot if you would."

Mitch salted the corn, shaking his head in amused disbelief. "It fascinates me the way women consider men a subspecies when it comes to matters of emotion and romance. No, I don't believe that, and I won't pretend to so that Glenna can hide behind me.''

"She just wants to be left alone, Mitch."

"That might work for you," he said brutally, dropping the salt shaker on the table with a bang. "And I can't do anything about that. But it won't work for her, and there I have some influence. All her life, Glenna has helped this one in our family, cared for that one, lived her life through somebody else's. I don't know if she's afraid to live her own life or if it just hadn't occurred to her that she has a right to.''

He paused to take a sip of wine and study her, a challenge in his eyes. "We've managed to foul up our relationship beyond saving, but maybe we can do something for her. What did she really tell you?''

Feeling as though he had slapped her, Judy sat back against her chair. "I promised."

"I could go upstairs and bully it out of her."

"That would be cruel," she accused.

He agreed. "Yes. It would be simpler if you'd tell me."

Feeling as though she'd run out of options in every phase of her life, Judy sighed and answered traitorously, "She doesn't want to leave you and the kids. She doesn't think you'd be able to cope—no, that's not quite right. She doesn't think anyone else would understand how well you deserve to be treated." She gave him a dry glance as she picked up her wineglass. "Of course, she didn't know then that you'd have bullied an answer out of her.''

Mitch nodded grimly. "Too true. Wernher suspected that was the reason."

Judy frowned in surprise. "She never told him."

"Like I said, we're not as dumb as you think we are.''

Judy glowered at him. "So you're going to confront her."

"No," he said, dipping his fork into his baked potato. "I'll leave that to Wernher. He sounds like the kind of man who'll come after her."

"If he does, what will you do without her?"

He shrugged. "I'll cope. That's what life's all about, remember?" Dropping his fork as though he'd lost interest in his food, he fiddled with the stem of his wineglass. "If Wernher is half the man he sounds like he is, Glenna goes with my blessing. They'll have each other. And the kids and I will always have each other." He looked up at her, his eyes penetrating and sad. "But what will you have, Judy?"

"I'll have my degree from Oxford." Judy looked into his eyes, turning her back on what it cost her and concentrating on what she would gain. "I'll be smarter and stronger than I was before. I'll have what every woman from the past would envy me for. I will have done what I've always wanted to do. And I'll be a better woman."

While knowing that he would never understand her, Mitch acknowledged to himself that despite what he had told her the other night, he would always love her. And he would never, ever sit outside on a warm summer evening without imagining her beside him, the scent of her hair and her body in his nostrils.

He picked up his wineglass and toasted her. "Then more power to you."

WITH THE ARRIVAL of the children, the long silences of the past several days were replaced by giggles, laughter and intricately detailed recountings of horseback rides, visits to a ghost town, picnics, swimming and playing horseshoes. Within twenty-four hours there were the

usual arguments, protests about going to bed, noses
turned up at vegetables cooking. Normalcy had been restored to the Kramer residence.

Mitch seemed a little less grim. The soft smile he re-
served for his daughters and the dry grin he often shared
with his son were once more in evidence. He was polite
to Judy, but carefully professional, and she bit down on
the longing she felt for their old camaraderie.

This was what life would be like from now on, she told
herself firmly. It would hurt. She was bound to Mitch
Kramer and his children with all the strings of loving at-
tachment she'd resisted for so long. As she tried to pull
away, she felt her emotions tear.

Glenna, delighted to see the children and warmly wel-
comed by them, became a model of domestic efficiency,
reclaiming all her old responsibilities.

"Go to the beach, relax, enjoy yourself," she advised
Judy. "You'll be working hard again soon enough."
Then as if remembering that there was much unhappi-
ness over Judy's departure, Glenna forced a smile.
"Have you been enjoying my pictures and all the tourist
information I brought home?"

They'd both been so unhappy since Glenna's return
home that poring over souvenirs and photographs had
held little appeal. "Very much," Judy said, giving her a
strong hug. They shared a lot, she thought grimly. Each
loved a man she couldn't stay with. "Why don't we look
them over together tonight? I'd really like your impres-
sions and suggestions."

Glenna nodded. "Right after dinner. Now go enjoy
yourself."

"That would be great." Gathering up towel and book,
Judy found herself trailed out the door by Liz and Katie, also carrying towels.

"Can we come?" Liz asked. She studied Judy closely, as though sensing something different about her and feeling uncertain as to what it was.

"Of course. You can tell me all about your trip again."

Judy had heard about it over and over again, but it was a safer subject than what she suspected was on Liz's mind. She couldn't discuss that with the child now, or she would fall apart.

Lying on her towel in the afternoon sun, with Liz on a towel beside her and Katie sitting Indian-style at her feet with a small shovel and bucket, Judy listened patiently to Liz's stories.

"This horse was named Rufus, and he was a piebald. That means that he has a white mark on his nose," she explained matter-of-factly. "I rode him all the time. He took apples and sugar from my hand, and he bumped my shoulder when I talked to him. That means he liked me. We took rides around this lake, and we saw jackrabbits and prairie dogs and a coyote. But I'm glad to be home again. I missed you and Daddy."

"He missed you, too," Judy said from behind her sunglasses.

"Did you guys...talk a lot while we were gone?"

"Yes," she replied quietly, sensing that Liz was not going to be diverted from her purpose in coming along to the beach. "Quite a bit."

"Did you...kiss and hug and stuff?"

Judy lifted her glasses to look at the child. "Elizabeth..."

"Dan thinks you're gonna get married."

"Lizzie, we're not," Judy said firmly. "I just came to work here while your aunt was gone." She sat up and removed her glasses, smiling gently at Liz. "I explained that to you."

"But things changed," Liz insisted, worry beginning to fill her eyes. "Didn't they?"

Her smile weakening, Judy wondered how she could explain the complexity of her feelings and dreams to a child.

AFTER WORK, MITCH HEADED for the beach to take a long walk to clear his head. Before he faced Judy and his children, he had to sort his thoughts, settle his ragged emotions, make some decisions. They all needed so much from him at a time when he seemed to have barely enough character to sustain himself. There was so much at stake here, so much required of him that hadn't been asked before.

At least he had one problem almost solved. All hell would probably break loose tonight, but that was all right. A good skirmish might relax the tense atmosphere in the house.

He took the concrete steps that led off the sidewalk and onto the sand and started for the water line. Then he saw them—two little blond heads and a dark one in what appeared to be grave conversation. For a brief instant he considered turning back.

But he saw a look of such despair on Liz's face and a slump of Judy's shoulders so abysmally forlorn that he knew he simply had to stretch whatever reserves of strength he had to cover all of them. He continued walking in their direction.

"SOME THINGS DID CHANGE, Liz," Judy admitted. "Your father and I are very good friends now."

With an insistence that was alarmingly adult, Liz shook her head. "No. You look at Daddy the way my mom used to, like she was always so glad to see him. And he looks at you the way he looked at her, the same way he looks at us, even when he's been mad at us. Like . . . like we're somethin' so special.''

Judy felt as though someone with a blunt instrument was working her over. "Liz, I have to go to England.''

She shook her head, her eyes suddenly brimming, filling with anguish, her pink mouth quivering. "But I want you to stay with us!''

Judy felt the stiffening leave her as she pulled Liz close and rocked her back and forth.

"What's the matter with Lizzie?'' Katie abandoned her shovel and bucket to investigate the cause of her sister's sobbing.

When Judy could not force an explanation past the lump in her throat and Liz continued to sob, Katie put an arm around Judy's neck and sat on her free knee. Tears spilled from Judy's eyes.

Liz's sobs deepened, and she wound her arms around Judy's neck, her grip desperate. "I don't want you to go, Judy,'' She wept. "Please don't go! Please stay with us.''

Katie, unclear about the source of her older sister's distress but frightened by it, began to sob also, her chubby fists clutching at Judy as she took up the cry. "Don't go, Judy! Don't go!''

Judy held the girls to her, every nerve and emotion screaming as pain ripped through her, leaving wounds she knew would never heal. The sound of her own sobbing finally forced her to calm herself so that she could calm the children. "Lizzie, please listen to me,'' she said firmly, rubbing the child's back, trying to penetrate her hysteria.

"No.'' Liz continued to weep. "Not unless you promise to stay.''

"Liz." Judy pulled the child away from her to look into her eyes. The agony there prodded at her open wounds. She made a sudden decision. "Lizzie, I have to go to England for a year, but I'll come back."

Liz shook her head, tears streaming down her cheeks. "My mother never came back. She went to the hospital, and she promised she'd be back in a week. But she didn't come back. She never will."

"Liz, I'm not going to die," Judy said, wrapping the child in her arms again. "I'll come back, I promise. But I have to do this. It's something I promised *my* mom."

Liz and Katie continued to cry, and Judy hugged them and rocked and spoke with calm conviction. "When I was a little girl, my mom worked very hard and gave up a lot of things so she would have the money to send me to college so that I could be the best teacher there was."

Quieting a little, Liz pulled back to look at Judy, her face red and puffy. "But you are."

Judy went on quietly, gently pressing her advantage. "When I go to England, I will learn more and be an even better teacher."

Liz asked in a choked voice, "Can't you ask your mom if it would be okay if you did it later?"

Judy shook her head, emotion strangling her. "My mom's in heaven, too, Lizzie. I'll be back in a year, I promise."

Judy felt Mitch, still dressed in his work clothes, come down beside her on the sand, and for the first time in her life, she wanted to hand over the responsibility for something she couldn't handle to someone else.

"Daddy!" Katie flew into his arms, but Liz refused to release her grip on Judy.

"Judy's going away," Liz sobbed.

Mitch looked into his daughter's tearful face, to the misery in Judy's dark eyes, and he pushed his own anguish aside. "Lizzie," he said, gently scolding, "I explained that when Judy first came, remember? She has very important things to do, things that will make a difference to a lot of other children, not just to you and Katie and Dan. We have to be brave and let her go."

With the selfishness of children, and an attitude he could easily identify with, Liz looked stubborn and said, "I don't want to. I want her to stay." Then with a generosity that made him feel very small, she swallowed, sat up, and looking into Judy's eyes with complete adoration, she said raspily, "But she promised her mom."

"I know." Mitch gently rubbed his daughter's sandy knee. "And she'd stay with us if she could. But she had things to do that are more important than us."

Judy looked into his eyes. "But I'm coming back. I promise I'm coming back."

Lacking words, Mitch put an arm around her and pulled her close. For several moments the four of them wept together in the sand.

Then, balancing Katie on his hip, Mitch stood and pulled Liz to her feet. "Let's go home. We're having company for dinner."

Surprised that Glenna hadn't mentioned that to her, Judy told Mitch and the girls to go ahead. "I'll gather up our things and be right behind you."

Mitch gave her a quick look of concern. "All right. But don't dawdle. Glenna will need help."

"I'll hurry."

A few moments later, Judy trudged the block back to the house with three towels and Katie's bucket and shovel. Stopping at the bottom of the steps, she looked

up at her newly repainted KRAMERS sign and fought a
fresh bout of cowardice.

Mitch watched Judy coming up the walk and felt love
and pain rise inside him with equal force. The line from
the classic poem ran through his mind. "'Tis better to
have loved and lost, than never—" Bull! he thought. He
didn't like to lose, especially if he had a choice. Personal
pride was not going to force him into losing this woman.
If he couldn't have her his way, he'd accept her in whatever way she'd come to him. He may never understand
what drove her, but he knew what she was made of. If he
had to let her go to have her, he could do that.

The screen door opened, and Judy looked up into
Mitch's eyes. He took the towels from her, tossed them
into a corner and offered her a hand up the last few steps.
On the porch, he closed the door that separated it from
the living room and pulled Judy toward the swing.
Pushing her onto it, he sat beside her, his eyes dark gold
and earnest.

"I'm sorry about the children...." she began, unable
to continue when her voice cracked.

Mitch pulled her into his shoulder and let the gentle
motion of the swing rock them. "You don't have to be
sorry about anything. You gave us everything you were
able to give, and we all love you for it. I—" he paused,
smiling at her as she lifted her head to look at him, her
eyes filled with love "—like to have things my way. Bad
habit. It was hard for me to come to terms with the fact
that you have more important things to do than be with
me, but I'm trying hard."

Judy felt his understanding wash over her like a cleans-
ing water. After the week of bitter silence, she melted
against him as he planted a kiss on her neck.

"I don't want you to cry over us, and I don't want you to feel badly," he said, holding her. "And when you've done what you have to do, we'll still be here."

"Mitch?" She lifted her head from his shoulder, her eyes wide and dark. "I won't let you pay off the school district, but when I come back, what if we took a loan or something? I could teach night classes, too. Then the money wouldn't have to come out of the business."

Just knowing that she wanted it made it possible. "We'll find a way." He pulled her close, stroking her back. "I love you, Judy. We'll do it. Everything will be all right." Then he drew her up and smiled. "Now come on. Let's get cleaned up."

THEIR DINNER GUEST was tall and robust, with a thick shock of graying blond hair and a full mustache. His cheeks were ruddy, his voice booming, as he said, "Glenna! *Liebling!*" and took the shocked woman who had answered the door into his arms.

Judy, who was helping the girls set the table, stopped to stare.

"Wernher Schmidt," Mitch whispered in her ear.

Openmouthed, Judy noted that Glenna's instinctive reaction was to put her arms around him and cling, taking his enthusiastic kisses with a provocative shifting of her body against his. She said his name with a sigh. "Oh, Wernher."

Judy turned to Mitch. "How...?"

"When I talked to him on the phone after Glenna refused his call, I gave him my number at the site. He called me a couple of hours ago from the airport and said he was on his way."

When Judy turned back to the door, Glenna had stiffened and pushed away from Wernher. He looked over her head at Mitch with an expression that acknowledged they had both expected as much.

Mitch went forward, hand extended. "I'm Mitch Kramer. Welcome to my home." He pulled Judy and the children forward, introducing them. "I've looked forward to meeting you."

"Looked forward..." Glenna repeated, placing her hands on her hips. Then she turned to Wernher in accusation. "What have you done?"

"Fallen in love with you, *liebling*," the man replied with disarming candor. "You wouldn't talk to me, but your brother did. We decided between us what the problem was and how to solve it. You are coming home with me."

"This is not Europe!" Glenna said, with pink cheeks and bright eyes. The children looked on in fascination. "Women do as they wish in America."

"What you wish," he said calmly, "is to be married to me." And before Glenna could protest, he asked quietly, "Would you lie in front of the *kinder*?"

Glenna folded her arms. "You cannot stay."

"I've been invited to dinner."

Glenna turned to Mitch with a glare. "Collusion?"

Mitch looked back at her, unrepentant. "Absolutely."

Glenna's eyes shifted to Judy, who tried desperately not to look guilty but felt partially responsible all the same. "You promised," she accused softly.

"She kept her promise," Mitch defended. "Wernher and I talked on the phone. Comparing notes, we came to the conclusion you seemed so sure we wouldn't see. Now let's have dinner and talk about it."

Glenna tore off her apron and threw it at her brother's midsection. "You've made your plans without me, you can have dinner without me, as well."

As Glenna disappeared in high dudgeon, Mitch pulled Wernher toward the living room, smiling apologetically. "I'm sorry about that."

"Don't be." Wernher's big voice boomed. "She's a strong woman, that's why I love her. But I must talk to her."

"Let me talk to her first," Mitch said, dispatching Dan to hang up the gentleman's coat, and Judy to the kitchen to get Wernher a glass of wine. "Girls, keep Mr. Schmidt entertained while I talk to Aunt Glenna."

"Ah!" Wernher scooped a little girl onto each knee. "I've brought you dolls from Germany and a stein for Daniel. But you must have only root beer in it," he cautioned the boy with a hearty laugh.

Running up the stairs, Mitch took a moment to wonder what in the hell he was doing. Now that it came down to it, what was he going to do without Glenna? She wasn't just the mainstay of his household and the guardian of his children while he was away, she'd also been one of his dearest friends since he'd been old enough to recognize her face.

With that bleak humor that seemed to appear to save him at the damnedest times, he realized that he was caring for the two women in his life he loved the most by sending them away from him. He hadn't guessed that there was that kind of nobility in him. And he hadn't guessed that nobility could be so painful.

He knocked authoritatively on Glenna's door.

"Who is it?" Glenna demanded with ill humor.

"Mitch," he replied. "I've come to help you pack."

The door was yanked open, and he stood looking down at Glenna's flushed face more miserable and angry than he'd seen it in a long time.

"Very funny," she snapped at him, turning away from the open door to march to the window and stare out at the breezy, waning afternoon. "I'm not going anywhere, and you should be ashamed of yourself for taking charge of my life like this. I made it plain that I didn't want to see Wernher."

Mitch took Glenna by the shoulders and turned her to face him. "Well, if you're going to fling accusations, how dare you presume that I'd be willing to sacrifice your happiness for my own comfort. And what makes you think I can't get along without you, anyway?"

Glenna shifted her weight and looked up at him with a long-suffering shake of her head. "Because when I was sick for three days last year, you took Dan to Lizzie's ballet class, Lizzie to Dan's baseball practice, and you lost out on two jobs because you never write a message down, you trust me to remember it. Need I continue?"

Mitch rolled his eyes. "That's because you remember things longer than anyone I know, particularly my mistakes. Well, let me tell you something." He tightened his grip on her when she sighed impatiently, giving the appearance of losing interest in what he had to say. "Monday morning I'm calling Summer Nannies to see if they have winter nannies, or if they can refer me to a kind, efficient woman with a sense of humor who's willing to work full-time. And you are going to Germany with Wernher."

"No."

"Yes."

"The children—" Glenna began, her eyes misting and her bottom lip beginning to quiver.

"The children will miss you like hell," he interrupted her, giving her a firm shake. "And so will I, but we will be just fine."

A tear spilled out of her eye, and she put a hand to her mouth, asking in a small voice, "And how will I be without all of you?"

Smiling, Mitch enveloped her in his arms. "You're going to be happier than you ever thought possible, because that man loves you and is determined to have you. And before you had time to get mad about it, your instinctive reaction to the sight of him was to fall into his arms. You're in love, Glenna. Life is just opening up for you. Don't be afraid."

"I'm fifty, for heaven's sake!" she said, half laughing, half distressed. "I'm overweight, and I have wrinkles!"

"You're also a nag," Mitch added with a bear hug that made the criticism more affectionate than serious. "But if Wernher isn't bothered about the other stuff, we'd better not tell him. Now, can we go down and have dinner before he concludes that we're completely ill-mannered and uncivilized?"

Glenna held on to Mitch and looked up at him earnestly. "Will you really be all right?"

Mitch pulled her close again and kissed her forehead. "Of course we will. You saved my life and my sanity by coming to help us when Mandy died. But I've got control of the situation now." He struggled valiantly to keep the irony out of his voice there. "And I can handle it. From now on, all I want you to think about is Wernher."

Glenna frowned as though she hated to bring up the subject. "But Judy's leaving, too."

"Judy will only be gone a year," he said with false bravado, tucking Glenna's arm under his and heading for the door. "When she comes back, we're going to pay her school district off so she can stay here."

"How? That's a lot of money."

Mitch shrugged as though it didn't matter. "I've got a whole year to work on that."

"YOU WERE RIGHT about Wernher," Judy said later that night, finding Mitch on the front-porch steps when everyone else had gone to bed. Mitch had vacated his room for Wernher and was sleeping on the sofa. "He seems like a wonderful man. The kids love him already."

"Mmm," he replied as Judy sank down beside him. "It'll be great to have a brother-in-law in the restaurant business. It's just too bad he'll be so far away."

"He won't be that far away from me," Judy said brightly. "I'll go to Munich on some long weekend and have him ship you knockwurst and sauerbraten."

"And hot mustard."

"Right. Hot mustard."

Silence fell between them, and with it, Judy felt an overwhelming sadness, a sense of having lost something without which she would always feel only half-fulfilled, half-committed, half-alive.

"It's getting chilly," Mitch said absently. "You can smell autumn in the air." As though to confirm his words, a gusty breeze swept up the walk and circled them before moving on. In its wake was the cold, salty smell of the ocean at night, the tang of evergreens and the northwest perfume of wood smoke—fall.

Feeling a pain so strong it was all she could do not to cry out, Judy leaned her head against Mitch's shoulder. "The year will seem like an eternity," she said.

He put an arm around her, pulling her close to him. "We'll write often."

She wondered how he would ever be able to translate into words the wonderful warmth of his smile, particularly when it was meant for her. Or his wry, scolding look when she was being difficult. What words could convey the touch of his hands—strong, tender, magical? How could she commit to paper what she felt when he wrapped his arms around her, when he stroked her back and ran his fingers through her hair.

"God," she said, her voice frantic as she clung to his chest. "Can I live without you for a year?"

He kissed her hair, his voice quiet but strong. "Of course you can. You'll have so much to do and so much to see."

Holding fast to his waist, Judy tried to understand why she felt so miserable. She was getting everything she wanted. How could everything not be enough? she wondered.

She could live a year without him, Mitch knew. She had the determination, the dream. But how was he to survive a year without her? He was sure he could find someone competent to care for the children, but he wouldn't feel as comfortable as he had leaving them with Judy.

And what of himself? All the light that had gone out of his life when Mandy died had returned with Judy. It had a different color, a different intensity, but it was the same brilliance of love given and returned. It made the day dawn and took every fear out of the night. And he understood that he was as responsible for keeping it burning as she was. And now, that meant letting her go.

"I love you," he said, crushing her to him, committing himself to the difficult task of loving a woman who had things to do.

Chapter Fifteen

At the kitchen table, Wernher conducted a transatlantic telephone conversation with his daughter, in loud, rapid German. Liz and Katie, sitting on either side of him, listened with rapt attention. When Judy tried to shoo them away in the interest of the man's privacy, he stopped her with a wave of his hand.

"I think we're going to have to take the girls to Germany with us," Glenna laughed. "He's crazy about them."

"Schön gut!" Wernher exclaimed, getting to his feet to hang up the phone. "My children agree to forgive us for being married here, if you will suffer a large reception when we get home next week."

"Next week?" Glenna paled.

Judy stood back and admired the man's style as he methodically dispensed with all of Glenna's objections. He'd had the foresight to bring his birth certificate. He'd been in touch with his consulate on the chance that the American government needed more proof of his identity, and he was financially prepared to handle everything.

"But there's so much to do!" Glenna protested.

Calmly, Wernher kissed Glenna's brow. "Then we will do it. Now, come. Show me your church, and we will begin to make arrangements."

Mitch's only say about the wedding plans was his insistence that he pick up the bill.

Wernher had tried to stand firm. "But you have little ones, and Glenna and I are not children who need—"

Mitch shook his head, put an arm around Glenna's shoulders and gave her an affectionate squeeze. "I insist, Wernher," he said. "Glenna's my only sister, and she's done so much for me. Let me do this for her."

Wernher finally nodded. "But I am sending for the wine. It comes by air from my restaurant. The finest Rhine."

"Agreed."

For six days the house was chaos. Invitations were made by telephone since there wasn't enough time to get them printed and mailed out. Janet Norgaard volunteered to round up the wives and girlfriends of Mitch's crew to handle refreshments following the wedding.

A shopping trip to Astoria yielded a classic white suit for Glenna and ruffly blue dresses for Judy and the girls. Tuxedos were rented for Wernher, Mitch and Dan.

As Glenna resigned club memberships, paid off charge cards and notified everyone of her change of address, gifts began to arrive and take up a substantial part of the living room. Crepe-paper streamers and honeycomb wedding bells were everywhere. And Mitch's cast was removed.

On the seventh day, as with the miracle of creation, Glenna was rested. In the bride's room of the Seafarer's Chapel, Judy reached up to adjust the netting on Glenna's small white hat.

"You look beautiful," she said.

"And I'm calm." Glenna looked at her own smiling face in the mirror and repeated with a little laugh, "I am so calm. I'm leaving the family I love to go across an ocean with a virtual stranger and I'm not the least bit frightened."

"You've got Uncle Wernher to protect you," Liz said, doing a pirouette so that the yards of chiffon in her skirt flared out. "He wouldn't let anything hurt you. I heard him promise Daddy."

"Isn't he wonderful?" Glenna beamed radiantly. "I feel as though I've loved him forever."

When the music began, Judy shushed the girls and opened the door to the body of the church, falling into line behind Liz. She remembered Gina Ferrero saying "That's how it is when it's right," in the darkness on the front porch of the old Queen Anne house.

Following Katie's and Liz's confident steps up the aisle, the pews on both sides filled with smiling guests, Judy caught Mitch's gaze over the girls' heads. He stood tall and straight beside Wernher.

As clearly as though he were shouting the words, his eyes said, "This should be us."

And Judy's heart accepted that as truth. It was right. But what did a woman do when the man was right but the time was wrong?

EVERYONE WEPT at the airport.

"Don't forget to write things down!" Glenna sobbed on Mitch's shoulder. "And if you can't remember the kids' appointments, ask Lizzie. She knows everything."

"We'll be all right," Mitch promised, rubbing her back.

"I know the kids will be fine," she said, pulling away to look at him doubtfully, a hanky pressed to her mouth. "It's you I'm worried about."

"You have someone else to worry about now. I will be fine. Now, come on." He pulled her back into his arms and hugged her fiercely. "Give me a loving, sisterly hug, then get on that plane before you have to chase it to Germany."

Wernher hugged Liz and Katie, who clutched the red-cheeked porcelain dolls he had brought them. Hoping to stem their tears, he promised to send them each another. Katie, effectively bribed, stopped crying, but Judy recognized Liz's forced smile as the result of strong character and an uncannily adult understanding of what others needed of her.

Judy stayed close to the two, and Mitch put an arm around Dan, who emerged from his aunt's embrace with a decidedly forlorn expression and a desperate attempt at calm. Glenna hugged Judy, and Wernher reached for Mitch's hand.

"I will take good care of her, I promise you," Wernher said.

"I know you will." Mitch clapped his shoulder. "Make sure she writes."

"We'll call," he promised. "Once a month."

Smiling brightly, the five waved Wernher and Glenna onto the plane, then stared for a moment at the doors as they closed behind them. The girls sniffed, Judy gulped, and Dan drew an unsteady breath.

Mitch was the first to move, ushering Judy and the girls away from the boarding gates. "Okay," he said briskly. "On to lunch. Where'll we go? Elmer's? Clackamas Town Center?"

"McDonald's?" Katie asked hopefully.

Getting nods from the other two children, Mitch looked at Judy. "I'm a pushover for McNuggets," she admitted, needing a reason to grin. "With sweet-and-sour sauce. And a chocolate shake."

"No wonder you exercise every morning," Mitch murmured, leading them away.

Dan fell into step beside his father, glancing over his shoulder at Judy and his sisters, who were trailing behind. "Lizzie says you guys aren't getting married."

Mitch kept walking. "That's right. At least not yet."

"You wanted to, though."

Turning to his son, Mitch saw the first glimpse of manhood in his eyes. The boy had detected something in his eyes he thought he had hidden. "Yes, but she has things she has to do."

"Oxford."

"Right."

Dan put a hand on Mitch's shoulder. "I'd have liked it if she stayed. She's neat. But at least she's coming back. It's gonna be rough for Katie and Liz when she leaves at the end of the week. Especially with Aunt Glenna going to Germany."

Mitch grinned down at Dan. "But not rough for you?"

"Sure." Dan returned the grin and squeezed his father's shoulder. "But I figure you got us through and over Mom. We'll be okay. And now I'm old enough to help you. If you get upset or depressed—" he frowned in imitation of a serious adult "—we'll go have a beer or something."

Mitch gave his son a playful shove. "You're such a comfort to me, Dan."

"We could talk about a motorcycle."

Mitch caught Dan's shirtsleeve. "Do you want to end up on a jet to Marrakesh?"

Dan walked on tiptoe in exaggerated reaction to his father's grip. "Do they have girls there?"

"Camels. Lots of camels."

"And we're not talking a good smoke, are we?"

"We're talking dromedaries."

"Forget the motorcycle. At least for now."

Mitch released him, then pulled him to his side with a hand on his shoulder, thanking God he had him. "Wise decision."

IN A GRAY WOOL SUIT with white pinstripes, Mitch looked bigger, darker, more dramatic than usual.

"How come we can't come?" Katie asked for the tenth time while Mitch paid off the young man who had delivered the children's pizza.

"Because it's an auction," Judy explained patiently, shooing the girls toward the table, where Dan was pouring milk into two glasses and Katie's cup. "It's just for adults."

"Brenda says they're gonna make lots of money from the trunk you painted." Liz sat down in her chair, sniffing the air as Mitch brought the pizza to the table. "That smells delicious. Tell Dan not to pick off all the pineapple this time."

"Stick to your half of the pizza," Mitch ordered him. "The works for you, Canadian bacon and pineapple for them."

"Blabbermouth." Dan pretended to snatch a piece of pineapple, and both girls screamed in protest.

Mitch rolled his eyes, took Judy's arm and pulled her toward the door. "Let's get out of here before I have second thoughts. Dan—"

"I know. The number of the school auditorium is on the refrigerator, and before the auction you'll be at Cliffside Inn with Lee and Brenda. Don't worry, Dad. I'm in control. Just tell them to go to bed on time."

"They promised," Judy reassured Mitch.

"Have fun, you guys." Dan waved them off, pulling a piece of steaming pizza out of the box for Katie and warning her that it was hot.

On the way to the restaurant, Judy and Mitch talked about the telephone call they had received from Glenna and Wernher two nights before, letting them know that they had arrived home safely.

"She sounded so happy." Judy looked out at the golden evening and turned to smile at Mitch's profile. "You *did* know what you were doing."

He shook his head. "Silly woman to doubt me."

"And Lee and Brenda are acting like newlyweds. For a while there, I thought Lee wanted your scalp."

"I guess the crew set him straight. Then when you convinced Brenda to have it all out with him, they talked." He shrugged at the solution that seemed so simple yet required real courage. "Each had hurts and resentments the other had never understood because problems had been brooded over rather than discussed. Your encouraging her to talk turned the tide for them."

"We're a fine pair of fix-its," Judy said quietly, trying to make it sound like a joke. Instead her tone carried an element of despair. They had helped Glenna and Wernher, and they had helped Lee and Brenda. But there was little that could be done about the separation they faced.

Mitch struggled against his own misery. "It'll be next June before you know it." He patted her knee and pulled her closer to him. "We're not going to spend our last evening together in a glum mood. We're going to eat, drink and spend a fortune at the auction. Then we're going to make love all night long. So what if you fly to England with your eyes closed. What time is Dale due to pick you up?"

She laughed, leaning her head against his shoulder. "His letter said 9:00 a.m. But he tends to lose track of unimportant things like time."

Mitch shot her a doubtful glance. "You're sure he's a safe traveling companion?"

"Sure. He's great company. But I'll be in charge of schedules."

Mitch concentrated on the road, biting back all the cautions on the tip of his tongue.

In the Cliffside Inn's candlelit dining room, Lee and Brenda gazed into each other's eyes, hands entwined on the table, looking as though their marriage had a new lease on romance.

"That's almost disgusting," Mitch whispered to Judy as the waiter gathered two menus and led them to the table.

Judy shook her head at him, knowing he lied. "It's beautiful, and you know it. Hi, you two."

The more formal dress did the same for Lee that it did for Mitch except that his fairer features made him look cooly dangerous. Brenda, in a shimmery red dress, her hair swept up in a complicated knot, looked bright enough to light the night. Until she looked into Judy's eyes and seemed to see the misery she herself had known a scant few weeks ago.

Lee poured zinfandel into their glasses, asking, "What'll we drink to?"

"To friendship," Judy responded, lifting her glass.

Brenda clinked hers against the other three, catching Judy's eye. "And to love."

Lee, whom Judy had always thought so quiet, kept the conversation moving through dinner. Mitch had a tendency to slip into lapses of thoughtful quiet. Judy, fighting a hardening lump in her throat, had difficulty catching the convivial atmosphere Lee and Brenda tried so hard to create.

"You're sure leaving is the right thing to do?" Brenda asked Judy as she reapplied lipstick in the ladies' room.

Judy, running a comb through her short, springy curls, nodded at Brenda's reflection. "I'm sure. It's a long story, and there are lots of reasons. But I've looked at it from all angles, and I have to go. Mitch understands."

"I've never seen two people look more miserable," Brenda insisted.

"If there was any way around it besides leaving Mitch for a year—" Judy dropped the comb into her small evening bag and snapped it closed "—I'd do it. But there isn't. All the preparation that went into this from everyone—from me, from the friend I'm going with, from the school I worked for and from Oxford—took months, even years. I'm committed. I have to go through with it."

Brenda frowned as Judy sank onto the low stool beside her. In the harsh light of the bulbs surrounding the makeup mirror, Judy looked pale and drawn. "Who are you trying to convince, Jude?"

Judy sighed, wishing she were home with the children or in bed or in Spokane—anywhere but here. "Please, Brenda—"

"You told me that there is an answer to everything if you just study the problem. And talk about it," Brenda said calmly, putting her hand over Judy's.

"We've talked about it." Judy said decisively, hoping to terminate the conversation. "Mitch sees it my way. He knows I have to do this, and he's willing to wait for me."

"I know that." Brenda nodded, turning Judy to face her, pinning her with her clear blue eyes. "But I think the person you need to talk to is you. And maybe your mother."

Judy responded with a look of complete confusion, and Brenda decided to quit. Handing Judy her purse, she pulled her to her feet. "Come on. The guys are probably eating everything."

PANDEMONIUM REIGNED at the auction. Unlike the silent auctions Judy had attended once or twice at home,

gestures here didn't count as much as loud voices, and
they seemed to be out in force. They also seemed to be
attached to generous souls, determined to make money
for the hospital. Scores of items went for prices higher
than would ever be paid in a store, and personal services—meals cooked, houses cleaned, lawns mowed—
were at a premium.

"We've saved the best for last," the auctioneer announced as two men carried out the trunk Lee had built
and Judy had covered with rosemaling. A respectful
"Oh!" rose from the audience.

The bidding began at a figure higher than anything
sold so far. It rose steadily, animatedly from all around
the hall, finally narrowing to two men who stood at opposite sides of the room. One was young and dressed in
casual designer clothes. The other was older and portly.
Clinging to his arm was a middle-aged woman staring
determinedly at the chest.

"They're Dr. and Mrs. Flynn," Brenda whispered to
Judy. "She's head of the hospital auxiliary."

Judy recognized the woman as the evening's hostess.

When the figure climbed to $2,000, the younger man
backed out, and Mrs. Flynn let out a little squeal of delight. There was loud applause as Mrs. Flynn made her
way to the microphone.

She quieted the crowd, most of them apparently her
friends, with both hands raised in a shushing gesture.
"Are Lee Madison and Judy Cassidy here?" she asked
the crowd.

Judy shrank against Mitch as Lee began to take steps
away from the stage. "Oh, God!" they said simultaneously.

Brenda caught Lee's arm, and Mitch raised his hand,
shouting, "Here!" He pushed Judy forward, then Lee.

"These are the two artists responsible for this beautiful piece," Mrs. Flynn said, her voice filled with excitement over her acquisition. "Lee constructed the trunk," she explained to her audience, "and Judy painted it in the beautiful art form learned from her mother." There was more applause, and she went on to explain about rosemaling, adding details that could have been known only to someone with a knowledge of the art, or someone with access to a book on the subject.

"I'm sorry about this," Lee whispered to Judy as they stood side by side on the stage in total mortification. "I suspect my wife had a hand in this. She belongs to the auxiliary."

"This cannot go unpunished," Judy said out of the corner of her mouth.

"You can trust me to take care of it," Lee promised.

"The most visible trait in this outstanding piece," Mrs. Flynn was saying as she stepped back, offering her two artists to the audience for admiration, "is that it was done with love. And for Manzanita Hospital. We can't thank you enough."

As the assembled group applauded once again, Mrs. Flynn hugged Judy, then Lee, and escorted them to the stage steps.

"How *could* you have done that?" Lee demanded of Brenda after the auction. The four of them stood in the dark in front of Mitch's car.

Brenda shrugged, unimpressed with her husband's indignation. "Mrs. Flynn was so taken with the trunk, she wanted to know something about the artists. I remembered some things Judy had told me, and Mitch added a few pertinent details. You did notice that it brought at least twice the price of anything else tonight?"

"Don't change the subject."

"You two did a great job," Mitch interceded calmly. "You deserved to be recognized."

Judy looked up at him, her expression deadpan. "I could fix it so that *you* are never recognized again—by anyone."

"Now, are the four of us going to part company tonight on a note of violence?" Mitch laughed.

The teasing atmosphere evaporated instantly, and Brenda put her arms around Judy, tears filling her eyes. "Remember what I said." She pulled away and looked Judy in the eye. "Have that conversation."

Lee reached down for Judy's hug. "Good luck, Judy. We both wish you the best." He pulled Brenda toward their car, both of them waving as Mitch and Judy got into hers.

At home Judy checked the sleeping girls for the last time, pulling their blankets up, smoothing their hair back, thinking with a pain that ripped right down the middle of her how much they would change in a year, how much they would learn and grow, mentally and physically. She had loved them from the very beginning, but now it was more than that. Over one beautiful coastal summer, their lives had been woven into hers. They had explored things together, laughed a lot together, learned together. They were tied to one another; they would be torn by the separation.

Hearing Mitch in the kitchen returning a call Dan had taken while they were gone, Judy wandered into the dark living room, needing a moment of solitude to pull herself together. She went to the porch doorway to breathe in the night and heard a rustle of sound from the sofa.

"Judy?" Dan's voice groggy with sleep, came out of the dark. She went to sit on the edge of the sofa as he sat up, rubbing sleep from his eyes. "Where's Dad?"

"Returning the call you took." As Judy's eyes adjusted to the dark, she saw the boy's embarrassed smile and the troubled look in his eyes. "What are you doing up?"

"I knew you'd be leaving early in the morning, and I wanted to tell you—" he paused on an audible constriction in his throat, and Judy felt her own close and tighten "—how great it's been having you here. It's been almost like...as good as...before Mom died. I'm gonna miss you."

Dan stood up, ready to walk away, but Judy stopped his escape by rising and catching his arm. She wrapped her arms around him and simply held him, too full for a moment to speak.

"I love you, too, Dan," she said finally. "And I'm coming back." He'd grown over the summer, Judy thought as he hugged her, and she realized he had an inch on her she hadn't noticed before. How tall would he be in a year?

"It'll be a year that'll seem like forever." Dan pulled out of her arms and smiled. "I'd better, I mean, I know you and Dad..." He laughed softly at what he couldn't say. "Good night, Judy."

Turning to the stairs, he passed his father coming from the kitchen and slapped a hand to his shoulder as he passed. "Good night, Dad."

"Good night, son." Mitch looked from Dan's retreating figure to the grief in Judy's eyes and guessed what had passed between them. Gently he led her toward his bedroom.

Wordlessly, on a note of heartache, they made slow, lingering love to each other. Every sense was explored, every inch of skin caressed, every nerve ending aroused and then soothed. They devoted hours to the reverence of each other's body.

In the small hours of the morning, as darkness raced toward dawn, they made love feeling the urgency of borrowed time. Climax came upon them almost without need for preparation, holding them at its apex, torturing them with its perfection. Then they lay together in the middle of the big bed, pulling on another blanket as fall chilled the night. Judy's head was pillowed on Mitch's shoulder, and he held her close, one rough hand absently rubbing the naked arm that lay across his chest. They were both awake, but neither spoke.

Judy was trying to remember Brenda's directive. "Maybe you should talk to yourself," she had said. "Or maybe to your mother." Talk to herself? As though she were both proponent and opponent? But hadn't she been doing that for a month? Hadn't she still been unable to find a solution?

It all came back to the very basic problem. She had to go; Mitch had to stay.

But it was only for a year. And she was living in a new age where women followed their own paths—not out of selfishness, but because of an inherent right to find the limits of their capabilities and their dreams.

"You told me that everything has an answer," Brenda had reminded her. Judy shook her head restlessly. The problem was too basic, too strong for a solution. Mitch couldn't ignore his business for a year. He had contracts, employees, children.

Finding no answer there, Judy tried to conjure up an image of her mother, pale blond hair in a bun, eyes bright blue, smile always in place, good humor emanating from her like warmth from the sun. "You can do anything," she had said so often. "You can be anything. I want you to live your life doing what you love most. You must go as far as you can, do as much as you can."

"You're hungry for some knowledge of your past that will legitimize Judith Cassidy," Mitch had said. Was that true? Was she on some search to find herself? Yes, she decided. Perhaps. She had never felt inadequate, but she had felt driven, pushed by something to be the best, to do the best. Was it really as simple as Mitch's suggestion? Was she trying to legitimize the fatherless Judy Cassidy by trying to be the ultimate woman?

Then, out of a corner of her mind came the unbidden memory of Mrs. Flynn pointing to her and Lee and their trunk. "Its most outstanding quality," she'd said, "is that it was done with love."

Her mind was wandering because she was exhausted, she thought. It had been a long day, a difficult evening and a night filled with love and with grief. As she shifted restlessly, Mitch pushed the hair out of her eyes. She looked up to smile at him and noted the light blue of dawn through the window behind his head. Then she fell asleep.

When she awoke the sun was high, the place beside her in bed was empty, and the mellow chords of a guitar came faintly from the other side of the house.

Her first thought was that it was too late. She hadn't found the answer, and it was now too late to search for it. Her plane left for New York and London in...she glanced at her watch and felt her heart jolt. Four hours! It would take two and a half hours to get to the airport.

With a sense of urgency she tore open the bedroom door and found herself face-to-face with Mitch holding a mug of coffee in his hand. He offered it to her with a teasing smile.

"I was beginning to think I was going to have to toss you out of bed. Dale's here."

She nodded, taking a long sip of coffee, letting it burn a path of caffeine down her throat and into her veins. "I heard the guitar."

Then she looked into Mitch's eyes. They were as filled with pain as she knew hers were. He said nothing, because there was nothing to say. They had said it all last night in each other's arms—the affirmation of love, the promise to wait.

Instead of flinging herself at him as she longed to do, Judy placed the half-empty cup on the dresser, grabbed her robe and put her hands up to smooth her rumpled hair. "I'd better say hello to Dale and get ready." She'd finished packing yesterday afternoon but had had little heart for attending to the little treasures she'd gathered during her summer in Manzanita.

"I put your car in the garage," he said. "And I'll run it once a week till you come... home." The word almost stopped him but he added briskly, "Dale's on the sun porch with the kids."

Turning off all feelings, Judy hurried out to the porch, belting her robe. She found Dale on the swing with his back to her, Dan beside him, leaning close to watch his hands as he plucked out a cheerful Dolly Parton tune. Katie and Liz sat opposite him on the edge of the coffee table, Katie animated, Liz grim and remote.

"Dale!" Judy exclaimed, stepping onto the porch. He handed the guitar to Dan and stood, his blond good looks beaming as he wrapped her in his arms for a quick hug. Then he held her at arm's length and looked at her.

"You look wonderful," he said, his eyes lingering on hers. "Different," he added thoughtfully, "but wonderful."

Mitch, observing their embrace from the doorway, found the expression on Dale's face ambiguous. He couldn't decide if the man's enthusiasm denoted romantic interest or simply friendship. Judy went into Dale's embrace eagerly, though her pleasure at seeing him seemed totally sisterly.

With the imprint of her body still warm against his own, Mitch felt a dark and bitter jealousy fill him as Dale held her close. With a ragged sigh he forced the sharp emotion aside and tried to observe them dispassionately. She had sworn her love for him all night long, but now she leaned against Dale for the kind of comfort he, Mitch, couldn't offer. Dale was good-looking, apparently open and caring, with feelings for Judy he suspected were far less platonic than she had ever guessed.

She would be with Dale for a year in a foreign environment, exploring places he could only imagine. Dale would be there for her while he was separated from her by a continent and an ocean. And a year was such a hell of a long time. Pain gripped his stomach in a fist and refused to let go.

Dale grinned, appraising Judy's robe and slippers. "I hope you're more ready than you look. We should leave in forty-five minutes."

"I'll be down in thirty," Judy promised, hurrying across the living room and up to her room.

Piling things into her tote with more speed than care, she looked up at the faint sound of a knock on the door. "Come in."

Liz entered the room, a smile firmly in place. She was wearing a blue sweatshirt that darkened the shade of her eyes, and well-worn corduroy pants, and she held a wild daisy on a fragile stem out to Judy.

"This is from the baseball field." She gulped but retained her smile. "I thought you could wear it on your blouse, then press it in a book when you get to England." She swallowed again, the smile wavering. "So you won't forget me."

Her emotions frayed to a fringe, Judy sat on the edge of the bed and pulled Liz to her. Firmly she swallowed back the emotion that would cripple her today if she let it take hold. "I could never forget you, Lizzie," she said, straining to maintain her composure, shamed by how firmly the child held to hers. "And I'll be back in a year."

"A year," Liz said with quiet emphasis, "is such a long time."

"It will go by fast," Judy heard herself say, wondering who she was kidding. "You'll see. Then I'll be back, and we'll do all the fun things we did this summer."

Liz looked into Judy's eyes with an expression so direct and honest that Judy felt unnerved. With her eyes brimming, the child smiled bravely. "Sure."

"I'll put this right here," Judy said quickly, before tears rose to fracture her voice. Slipping the stem of the daisy into the buttonhole on the pocket of her pink shirt, she stood to look into the mirror. In the glass she saw the jaunty window box she had painted and the flourishing philodendron. Beside it in its round pot was Katie's plant, smaller and a little less lively because she often forgot to water it. Judy forced herself to turn with a smile. "How does that look?"

"Very pretty." Liz sniffed. "Can I do anything to help?"

"Yes. You can carry this." Judy handed her the jacket that matched the tailored twill slacks she wore. "And this." She pointed to her paint box on the floor. "And I'll take the cases."

"Daddy said to call him to carry your stuff."

"I can do it," Judy insisted, heading for the door. Emotion was choking her now, clouding her eyes, numbing her brain, causing a ringing in her ears.

Halfway down the stairs, Judy stopped, thoughts, memories, elusive insights whirling around in her mind with cyclonic force. "I want you to do what you're best at," her mother had said. "Go as far as you can. Do as much as you can." Then, came Mrs. Flynn's voice. "Its most outstanding attribute is that it was done with love." But the more she tried to sort out and analyze, the more confused she became.

There's something in that confusion, she thought with a feeling of desperation, that I should get a grip on, something I should understand.

"Judy?" Mitch was standing beside her on the steps, saying her name forcefully as though it was not his first attempt to break through her thoughts.

"Yes?" She concentrated on his face.

"Are you okay?" he asked in concern.

She didn't know how to explain the confusion in her mind, the firm tug she felt in several directions. All summer—all her life—she'd been so sure. "I'm fine. It's just..." Looking into his eyes, level with hers as he stood on the lower stair, she saw all his kindness reflected there. She saw his caring, his wit, his grudging though stalwart understanding of what she had to do, and she felt a scream rising in her throat. Swallowing, she finished in a whisper, "The summer went so fast."

He, too, swallowed, struggling for composure. "We can only hope winter does the same. Let me take those." He picked up her cases and preceded her down the stairs.

The children were gathered on the porch, the breeze a little less warm, the sun a little less golden than just a few days ago. Dale offered his hand to Mitch, then to Dan, and he ruffled the girls' hair. "Thanks for your hospitality this morning," he said. He turned to Judy, studied her pale cheeks and dark eyes and frowned. "I'll put your cases in the trunk while you say goodbye."

Pain snapped open inside her like a broken spring. She put her big purse on the floor beside her feet and leaned down to hug the girls. Liz and Katie began to cry, and Judy lost all semblance of control. Falling to her knees, she held the sobbing girls close to her. Liz clung, the courage she'd tried so hard to hold on to evaporating.

"Promise you'll come back," Liz begged. "Promise!"

"I promise, Lizzie," she said as she wept. "Katie, I promise."

Mitch peeled them off her, and she hugged Dan, feeling his wet cheek against hers. He then busied himself with comforting the girls while Mitch took Judy in his arms.

She held him with the strength of all she felt for him, her ears filled with the sobbing that surrounded them. "You know I love you," she said, tears streaming down her face.

"Yes. I love you, too. And I'll be right here waiting for you." Mitch frowned, and he expelled a breath, in the grip of burning pain. "Write often, will you? And call collect if you need to talk about something, anything."

They shared one last, hard kiss, and she tore herself away, picking up her purse. Looking into his eyes, she whispered, "Bye."

He nodded and swallowed again, unable to form the word. Goodbye was so permanent, and he couldn't rest the fear that that was a stronger possibility than even she realized.

Shouldering her purse, Judy turned her back on Mitch Kramer and his children, went down the steps and started down the walk to the car. Afraid to turn and wave, Judy slid into the passenger seat, and Dale closed her door. In a moment they were moving up Beachfront Lane, turning the corner and driving up the long hill that led to the highway. Dale, frowning in concern, patted Judy's knee as her breath came in tearing gulps.

I'm doing the right thing, she told herself over and over. I'm going to Oxford to follow my mother's directive to do what I do best. It wasn't until they reached the highway and Dale flipped on his turn signal that something finally clicked in Judy's mind. Awestruck, she reached out for the steering wheel, shouting, "Dale, stop!"

"Judy!" Dale brushed her hand away, straightening the car with a pithy oath, then pulling over. "What?" he demanded, but she was staring ahead of her, not seeing the highway, not hearing him.

The riotous confusion Judy had tried to make sense of all morning finally slowed its furious circling. At last she could clearly see the truth, and with that understanding and acceptance.

Until June of this year, what Judith Cassidy had done best was teach. Then she had come to this beautiful stretch of beach to work for the summer, and she had discovered depths to herself she hadn't known were there. She had learned to love and care for children twenty-four hours a day, rather than just during the tidy periods of a school day. And she had learned to love a man, something she had thought a busy woman with plans didn't have time for. And that man taught her that there was no such thing as a right time or a wrong time, only time itself.

The simple truth was—and she turned to Dale as the exquisite clarity of it washed over her—that what Judith Cassidy now did best was love Mitch Kramer and his children. Loving, as she understood it, meant meeting someone else's needs. That was a truth she had learned from her mother and seen proven again when Mitch gave her his blessing to leave him. She saw it as a requirement of what she now did best.

She loved Mitch and his children, and she had to stay with them. She couldn't walk away in search of her own dream and return when it was convenient, because they needed her now. Sometimes love's demands were very immediate. Strangely, instead of feeling the burden of it, she felt elation.

"I've got to go back, Dale," she said, smiling at last. Dale looked into her eyes, and he must have seen there was no point in asking her if she was sure, because he simply executed a probably illegal U-turn and headed back to the Kramers.

They found Mitch and the children sitting on the steps, Liz sobbing in Mitch's arms while Dan held Katie. The boy had an arm around his father, as though offering comfort. Judy groaned aloud at the sight of them and knew her heart would have broken were it not so full.

She turned to Dale, who waited quietly behind the wheel, and threw her arms around his neck. "You're going to have to do this without me, old buddy," she said, grinning from ear to ear. "Send lots of postcards."

Dale put a hand to her face and shook his head at her. "I knew you wouldn't be able to leave. I saw it in your face at the house. They've got you all trussed up with strings."

Judy laughed. "Sometimes strings tie you down, and sometimes they hold you together. Bye, Dale."

From the porch, Mitch saw Dale pull up to the curb, then step out and remove Judy's luggage from the trunk of the Volvo. Then he hugged her and walked around to the driver's side of the car. Mitch felt Dan stiffen beside him and Liz turn in his arms. With a swiftly spoken order to Dan to keep the girls on the porch, Mitch jumped off without using the steps and covered the length of the walk in six strides. Dale was pulling away when Mitch reached Judy.

With a shrill whistle, Mitch called him back. The Volvo screeched to a stop. He took Judy by the arms and shook her. "What are you doing?"

She looked calmly into the depths of his eyes. "I'm staying."

"Oh, no, you're not," he said firmly. "You've worked so hard—"

"That's true," she admitted quietly, "but I love you and the children. I don't live for me anymore. I'm staying." She ducked down to smile into the car at Dale. "You can go, Dale."

"No!" Mitch shouted. The Volvo rocked as Dale accelerated then braked. "Judy, you'll be sorry tomorrow."

"I will never be sorry," she said with such genuine sincerity that the power went out of his protest. "Besides, the moment we have enough saved and you can clear your work schedule for a year, or put Lee in charge of it or something, the five of us will go to Oxford for a year. You and the kids can explore while I'm studying."

For a moment Mitch could only stare at her. Then he felt as though God Himself had leaned down from heaven and patted his shoulder. "But you'll have to wait a year, maybe two," he made himself remind her.

Judy nodded. "I think I'm big enough to do that."

"I wouldn't ask it."

"You didn't. I offered it." Her soft dark eyes searched his, the woman she had become looking for her place in him. "I need to give to you, as well as take from you. And even more than that," she added, "I need to be with you. I'm staying."

Too full to speak, Mitch took her in his arms. Then he raised his head and caught the scent of September in the air as a breeze drifted by. September, he thought in humble amazement, and she's still in my arms. He pulled away from her, and retaining his hold on her hand, looked into the Volvo. "You can go, Dale," he said.

Dale leaned out of the driver's-side window. "You're sure?"

Judy nodded. "We're sure."

With a grin and a shake of his head, Dale waved and drove away.

Mitch turned Judy to face the porch. "You'd better brace yourself for this," he warned.

Dan and the girls watched as Dale disappeared down the street, obviously afraid to hope. They turned to study their father standing hand in hand with Judy. Hesitantly, Liz took a step down, but Dan reached out to stop her, still waiting.

"She's staying!" Mitch called.

As though shot out of a cannon, Liz broke free of her brother and flew down the steps, screeching in delight, colliding with Judy halfway up the walk. Dan and Katie followed behind. Mitch lifted Katie and put his free arm around Judy, who was being sandwiched between his other two children. Tears and laughter bubbled out of their tight knot.

Caught in the middle, unable to move, Judy clung to the children and reached up for Mitch's kiss, happily trapped, forever entangled in love.

Epilogue

Judy and Mitch stood in silence in the center of the main quadrangle of Christ Church, the largest of the thirty-seven colleges of Oxford University. A cold wind blew and a pewter sky threatened rain. Around them, tourists wandered, staring in awe at the Gothic grandeur of their surroundings.

"We're here," Judy whispered to Mitch, clutching his arm in her two hands. Joy made her want to shout, but reverence and awe forced her to whisper. "William Penn studied here. Lewis Carroll taught mathematics here. And tomorrow, Judy Kramer begins to study European history here. Mitch!" She looked up at him, her eyes brimming and bright with the fire of a dream realized. "We're here!"

Disengaging his arm, Mitch put it around her shoulders and held her close. He was as pleased to be here as she was. In the two years he'd been married to her, he'd learned to understand and respect her passion for education, and particularly her love for history. He'd worked twelve-hour days and seven-day weeks, dreaming of the day he could stand here with her on the threshold of her dream. Unlike many things in life, the reality of it was even sweeter than the anticipation.

"You made it," he said, pulling her jacket collar up against the wind. "I don't have to ask you how it feels. You're glowing like a candle."

"*We* made it," Judy corrected him, wrapping her arms around his tweed-jacketed middle. "That's what's most important to me, Mitch." Her eyes grew grave and dark, her expression a little desperate, as though she were afraid he didn't really understand. "Had I made it alone, it would have been an accomplishment I was proud of, and I'd have been happy. But having you and the children with me, it's...it's more than I dreamed. It almost hurts, it feels so wonderful. Do you have any idea how much I love you?"

"Yes," he replied firmly, instantly. She had shown him a hundred times in big and little ways. He was so happy with her, he sometimes couldn't believe she had happened to him.

"Come on, Mom, Daddy!" Liz came running across the courtyard, followed by Katie. "There's a bell tower over there with a bell called Great Tom. It weighs seven tons!" She was reading from a guidebook, encouraging them to follow her as she led the way. "Every evening at five minutes past nine it rings 101 times, once for each member of the original college."

Katie held her arms outstretched. "It's really big!"

"Good-looking women here, Dad," Dan said, indicating a group of short-skirted girls walking across the quadrangle. Now sixteen, he was as tall as his father and, though still dating Chelsea, had a healthy interest in all members of the opposite sex. "Doing my junior year in England might not be bad at all."

"I'll have to take your word for it, son." Mitch grimaced as Judy turned him in the other direction. "Judy doesn't allow me to look."

Dan followed, walking backward to keep his eye on the shapely legs. "I'll give you detailed reports—oof!" Colliding with Judy, Dan looked down into her feigned frown and laughed sheepishly. "Later. I'll give him my report later."

"He doesn't want to hear your report," Judy assured him stoutly. "Do you, Mitch?"

"Ah, well, later, maybe." Judy grabbed the lapels of his jacket, and he stammered, "Just a few... pertinent details. One or two. Nothing much. Hardly anything."

As Dan watched, Judy's mock glare turned to laughter, then to that something that Mitch cherished, something that made her eyes brighten and her cheeks flush, and always stopped him in his tracks. Smiling, Dan turned to catch up with his sisters. He must have realized that Judy and his father didn't need him right now. They needed only each other.

HOW TO ROSEMAL—

Rosemaling is a Norwegian folk art used to beautify everyday objects. Examples are on display at the Norwegian American Museum in Decorah, Iowa.

To rosemal a flowerpot as Judy did for Elizabeth:

1. Seal the object with shellac. When dry, sand, dust and select a pleasing color of oil-based, semigloss enamel for the background.

2. Draw your design on tracing paper (use the scoll band pattern on this page, or your own). Chalk the back, then place the paper—chalk side down—on the painted object. Retrace the design with a firm pencil. Remove and you're ready to paint.

3. Place small amounts of yellow ocher light, Prussian blue, cadmium yellow and red light and burnt umber on a pallet.

4. Using three parts yellow ocher, one part blue and a little umber, mix green. To tone, add some umber to the cadmium red.

5. With an outline brush, paint the spine umber. Then with a #4 brush, paint the swirls by applying a band of yellow, overlapping with green, and again with umber, keeping the dark color on the inside and the light to the outside curve of the scroll. Clean your brush and apply the yellow toward the inside of the design. Continue with green and umber until you've created the rainbow effect characteristic of rosemaling.

AR267-1

ATTRACTIVE, SPACE SAVING BOOK RACK

Display your most prized novels on this handsome and sturdy book rack. The hand-rubbed walnut finish will blend into your library decor with quiet elegance, providing a practical organizer for your favorite hard-or soft-covered books.

Only $9.95

Approximately 16" x 8" when assembled

Assembles in seconds!

To order, rush your name, address and zip code, along with a check or money order for $10.70* ($9.95 plus 75¢ postage and handling) payable to *Harlequin Reader Service*:

Harlequin Reader Service
Book Rack Offer
901 Fuhrmann Blvd.
P.O. Box 1396
Buffalo, NY 14269-1396

Offer not available in Canada.

BKR-1A

*New York and Iowa residents add appropriate sales tax.

TaylorHouse

by Leigh Anne Williams

One house . . . two sisters . . . three generations

Harlequin American Romance introduces the TAYLOR HOUSE trilogy in October 1988

The Taylor family of Greensdale, Massachusetts, had always been "the family on the hill." Grammy Taylor and her two daughters, Katherine and Lydia, were admired more than they were known and loved. But the passing of the matriarch brought with it a unique test for the two sisters—could they save Taylor House . . . and save the town?

—Meet Katherine, who is determined to bring her dream to life.

—Meet Lydia, who hopes to keep that dream alive.

—And meet Clarissa, Katherine's daughter, whose wish is to carry on the traditions of Taylor House for a new generation.

A story of family, home and love in a New England village.

Don't miss the stories of these three women in the October, November and December Harlequin American Romances for 1988:

#265 *Katherine's Dream*, #269 *Lydia's Hope* and #273 *Clarissa's Wish*

TAYLR-1